"Form up, y

Doomsday pe
with him to hit
and control sector several hundred clicks from the landing areas, other fighters and bombers turning off seconds later to hit their assigned targets.

Light cloud cover was ahead, high in the atmosphere. He punched through and below him, clear in the shimmering desert heat, was his target, the base clearly visible in the middle of a high plateau. He went into a dive, aiming for a canyon cut into the side of the plateau. Just as he entered the canyon a missile streaked by straight overhead and slammed into the far side of the crevice, the concussion rattling his ship. He wove down the canyon for half a dozen kilometers, mentally calculating the moment, and then popped back up and turned straight in at the base.

He released a missile which streaked away and several seconds later was broken into half a hundred sub munitions, each of the small arm-length bolts locking on to individual radar and comm link targets and tracking them in. Skimming in low, less than fifty feet off the ground, Jason watched as the volley of shots leaped ahead. Several seconds later the first round hit, the matter/antimatter explosive heads mushrooming out. The entire top of the plateau suddenly seemed to lift into the air as all fifty warheads found their marks and cut loose.

The Wing Commander Series

Freedom Flight
by Mercedes Lackey & Ellen Guon
End Run
by Christopher Stasheff & William R. Forstchen
Fleet Action
by William R. Forstchen (forthcoming)

WING COMMANDER™

END RUN

CHRISTOPHER STASHEFF
WILLIAM R. FORSTCHEN

END RUN

A Baen Books Original

Baen Publishing Enterprises
P.O. Box 1403
Riverdale, N.Y. 10471

ISBN: 0-671-72200-X

Cover art by Paul Alexander

First printing, January 1994

Printed in the United States of America

Distributed by
SIMON & SCHUSTER
1230 Avenue of the Americas
New York, N.Y. 10020

For Lt. General "Jimmie" Doolittle, who did the end run first. Thank you, Godspeed, and safe journey.

PART I

MILK RUN

by Christopher Stasheff

"Viking at two o'clock!" As an afterthought, the duty officer hit the "battle stations" alarm. The klaxon quacked feebly throughout the ship—well, most of it, anyhow. At least, they heard it in the wardroom.

"Oh, yes sir, right away, sir!" Flip leaped up jogging, knees punching high in parody as he headed for his gun turret.

Jolie watched him go as she ground out her cigarette under a smoking lamp that no longer quite cleared the atmosphere. She heaved a sigh. "Flip he's called, and flip he is. Come on, Harry—get cannonized."

"I'll leave that for the Kilrathi, if you don't mind." Harry rose from the seat across from her. "I just shoot 'em, I don't catch 'em." *I hope*, he added silently, the old familiar fear chilling his core. "Have fun in the tail gun." He took one last drag, then rolled the coal carefully off his cigarette, blew out the last of the smoke, and tucked it away for future reference. He leaped into a run, jogging toward his gun turret.

On the bridge, Captain Harcourt asked, "What's it look like, Billy?"

"Private enterprise, Captain," the lookout answered.

Harcourt grunted. They had all had more than

enough experience with the lightly armed, privately owned raiders who kept appearing out of uncharted jump points to raid the Confederation colonies along the edge of the war zone. At least, they thought their jump points were uncharted—but after two years on picket duty, the crew of the Venture-class Corvette *Johnny Greene* knew where all three of them were, so well that everyone on the crew could recite the coordinates in their sleep—and frequently did.

They didn't get very excited about the Vikings any more.

To an outsider, the crew might have appeared to be anything from informal to slapdash, but they worked together smoothly and efficiently, affecting a boredom that they almost always really felt—except when one of the privately-owned raiders showed up for a quick try at easy meat. Then the appearance of boredom masked the old, familiar fear of violent death. There was always the chance that one of the Vikings might be a match for the *Johnny Greene*, always the chance that a jump point might disgorge something bigger.

"All battle stations green, Captain," Lieutenant Janice Grounder reported.

Billy killed the klaxon, what there was of it.

"Right, Number One. Set course for intercept."

"Already on it, Captain. Skoal," answered Morlock Barnes, the astrogator.

Harcourt settled back in his acceleration chair, satisfied, surveying the bridge—pools of light in a chamber of gloom, each pool with a person huddled over a console. The atmosphere was quiet, feeling something like a neighborhood library—if a library had the underlying tension of a life-or-death fight. It was a nice, cozy place for four people.

Unfortunately, they had five in it.

Harcourt looked for something out of order. He had a lot to choose from; the room was a monument of ingenuity, with every screen illuminated by a clip-light, the backlighting having burned out months before. In front of Grounder, who doubled as helm, were two gyroscopes with extended axes, very obviously cobbled out of bits and pieces of metal. Mounted at right angles in universal gimbals, they were substitutes for the attitude gauges, which had burned out even sooner than the screen lights. The helm itself still responded well, but only because Coriander, the damage control officer, had gone EVA and replaced the thrust tube that had been shot off by a Viking six months before. She had used the casing of a dud missile that, fortunately, they had been able to reclaim from the wreckage of the raider at which it had been aimed.

It was ironic that because the missile hadn't fired, the ship had still been intact to be captured after Flip and Harry had shot off *its* thrust tubes. The Kilrathi had tried to escape in rescue pods, and were now comfortably interned on the surface of the planet they had tried to raid. Of course, they were doing hard labor, helping to strengthen the planet's defenses, but that was one of the fortunes of war. The flip side was that their ship had furnished a surprising number of spare parts that had helped keep the *Johnny Greene* moving. For example, other Venture-class Corvettes did not have tail guns.

The dud missile had also furnished a computer lock-on, which Coriander had jury-rigged to aim Harry's laser cannon, his own aiming computer having melted down during a particularly heavy engagement. Flip aimed his laser cannon with the lock-on from the Kilrathi missile that their own dud had sheared in half on its way through the Viking's side.

They no longer noticed the stink in the air, the aroma of bodies that were washed too seldom—the water purifier was still functioning, sometimes—and the air regeneration system had interesting green growths here and there, plus filters that were nearly clogged.

The occasional Kilrathi raider did, at least, relieve the boredom. Never mind the fact that every single one of them could be killed—not very probably, because the Kilrathi were very much more lightly armed than the *Johnny Greene*. They were desperate fighters, though, and there was no way of telling when one of them might get it right.

Never mind that, indeed—and Harcourt tried not to. They had all grown so used to the routine that the others were pretty good at ignoring the danger, too—or, at least, pretending.

"Retract scoops," Harcourt ordered. "Full thrust."

"Full thrust," the intercom confirmed. CPO Lorraine Hasker was in the midsection of the ship with her own console, monitoring the health of the engines that were her babies—even if two of them were cuckoos in her nest.

The ship accelerated—surprisingly, much faster than it was supposed to be able to. Coriander had made a few modifications of her own. If they kept it up for any length of time, the engines would burn out—providing they didn't shake the ship apart first; the two original engines weren't quite in tune any more, and the Kilrathi add-ons weren't exactly balanced. But they wouldn't need to keep up that speed for long.

The Kilrathi apparently hadn't been expecting either the *Johnny Greene* or its speed; they changed course, paralleling the Confederation ship's vector, and shot away, accelerating at maximum thrust.

"He's running," Billy reported.

"Don't they always." It wasn't *quite* boring, Harcourt considered—at least it was action. But they always followed the same pattern. "You'd think the blighters would tell each other what happened when they tried any given maneuver. They could at least spread the word that it doesn't work."

"How?" said Grounder. "None of them ever make it back."

"Well, that's true," Harcourt allowed. "But there must be thousands of them doing this all along the front. *Some* of them must get back."

"Maybe the other ones don't try to run," Grounder suggested helpfully, "like that first one we fought. Remember? *They* charged *us*."

"Yes, and their engines have been coming in handy ever since." Harcourt looked over at CPO Coriander. "Nice job, Chief. Don't know how you ever managed to tie them in with our control system."

"I didn't," Coriander answered, "quite."

"Good enough for me," Grounder said. "They roar when I push the stick."

"Thanks, Lieutenant—but we'll need everything we've got," Coriander said. "The bastards keep chipping away at us. Every one we blow up, takes a little bit of us with it."

"We're at maximum velocity," Grounder reported. "Estimate two minutes till we're in range."

"You think they'd look up the specs on a Venture-class Corvette," Coriander sighed.

"They did, Chief, but you weren't on the chart," Billy called over.

That, Harcourt reflected, was nothing but the unvarnished truth. A corvette was a very uneasy compromise; it sacrificed the agility of a fighter-bomber for not as much firepower as a destroyer. But if you couldn't afford to put a destroyer out on guard duty, a corvette was better then nothing. *And*, he reflected, *if you're losing the war and running short of ships and men, you have to keep that corvette on station for two years in a row, without leave or refitting.*

Better than nothing? Maybe—but not much. At least, not enough to give its crew any feeling of security.

Under circumstances like that, you either went crazy and tore each other apart, or you became extremely close. The crew of the *Johnny Greene* hadn't torn each other apart—yet.

It never occurred to Harcourt that he might have had something to do with that.

"Viking is turning," Billy reported.

Harcourt nodded, gazing at the illuminated grid of the battle display in front of him in frustration. Light, it had—lines, it had. Blips, it had none. The hit they had taken eighteen months before had knocked out the relay circuit from the battle computer. Billy could see where the foe was, but nobody else could. They just had to trust him.

They did.

Still, the battle display did lighten the gloom of the bridge nicely.

Harcourt felt the tension building. "Now we'll see if this Viking can think of anything new and different."

"How many things can you do in a space dogfight?" Grounder countered.

"Come now, Lieutenant!" Harcourt reproved. "You show a singular lack of imagination. Now, if I were him, I would . . ."

"He's diving!" Billy cried.

Suddenly, Harcourt ached to be able to see, but the display in front of him stayed stubbornly featureless. He glared at the direct-vision port, but it showed only careless stars.

One of them was moving—but they were still too far away for the Kilrathi to show as a silhouette.

"He knows we don't have any armament underneath," Harcourt said. "He's going to try to come up under us and shoot off our belly armor."

"Well, at least it's something new," Grounder said—but there was a tremor of trepidation in her voice.

Harcourt hit "all stations" on the intercom. "Everybody stand by! We're going to flip!"

"I already did," the senior gunner answered.

"Yes, Flip, and we've all decided to join you. Now, hold tight—you're going to be hanging upside down relative to where you are now."

"So?" Jolie's voice replied succinctly. "We'll just think of it as, we're upside down *now*, and we're going to be right side up!"

With artificial gravity holding them down to their seats, it didn't really matter—but they all knew the unpleasant sensation that a roll could produce, gravity or no gravity, because Coriolis force is Coriolis force and fluid is fluid, especially if it's in the inner ear, telling you that you're rolling, no matter what the seat of your pants says.

Harcourt watched Grounder's two gyros in their universal mounts as the blue poles swung around and down to point at the console itself. Blue was up, red was down—and right now, down was up, so Harcourt knew they were upside down. At least, they were inverted in relation to how they had been a couple of minutes ago.

"Viking above us," Billy sang out.

"What's the range?"

"Five hundred kilometers," he answered, "closing at a klick a second."

"Taking his time, isn't he?"

"Hey, he wasn't expecting to see our top."

"Close enough," Harcourt decided. "Fire!"

The ship bucked as the two cannon fired, a quarter-second out of phase—one of the other little things that had gone wrong, and really should have taken them into repair dock.

Flip yodelled with glee, and, "He's hit," Harry decided.

"We got his tail," Billy reported, gaze glued to his screen.

"I never see any action," Jolie grumbled over the intercom.

"You will now," Billy told her. "He's rolling over and coming up behind. He still wants to get at our underside."

"I know how he feels," she griped.

"See if you can't fry him a little on the way," Harcourt suggested.

The skin of the ship delivered a muffled "whumpf" to them—the sound of the mass driver discharge, conducted through the hull. Then Jolie's voice on the intercom, disgusted: "Damn! Missed!"

"No, you didn't," Billy countered "You winged him on an attitude control tube . . . Wait! Missiles! He's firing!"

"Return fire!" Harcourt snapped.

"But he's not in range! We've only got two missiles left!"

"If we're not in range, *he's* not! Number One! Evasive action!"

"Aye, aye!" Grounder grinned, and the gyroscopes whined as they began to weave up, down, and crossways in some very interesting combinations.

It didn't work.

"His missile's locked on," Billy reported, "and we're flying into it!"

Grounder said, "We should come up behind it before it gets to us."

"Not even at top acceleration!" Coriander called out. "I keep telling you! Missiles are faster than ships!"

"Even with two extra engines?"

"Even with *ten* extra engines! Pull out of it, Grounder! Give Jolie her chance!"

Grounder looked up pleadingly at the captain, but Harcourt shook his head. "No time to experiment, Lieutenant."

"Oh, *all* right!" Grounder huffed, and the gyro slowly rotated.

"Closing!" Billy yelped. "Three hundred kilometers! Three fifty! Two hundred!"

"Fire, Jolie," Harcourt advised.

The hull delivered the "whumpf" again.

The sudden glow from the screen illuminated Billy's face. "Got him!" he whooped. "Nice shooting, Jolie! Now he doesn't have *any* tail!"

"Still bored?" Harcourt asked.

"No, not for the moment," she admitted.

"He's got to pull out now," Coriander said. "Got to steer with his nose thrusters, and run."

"No, he doesn't," Harcourt said. "He's Kilrathi."

"Still coming." Billy's voice was low and tense. "Wobbled a bit, but he's still coming."

"He's crazy! Jolie could shoot him into shrapnel!"

"Then he'll die trying," Harcourt said grimly, "or we will. *Now* give him our missile."

"Now?" Billy squawked. "He's flying straight toward us, Captain!"

"Then it will hit all the harder."

"Our last two!" Coriander wailed.

"That's what they're for, Chief. Launch Missile One."

Grounder hit a pressure patch. "One away."

"So is his," Billy called.

"Evasive action!" Harcourt snapped.

Grounder's gyros whined and described crazy loops with their poles as she swooped upward, then swung from side to side as the ship corkscrewed back toward the raider. The Kilrathi missile, not yet locked on, went blithely on its way . . .

Straight toward the *Greene*'s missile.

"They're going to lock on each other!" Coriander wailed.

"Line up on that ship and give them our last one," Harcourt ordered.

"No, wait!" Billy shouted. "Theirs *did* lock on our ship! It's coming straight toward us!"

"Well, good," Harcourt sighed. "Then ours might still lock onto them."

"It did," Billy reported. "Now, how do we get rid of theirs?"

"Flip! Harry!" Harcourt called. "A silver florin for the one who gets it first!"

"Mine!" Flip caroled, and, "What's a florin?" Harry asked, as the ship shuddered with the out-of-phase double blast again.

Once more, Billy's face glowed orange. "Got it!"

"My florin," Flip said immediately.

"What are you talking about?" Harry demanded. "That was my shot! Any dunce could see it!"

"I'm not just *any* dunce . . ."

"Okay, okay," Harcourt sighed, "a florin for each of you. What about *our* missile, Bil . . ."

Then he saw the yellow glow on Billy's face and sighed with happiness. "Ah. Score!"

"Hit," Billy confirmed. "The whole raider. Gone."

For a moment, depression seized Harcourt. A dozen lives, maybe more, snuffed out in a moment . . . brave men, probably, or at least bold creatures . . .

Then the whole ship shuddered, and the dull sound of an explosion echoed through the hull.

"Sorry, Captain, I couldn't see it closing!" Billy cried. "The glare from the raider going up . . ."

"They launched one more just before they died," Harcourt snapped. "Sound off by stations!"

"Sentry here!" Billy called.

"Astrogator here!"

"Damage Control working!"

"First Officer here."

"Gun Turret One here!"

"Gun Turret Two!"

"Tail Gunner here!"

"Engineer alive and feisty!"

Harcourt exhaled with relief. "We're all okay, then. How's the ship, Chief?" And, with a hint of anticipation: "Is it something essential?"

"Yeah, you could say that." Coriander was studying her board. "It's the oxygen fusion reactor."

A cheer rattled the intercom and blasted off the bridge walls.

"A hit, a palpable hit!" Grounder sang.

"O_2 generation is shot!" Flip whooped.

"Can't stay on picket duty now!" Lorraine warbled.

"Gotta go to repair base." Coriander nodded with full conviction. "Can't stay out in space now, Captain. We're stuck with the oxygen we've got in the system already. Sure, we can recycle it for two weeks, maybe a month—but after that, we're dead. Nope, gotta go to base."

"What a pity," Harcourt sighed. "Only two years on station. And here I thought we'd set a new record. Oh, well, I suppose we'll have to console ourselves with R & R."

His mind filled with visions of supple bodies, low lights, soft music, wine, *real* food . . .

And fresh air!

Stars shifted in the vision port, and Harcourt knew they had completed the last jump to Xanadu. He smiled in anticipation of a sandy beach under a clear sky. "Tell them we're coming, Number One."

"Yes, sir." Grounder pressed a switch. "CS *Johnny Greene* to Xanadu Base. Come in, Xanadu."

Harcourt pressed "All stations." "Gunners and engineer to the bridge." He knew he wouldn't be able to keep them away from the first sight of the paradise that awaited them, so he made it official. For himself, he stared at the port, trying vainly to pick out the star that was Xanadu. The jump point was one and a third AU's from the planet, which wasn't much larger than Terra, so of course it appeared as a star—but not yet a discernible disc.

The planet had been named for its climate. It was mostly water, with a few archipelagos. The largest island, of course, held the Fleet repair base. The second largest held the main R & R station, and vacationing spacehands dispersed from there to their own secluded lazy places on the smaller islands—if they wanted to be alone. If they didn't, the main station had casinos, restaurants, holo palaces, golf links, tennis courts, a shoreline that was one long beach where the surf rolled in perfect tubular waves, and a temperature that always ranged between sixty and eighty degrees Fahrenheit—all the amenities for a few weeks of sybaritic luxury before the tired spacedogs had to return to the lines. It may not have been Paradise, but it was close enough for Government workers.

The gunners crowded in through the hatch with Lorraine, the engineer, between them. Harcourt looked at his crew and saw the same glassy-eyed smile of anticipation on all their faces.

"Xanadu Base to CS *Johnny Greene*."

Grounder looked up, eyes glinting. "*Johnny Greene* here. Do you have a landing assignment for us?"

"'Fraid not, *Johnny Greene*. We have a message, instead—orders. Do not land on Xanadu. Repeat, do not land."

Grounder stared in shock.

Then she recovered. "Fleet base, our oxygen generation plant is shot—literally and figuratively. We have enough O_2 for a week's breathing, no more."

"We know, *Johnny Greene*, but orders are orders, and a week is enough breathing space."

"Let me double-check that supply with Damage Control, Xanadu." Grounder looked up at Coriander. "Chief?"

"Yeah, it'll last that long," Coriander grated. "They better have a damn good reason!"

"Damn good," Harcourt seconded. "Relay that up here, Number One."

Grounder hit the switch with a look of relief.

"Yeah, we have a week's oxygen left," Harcourt growled. "Captain Macmillan Harcourt here. We've been standing picket duty for two years, and my crew is going crazy for some R & R while their ship is being repaired. What's the problem, Xanadu?"

"Only orders, Captain Harcourt—signed by Admiral Banbridge."

Harcourt stiffened. That was coming from awfully high up. Why was Banbridge concerning himself with a lowly corvette?

"Orders are to divert to Hilo Base," Xanadu said.

"Hilo Base?" Harcourt turned to the astrogator. "Where's that, Barney?"

Barney scanned the chart on his screen, shook his head. "Nothing I ever heard of, Captain. I'll scan." He punched the name into the computer.

Harcourt decided to help him a little. "Coordinates for Hilo Base, please, Xanadu?"

"It's not on *any* of our charts," Barney reported.

"Thirty-two degrees right ascension, seventy-two degrees east," Xanadu replied. "Sixteen light-years outward."

"Thirty-two, seventy-two, sixteen," Barney echoed, punching the numbers into his computer.

Then tension on the bridge fairly thrummed. Everybody stared at the astrogator.

"Yeah, it's there." Barney shook his head. "I wouldn't call that much of a world, Captain. Says it has a couple of big lakes, though, and an inland sea. Plus a couple of R & R domes."

The crew let out one massive groan.

"Well, there goes our month on the beaches," Grounder sighed.

"They can't do this to us!" Flip erupted. "Two years on picket duty, *two years*!"

Grounder killed the audio pickup in a hurry.

"Two years!" Flip yelled. "We never griped, we never complained, we never said, 'The hell with this!' and headed for home! Two years! Fifty-three fights, our ship getting shot away piece by piece! We put up with the stink, we put up with the smoke, we patched and finagled and made things work somehow! We *earned* this leave, damn it!"

Everybody stared straight ahead, shaken. It was only the second time in two years that they had heard Flip raise his voice in anger. The first time had been right after their premier encounter with a Kilrathi raider, when a near miss had burned off the brand-new paint job on Flip's beloved ship. The rest of the time, he had always been cheerful to the point of being nauseating, always joking, always laughing. To hear *him* flare up shook them worse than Banbridge's orders.

"The domes will keep things warm," Harcourt sighed. He nodded to Grounder, and she opened the audio pickup again. "What're the rest of the R&R facilities, Xanadu?"

"Danged if I know, Captain," Xanadu replied. "Never heard of the place."

Flip had calmed down substantially; his voice had turned cold. "Mutiny, Captain. I move we desert."

Grounder stabbed frantically at the audio switch.

"Don't tempt me," Harcourt groaned. "I've got a wife and kids back on Terra."

The bridge was silent; everybody knew that Flip had married just before they left for this last tour of duty. His new wife lived on the same planet as his parents, Flip's home, which was now entirely too close to the front lines.

Flip sighed, like the air gushing out of a punctured tire. "Right, Captain. We go where we're told in this man's fleet."

"That's what we swore." Harcourt felt like doing a little of the other kind of swearing right then, though. He nodded at Grounder, and she turned on the audio pickup again. "Orders understood, Xanadu," Harcourt sighed. "*Johnny Greene* en route to Hilo. Signing off."

"*Bon voyage*." Xanadu said, the tone sympathetic. "Signing off."

Hilo loomed in the vision port, filling its center—bland, tan, and arid with only a few dots of blue and a crescent of azure at its rim.

The gunners and Lorraine jammed the hatchway. "I can almost feel that baking desert wind," Flip groaned.

"No, you can't," Coriander countered. "The temperature never gets above fifty there."

"And this is R&R?" Billy griped.

"Belay that, folks," Harcourt sighed. "Wake 'em up, Number One"

"CS *Johnny Greene* to Hilo Base," Grounder said. "Come in, Hilo Base."

"Hilo Base to *Johnny Greene*," a husky contralto answered him.

Every male head on the bridge whipped about to stare at the screen in front of Grounder. They saw a beautiful tanned face with a cascade of black hair, deep red lips, and long lashes over big dark eyes, giving them a collective wink. "Good to see you, *Johnny Greene*. We've been expecting you."

Grounder bristled. "Oh. This was *your* idea?"

"Lieutenant!" Harcourt reproved her.

The contralto just laughed, low and warmly. "It wasn't my idea, Lieutenant, but we have some hunks here who will claim it was theirs, once they get a look at your face."

Grounder stared, at a loss for words. She had never thought of herself as pretty—but she had been thinking about hunks. At least, until they hit Xanadu.

Harry stepped up for a look over Grounder's shoulder, Jolie crowding right behind him, eyes snapping. "Cat!" she hissed.

"You mean she's pretty?" Barney was stationed in front of Grounder; he couldn't see.

Lorraine groaned. "Just what we need, on leave—competition!"

Grounder finally managed to find her voice again. "What's the weather like down there, Hilo?"

"Outside the dome," the contralto said, "it's forty degrees Fahrenheit with a thirty-knot breeze, kicking up a lot of loose sand."

Coriander stifled a moan.

"*Inside* the dome," the contralto said brightly, "it's seventy-two degrees, water at sixty-eight. The slot machines are loaded to make sure you can't lose too badly, the croupiers have curves you never learned in Calculus, and the dealers look like Don Juan should have, with very soft, sensuous hands."

Jolie, Lorraine, and Grounder perked up, and began to look interested. So did Coriander, but she looked wary, too.

"Of course," the contralto went on, "we've just finished our second dome, where it's twenty-eight degrees, three different grades of slopes, three chair lifts, and two feet of fresh snow every morning. Skis supplied, of course. The chalet has a loaded bar, a hot band, and dancing all night."

"This . . . just might be . . . an interesting leave, after all," Billy mused.

The dark-haired beauty on the screen smiled and gave them another wink. "We don't promise anything but dancing, mind you. You'll have to do the rest yourselves."

Harry glanced at Coriander, thinking of all the passes he'd put off making for the last two years; emotional complications in a war zone were something none of them needed. Coriander glanced back at him, saw he was looking, and turned away quickly, blushing.

"Oh, I think we can manage," Harcourt said easily. "Where do we land, Hilo?"

Finally, after two years, they opened the *Johnny Greene*'s main hatch. The airlock equalized pressure, but they still wore their suits—Hilo didn't have all that much mass, and none of them were used to breathing thin air. The crew filed out, looking brightly about them. The sun was shining, the sky was a very dark blue, and . . .

The sand stretched for miles and miles and miles.

But the airbus was waiting, and an officer in a pressure suit stepped up, holding out a gauntleted hand. "Captain Harcourt? Captain Tor Ripley. Welcome to Hilo."

"Thank you, Captain." Harcourt took the hand, a bit surprised to see someone of his own rank for the welcoming committee—almost as surprised as he was by a handshake instead of a salute. "May I present my first officer, Lieutenant Grounder . . . my astrogator, Ensign Barnes . . ."

He made the rounds, each of the crew members

saluting, Ripley returning. Then, the formalities done, he said, "Welcome to Hilo! Welcome!" and ushered them onto the bus.

The doors closed; air hissed in; the green patch lit.

"Okay, we can crack our helmets." Ripley gave his headpiece a half-twist, then tilted it backward to bare his face. Harcourt did the same.

"Now, Captain," Ripley said, "I'd like to talk to you about getting off picket duty for a while."

As one, all the crew's heads swivelled, staring at Ripley.

"It's . . . certainly something I'm willing to consider," Harcourt said slowly, somewhat dazed—but instinctively looking for the worm in the apple. "What's the nature of the assignment?"

Ripley told them.

Grins broke out on all faces. The crew nodded.

"I volunteer, Captain."

"So do I."

"Me, too!"

"And me!"

"Guess I do, too," Harcourt said slowly. "We'll take the assignment, Captain Ripley."

Well, it sounded like a good idea at the time.

In fact, it sounded like a milk run. All they had to do was make an orbit or three around a small, insignificant planet the Kilrathi called "Vukar Tag." It was way out in the Kilrathi boondocks. Okay, so it was in enemy territory, but it was closer to the Fleet than to Kilrah, and they had the jump points very clearly mapped.

"One of our destroyers was chasing a Kilrathi raider home," Ripley explained. "He was following the cat just a little too closely through the jump point, and something in the turbulence got the angle wrong. When the stars stopped shifting, there was no sign of the raider—but they did spot a Kilrathi corvette going into Vukar Tag."

They were sitting at a poolside table, watching the rest of the crew with a few of their hosts and hostesses, disporting themselves like blowing whales and courting dolphins.

"You know," Billy said, "I never realized Jolie had a figure. . . ."

"Under combat fatigues, who would know?" Harcourt agreed. "But all the figures we need right now are the ones in your notepad." For himself, though, he was finding it difficult to keep his eyes off Lieutenant Grounder. Her swimsuit was very demure, but he would never have called it "innocent. . . ."

He wrenched his mind back to the topic. "That's how they found out the name?"

"Right—not that they could understand it, of course. Nobody aboard spoke much Cat. But the captain had the good sense to slap on the recorder, and when he got back to base, our experts deciphered it."

Billy glanced at Harcourt.

Harcourt nodded almost imperceptibly.

Billy turned to Ripley. "If you don't mind, sir—professional interest. What did they find?"

" 'Professional interest' is right," Ripley answered. "It was just the usual greeting and landing instructions—but they did pick out of it that the planet's name is 'Vukar Tag.' " He shrugged. "What it means, nobody seems to know. What's even more of a puzzle, is why there's a cruiser in orbit around the dustball."

"A cruiser." Harcourt had a nasty suspicion. "Any moons?"

"One, and small—but big enough to hold at least a wing of fighters, if that's what you're thinking." Ripley nodded. "I thought the same thing."

" 'Well guarded' is right!" Harcourt scowled. "What *are* they hiding there?"

"Well, I hope you're curious enough to want to find out, Mac," Ripley said. "I really hope you are."

"Minerals?"

Ripley shook his head. "It's mostly desert, and no sign of a mining operation, though they did see shuttles coming up to a transport ship. They may be exporting something, but according to spectroanalysis, the only thing it could be is high-grade silicon."

"Silicon isn't exactly rare," Harcourt pointed out. "There has to be a good supply on every Kilrathi planet."

"Has to," Billy agreed. "The sand from Vukar Tag must be very pure, or something."

"Or something." Harcourt didn't want to say it, but it was hard to keep from thinking of religious associations. "So it's a desert, and it's a backwater, and all we have to do is fly around it once or twice and get pictures." He looked up at Ripley. "That right, Tor?"

Ripley nodded. "That's the mission in a nutshell, Mac. Of course, since it's a reconnaissance flyby, you'll be carrying a specialist."

There was the worm in the apple that Harcourt had been braced for all along—if he didn't count a cruiser and a wing of fighters. "He's in charge of the cameras?"

"Yes, and you'll pretty much have to go by her direction, once you get near the planet."

Harcourt frowned, picking up on the correction in gender. "She knows navigation?"

Ripley shrugged uncomfortably. "She's had the same training as you and I, and she's had fifty hours combat flying time in a Sabre."

"That's just great," Billy groaned.

"Billy, you're out of line," Harcourt said severely. Inwardly, though, he was grateful to his sentry for saying what he had wanted to, but shouldn't. Just enough training and experience to make her think she knew what she was doing, but not enough to *really* know ... "Just so she understands she's under my orders, Tor."

"Oh, of course, Mac!" Ripley dismissed the issue. "Now, about your route in ..."

The route in, of course, should have been no problem at all. Intelligence had the jump points mapped, and there was no particular reason to think there should be any Kilrathi shipping near any of them—no raiders, since it was inside the borders of the Kilrathi Empire; no pickets, since the fleets were a dozen light-years farther out from Kilrah, waiting to skirmish with the Confederation. There might be the odd transport freighter, but that shouldn't pose much in the way of a problem.

"I don't understand, Tor," Harcourt said. "If all it is, is a ball of sand—why is it worth a close look?"

"Because," said Ripley, "for a worthless dust ball, it's amazingly well guarded."

"Oh, really?" Outwardly, Harcourt still looked relaxed and casual; inside, he was turning into a coiled spring. "What is it? A refitting base? An auxiliary shipyard?"

"Could be, but there really isn't enough traffic—just the occasional escort or transport." Ripley shook his head. "From what little we can see from a long way off, there's nothing there."

"So why all the ships?" Harcourt asked.

"That," said Ripley, "is what we want to know."

Of course, Harcourt should have turned down the assignment right then—or at least talked it over with the crew, and let *them* turn it down. But two weeks of watching bikinis while soaking up sunlight and alcohol had left him with a warm, ruddy glow that made the worst a Kilrathi could do, seem inconsequential.

Which was just what Ripley had intended, of

course—sun, water, and no news, no other crews in from the war zone to trade notes with.

No wonder they had been diverted—in more ways than one!

Ramona Chekhova was only thirty-two. It was an inconvenient age—young enough to have rash, hot-blooded impulses, old enough that she should have known better.

She carried her duffel bag up to the *Johnny Greene*, dropped it, and stood to attention, glaring at the crew who were drawn up in a semicircle to wait for her. They saluted. She returned the salute, then turned her glare on Captain Harcourt.

"Lieutenant Commander Ramona Chekhova?" he asked.

"The same," she confirmed. "I'm waiting, Captain."

Harcourt stiffened, his face wooden. "I'm afraid you're forgetting a point or two of military etiquette, Commander. I am the commanding officer of the *Johnny Greene*—and *I* am waiting for *your* salute."

Yes, a lieutenant commander outranked a captain—but not on board his own ship. There, the captain is the boss.

And Ramona knew it, too. She finally flipped her hand in something vaguely resembling a salute, seething inwardly.

Harcourt saluted crisply in response.

The crew looked a little relieved, thinking Harcourt had won the first round.

Harcourt knew better. "Lieutenant Commander Chekhova, my first officer, Lieutenant Janice Grounder . . . my astrogator, Ensign Morlock Barnes . . . my Damage Control Officer, Chief Petty Officer Darlene Coriander . . ."

Chekhova nodded at each in turn as he completed the introductions. Then she turned back to Harcourt.

"Permission to come aboard, Captain." She wasn't at attention, she wasn't at ease, she was just sort of slumping in place. Harcourt decided to ignore the insult and said, "Permission granted." He stepped over to the boarding ramp. Ramona hesitated for a moment, caught between military courtesy and old-fashioned courtesy—but she knew that a lady must insist on being treated as a lady, or she will sacrifice one of her strongest advantages, so she stepped up on the ramp.

Harcourt was relieved to see her snap to attention to salute the colors—and the salute was crisp, in perfect form. At least there was something that she *did* respect.

Harcourt was about to order the countdown for liftoff when movement at the corner of his eye caught his attention. He turned and looked.

Ramona stood in the hatchway, watching the activity on the bridge with an expression of guarded interest.

Harcourt had a brief struggle within himself. He knew it was possibly foolish, but the gentleman in him won out. "Would you like to come in to observe, Lieutenant Commander?"

"No, thank you, Captain." But Ramona made no move to go away.

Harcourt frowned. "Well, then, I must ask that you return to quarters."

She gave him a cold stare. "Protocol, Captain?"

Harcourt suppressed a surge of irritation. "Practicality, Commander. You would be welcome to join us for a few minutes, but then I'd have to ask you to leave anyway. We have a bridge crew of five, and five acceleration couches. After we're under way, you'll be welcome, if you deign . . . if you wish to join us. But while we're lifting off, I must ask you to stay in your quarters, strapped into your acceleration couch, in accordance with regulations."

She glared at him, then spun on her heel and stalked away.

Harcourt gazed after her, eyes narrowing. He should have insisted that she say, "Yes, sir," to acknowledge that aboard ship, the captain is always the senior officer. Even a lieutenant in command of a fighter-bomber can issue orders to an admiral aboard his craft, and be sure he was within his rights and would be obeyed. Of course, the admiral might bust him back down to private later on—but if the matter was really important at the time, the lieutenant could insist on it.

Of course, the lieutenant would be a fool to try to push an admiral around, unless it were a matter of life and death.

Harcourt decided to let it pass.

He turned back to the bridge crew—just in time to see them whisking their eyes back to their screens. He smiled thinly and said, "Commence launch, Number One."

"Yes, sir," Grounder said. "All stations, ready?"

"Go," said Billy.

"Go," said Coriander.

"Go," Lorraine said over the intercom.

"Go," Barney echoed.

"Initiating countdown. Ten . . . nine . . . eight . . . . seven . . ."

Ramona stormed back into her cabin, threw herself down onto her acceleration couch, and strapped in. How dare that idiot Harcourt order her around like an infant! She steamed, her whole body tense, then realized it was a horrible condition for lift-off, and tried to force herself to relax.

She had to establish her authority aboard this

ship—had to! If she couldn't, she might as well kiss this whole mission good-bye. *She* knew how closely they had to skim the planet in order to get clear pictures, and she knew as well as Harcourt how heavily-guarded the planet was. She wasn't about to throw her whole career away because some middle-aged idiot wouldn't listen to her, a middle-aged idiot who hadn't even been able to win commander's rank, and was still captain of a mere corvette, a job normally relegated to a lieutenant.

She would *not* be treated as a subordinate! She had fought for her rank, she had taken risks, she had endured hardship, she had brought back information under enemy fire—and she wasn't about to let anybody stop her from bringing this mission in successfully completed, either!

Ramona decided she would have to exert her authority as soon as possible.

Ramona waited until the graveyard watch, then came up on the bridge when most of the rest of the crew were asleep. She halted, staring at Grounder, wondering if the woman were on drugs, the way she was gazing about her with a happy smile.

Everything worked now—at least, until their next battle. That was why Grounder had been gazing around her in euphoria—at all the shiny new equipment that actually *functioned.*

But of course, Ramona didn't know about that.

Then Grounder saw Ramona. She started and looked up, surprised. "Good evening, Commander."

"Good evening." Ramona paced the bridge as though she had every right to be there, ignoring Grounder and Barney.

"Uh . . . begging your pardon, Commander," Grounder said, "but I don't think the Captain has authorized your presence on the bridge."

"Yes, he did." Ramona turned to confront her. "Just before we lifted off, remember? He said I'd be welcome on the bridge once we were under weigh." And she turned her back, inspecting the meters and the screens.

Her eye lit on the velocity readout. This was a place where she could give orders with no worry about disrupting the ship. "Only cruising speed?"

Grounder stared, puzzled. Then she said, "Well . . . yes, sir. That's standard operating procedure en route to a jump point."

"We don't have time for that," Ramona snapped. "Full acceleration! Right away!"

"Uh-h-h-h-h . . ." Grounder exchanged a quick glance with Barney. "I don't know if the power plant will take it, sir."

"What do you mean, not take it?" Ramona was instantly angry. "I know the specs on a corvette as well as you do, Lieutenant! This tub can take full acceleration for ten hours without any trouble!"

Grounder bristled at hearing the *Johnny Greene* called a "tub." "This *ship* can take full acceleration for about one hour, sir. Beyond that, maybe it will and maybe it won't—depending on how well they overhauled the engines."

"Overhaul?" Ramona glowered. "What was the matter with them?"

"A near miss from a Kilrathi missile. Jolie shot it down fifty meters from the ship, but some of the shrapnel chewed up the insides of the engines a little."

"Is that why you have those obscene Kilrathi monsters welded on?"

For the first time, Grounder really wondered about the woman. "I'd scarcely call them 'obscene,' sir. They're machines, and they work—and I think Chief

Coriander worked magic, managing to tie them in with our system."

"Well." Ramona's lips curved in a nasty smile. "With four engines instead of two, you certainly shouldn't have any trouble maintaining full acceleration from here to the jump point."

"Nothing except the stress on the structure of the ship," Grounder countered. "The *Johnny Greene* was built for only two engines; four puts in more stress than the ship will take, if it goes on longer than an hour or so."

"Don't try to tell me how a ship works, Lieutenant! How do you think I got to be a light commander? Just do as you're told! Retract your scoops and hit full acceleration!"

"But the fuel supply . . ."

"Do it!" A very ugly gleam came into Ramona's eye. "Are you refusing a command from a senior officer?"

Grounder's face became a flint mask. "No, sir."

"Then do as you're told!"

"Full acceleration, aye!" Grounder sighed. The silly shrew would have to learn for herself.

The little ship surged ahead.

Ramona grabbed at the back of an acceleration couch and held on until the surge had passed. The little chit had done that deliberately, she knew, to try to throw her off her feet—but she had obeyed orders, so Ramona couldn't really make an issue of it. Instead, she turned away to pace the bridge, her lips curving just a little in a smile of satisfaction. She wasn't about to take the chance of leaving the bridge, though; if she did, that snip of a lieutenant would try to ease the acceleration down again. No, Ramona had issued an order, and she meant to see that it was obeyed.

She kept watch for two hours, watching Grounder's face grow more and more pale, more and more strained, watched and glared until . . .

Until the klaxon blared, tearing at her eardrums.

Ramona slapped her hands over her ears, staring around, amazed. She adjusted to the loudness of the horn, took her hands away . . .

The ship lurched, then began to jolt forward in jumps.

Ramona stumbled, reaching out and catching herself against the top of a console. "Stop it, Lieutenant!"

"As you say, sir." Grounder pulled the acceleration control down.

"Not that! I said *full* acceleration, damn it!"

But Grounder kept easing off. "Sir," she said through stiff lips, "that alarm you hear is for the power plant overheating, and the shuddering you're feeling is the strain on the ship's skeleton that comes from four engines, not quite balanced in thrust, driving a ship that's only designed for two. I can't . . ."

Harcourt burst onto the bridge, his hair tousled, clothes in disarray, eyes still filmed with sleep, pajama cuffs still sticking out of the sleeves of his uniform blouse. "Status!" he snapped.

"Reactor overheated, Captain. Beginning to cool, though."

"*Overheating!* And the shuddering we've got going through the frame? What're you doing, Grounder? Running the ship flat out?"

"Yes, sir," Grounder said through thin lips.

Harcourt stared at her in disbelief. "*Flat out?* A two-engine ship with four engines?" Then he realized the order that had to be given. "Decelerate to cruising velocity!"

"Aye, aye, sir."

"All right. Cancel the klaxon."

Grounder toggled the alarm off.

Harcourt drew a deep breath, striving for calm. "What in the name of Heaven possessed you, Number One?"

Ramona realized she'd better acknowledge her error before Grounder could blame it on her. "She was acting under my orders, Captain!"

Harcourt grew very still.

Then, slowly, he turned, his eyes chips of ice. "Orders? Who are you to give orders aboard my ship, Commander?"

In spite of herself, Ramona felt a chill of fear at the sheer mayhem leashed in his eyes.

She couldn't let him see that, of course. She thrust her jaw forward and snapped, "We have to get to Vukar Tag ASAP, Captain! We need to get to that jump point *now*, and . . ."

"And in one piece, Commander!" Harcourt stepped closer, eyes iron, fists on his hips. "Everybody aboard this ship knows the modifications we made—*had* to make, just to keep this ship on station! For *two years*, Commander! And fifty-three Kilrathi raids! They know their ship, and you don't! I will comply with the orders that have been given me to the best of my ability, my crew's ability—and my ship's ability! Any interference from you will hamper our ability to execute this mission!"

"Interference!" Ramona felt a surge of anger coming to her rescue. "Captain, I am in charge of this mission!"

"And I am in command of this ship!" Harcourt turned to Grounder. "No one aboard this ship is to accept any orders from Commander Chekhova unless they have been cleared through me first! Is that understood?"

"Yes, sir!"

"Yes, sir!" Barney echoed.

"See that the order is promulgated to the entire crew at breakfast, Number One."

"You are not executing your orders to my satisfaction!" Ramona raged.

"Then you may file charges against me, in accordance with established procedure." Harcourt was suddenly icily formal. *"When this mission is completed!"*

"But at the rate you're going, this mission will never *be* completed!" Ramona knew it was untrue, of course, but all that mattered right now was winning the fight—and making this pigheaded captain realize who was boss.

"Forget about the breakfast announcement, Number One." Harcourt stepped over to his console and pressed "all stations." "Attention all crew! Wake up and hear this! All stations attend! No one is to accept orders from Commander Chekhova without my express approval! Signify understanding!"

Everybody was awake, of course. In fact, they had been halfway to battle stations when Grounder had cancelled the alarm. Now they responded from their cabins.

"Gunner A acknowledging, Captain."

"Tailgunner acknowledging, Captain."

"Gunner B acknowledging, sir."

When the roster was completed, Harcourt turned his icy gaze on Ramona. She stood, fists clenched, face dark with fury at the public humiliation. "Captain Harcourt, this is insubordination of the worst sort!"

"No, Commander. Your action took that honor."

"I am in charge of this mission, and you will have to maneuver as I prescribe in order for me to obtain the visual survey that I have been commanded to conduct!"

"And so I shall—within the margins of safety for this ship." He stepped closer, too close, crowding her. "But you will issue all your orders to me, and through me, Commander—or *I* will place *you* on report on the instant, and confine you to quarters until we have completed the jumps to the Vukar Tag System. Is that understood?"

Ramona glared at him. It was a standoff, and she knew she should stand her ground . . .

But she knew it was quicksand, and she was sinking fast.

"Understood, Captain," she grated. "I'll wait till we get to Vukar Tag."

The unspoken threat hovered in the air between them. They stood with gazes locked, every muscle tense.

Finally, Harcourt gave a curt nod. "Thank you, Commander. That will be all. Please return to your quarters."

He stepped aside. Ramona marched past him, head high, chin up . . .

Until she reached her cabin.

There, she secured the door behind her, toggled her audio pickup to "Off," then "Interrupt," so that it could not be activated from the bridge . . .

And threw herself on her bunk, the sobs tearing at her throat.

The moment of disorientation passed, and Ramona stood up from her acceleration couch, a gleam in her eye. It had been a month, a month of staying in her cabin when she could. When she couldn't, she had avoided the vindictive glances of the crew, enduring Harcourt's brittle courtesy at table, and swallowing her pride.

Now, though, *she* would be in charge. She went to the door.

The cabin speaker came to life. "Commander Chekhova to the bridge, please," Harcourt's voice said. "Commander Chekhova to the bridge."

It was a nice try at face-saving, but Ramona wasn't about to let him get away with it. She marched out into the companionway and swept up toward the bridge.

Retribution was coming.

But retribution stalled at the bridge hatchway. As she stepped through, she saw it—the battle display, repaired and working all too well, alight with colored symbols that showed her the situation.

At the center, a green circle represented the *Johnny Greene*. Halfway to the rim, a yellow circle that represented Vukar Tag lay at two o'clock—but at the rim itself was another, much larger, yellow circle—swollen, a fat yellow dot lying near it, with fireflies hovering about.

"We seem to have arrived during war games," Harcourt said, watching the display. "Makes sense, with a bunch of gung-ho pilots this far out in the boondocks, with nothing to do but chew their claws and go crazy aching to be back at the front lines, where they can earn some glory . . . Well, any commander would need to do *something* to keep their fighting skills up, not to mention keeping them from clawing out each other's throats."

"Yes." Ramona's mouth was dry. "He would." Then, "So they have fighters stationed on the gas giant's moon?"

"Artificial moon." Harcourt nodded at Billy, who said, "The readings indicate an orbital station, Commander."

Harcourt nodded. "At maximum velocity, they'd have no trouble at all cutting us off between Vukar Tag and the jump point, when we're trying for our exit." Finally, he turned and looked up at her. "Seems this planet is even better guarded than we knew."

"Yes." Ramona saw the chance to push a confrontation, and forced her attention sternly away from it. The mission came first. "Kind of strange, for a ball of sand and rock."

Harcourt turned back toward the display. "Has to be something going on in their furry little minds that we don't know about . . . Well, I guess we leave that to the folks in Psych."

"Right," Ramona said. "Our job is to bring in pictures of that world, every square foot. How can we do it, Captain?"

"Oh, we can get in there and take pictures, all right," Harcourt said breezily. "Four fly-bys, and you'll have the whole planet scanned—or do you need more?"

"Four is enough," Ramona agreed. "One polar orbit will do in a pinch, if I'm high enough up—the computers back at HQ can compensate for distortion and magnify the details, as long as I have million-pixel resolution on the crystal, which I do. They can plot a polar projection there, or magnify any square foot they want."

Harcourt nodded. "That's good, because we can get in there for an orbit, but the chances of our completing more than one without being shot down are miniscule. One, though, we might complete." He looked at her again. "What we *can't* do is get those pictures back to the jump point."

Her eyes sparked anger. She locked glares with him. "*Can't*, Captain?"

Harcourt shook his head with full conviction. "We can try, Commander. We can try like fury. But the Cat admiral who is commanding this little fleet only needs to be halfway intelligent to blow us up before we clear the orbit of Vukar Tag's moon—and even if we make it that far alive, he'll definitely cut us off before we get to the jump point."

Slowly and conscious of every ounce of dignity, Ramona turned back to the battle display, feeling a cold weight sinking within her. He was right, she knew; even a dunce would be able to keep them from escaping.

Of course, the odds that the cruiser wouldn't tear

them to pieces with its fighters, before they even completed one orbit, were miniscule, too, no matter what Harcourt said. Personally, she wouldn't even want to bet on their getting close enough for that orbit, without being shot to shreds.

But she heard herself saying, "I can't take any pictures from this far away. How long before *they* discover *us*, Captain?"

Harcourt shrugged. "Could be two seconds from now, could be an hour. It all depends on when they have a planned sentry-scan of the jump point. But we're not waiting."

"Oh?" Ramona didn't want to sound ignorant, but she had to know. "How are you going to stop them?"

"Barney?" the Captain asked.

Barney pointed at a faint, fuzzy line between Vukar Tag and the gas giant. "Asteroid belt. We can hide in there for a while, sir."

It was an old trick, Ramona knew, but it was almost always effective. With all systems shut down except life support, there was no external radiation to give them away, so any scanner would perceive them as just another piece of floating space junk. She nodded reluctantly, to hide a feeling of massive relief. "Do it."

"Cut all active sensors," Harcourt ordered.

"Actives dead." Billy leaned back, folding his arms and watching his screens. Only the passive sensors, the ones that received incoming radiation but didn't send any out, were still operating. Since the enemy ships were all putting out radiation with their own sensors—radar and its descendants—they still showed on his screen.

The asteroids didn't generate radiation, so they no longer showed—but their force field would protect them from even the largest piece of space junk they were apt to bump into. The force field was a closed system, so no radiation would leak from it to show their location.

"Let me know if anything starts moving toward us." Harcourt didn't have to say that he meant anything with a mind inside it. He turned around to Ramona. "Now. Any ideas on how we get close to the planet?"

Ramona started to say that was *his* responsibility, then bit the words off. If she was supposed to be in charge of the mission, it was exactly this sort of thing that she was supposed to be able to cover. She frowned, thinking.

Harcourt's tone softened. "Why don't you sit down, Commander? This might take a while." He looked up at Ensign Barnes. "Barney, do you suppose you could rustle up a couple of cups of coffee?"

"Sure thing, Captain." Barney headed out the hatch.

Harcourt turned back to Ramona. "Let's start by figuring how we would do it if there were no enemy in the way. Do that first, then we can make a few modifications to allow for Kilrathi stumbling blocks."

Ramona almost laughed at the idea of his "few modifications." "Left to our own devices, we'd make a slingshot around the planet—except when we got done with the horseshoe, we'd bend it a little farther and make it a complete circuit."

"You sure that's all you need, Commander?"

Ramona shrugged. "It wouldn't be, if there weren't any enemy—but there are, so let's leave it at one orbit. If we complete three hundred and sixty degrees, though, doesn't that send us off at the wrong angle for escape?"

"No, because we'd modify the angle of approach so that the angle of exit would sling us right toward the jump point." Harcourt's brows drew down in concentration. "Of course, if there *are* enemy there, we'd want to end the pass going in the wrong direction, to mislead them. Then . . ." He turned and studied the battle display for a few minutes. "We'd exit going toward the gas giant, and use it as a slingshot to alter our trajectory back toward the jump point. Tractor beam the planet."

In peacetime of course it would be highly illegal to use even a small asteroid that way, like a drunk grabbing a light pole and swinging around; the asteroid would take an entirely new—and potentially fatal—orbit, maybe even smashing into a planet. But this was war.

"We could keep that," Ramona said slowly, "if it weren't for that wing of fighters stationed on its moon."

"Right." Harcourt nodded. "I think I just found out why they chose to station them there. I've been wondering why, when they had a perfectly good moon right by Vukar Tag itself. Of course, they've got another wing there." He turned to Billy. "Any other planets?" But before Billy could answer, "No. It doesn't matter. Any rock sizable enough to hide us while we shift direction, they'll have an outpost stationed." He turned back to Ramona. "We'll have to expend fuel and realign our course once we're back in the asteroid belt."

"So we'll be coming back here?" she said slowly. "That makes sense. Now how do we manage that, if they get a few fighters in our way?"

"Shoot them down." But Harcourt's face showed that he wasn't quite as confident as he tried to sound.

Ramona nodded. "Okay, we've made a plan and allowed for a few enemy craft. Now, how about worst case? Let's say the cruisers scramble all their fighters, gun for us themselves, *and* call in the troops from the moon and the gas giant."

"Oh, we're not that important. Of course, whatever's on Vukar Tag, probably is." Harcourt turned to the bridge at large. "Anybody have any ideas?" He pressed "all stations." "Gunners and engineer to the bridge. Brainstorm needed. All and any ideas welcome, no matter how asinine, no matter how badly it won't work. Maybe it will give us a plan that will."

Ramona stared, unnerved. She had never heard of a captain depending on his crew this way. He was supposed to be alone and aloof, the source of all the ingenious plans, all by himself.

But she had learned the hard way about the closeness of this particular crew. She bit back a scathing comment.

"Capture an enemy ship," Barney said slowly.

"Oh, fine, if we're still alive when we're done!" Grounder said.

Barney shrugged and said defensively, "The Captain said *any* idea."

"I did, and it's a good one." Harcourt raised a finger. "But how do we split off the enemy ship alone so that we can grapple and board it?"

Flip, Harry, Jolie, and Lorraine came filing in. "Board a Kilrathi?" Harry said. "What is this?"

"The Dumb Idea Session," Billy told them, and they all nodded, understanding immediately.

Ramona only wished she did.

"So what do we do with it once we capture it?" Jolie asked.

"Take it in on a close approach to the planet," Grounder explained.

Billy snorted. "They'd still atomize us once they found out we wouldn't obey orders. For all they'd know, we could be a Cat psycho playing kamikaze."

"One of their own men?" Barney asked.

Jolie shrugged. "Every race has insanity. At least, we have to assume that."

"I haven't seen a crazy Cat yet!"

"Me neither—but I've never seen a Cat myself, eye to eye, anyway."

Grounder nodded. "Could be their mental cases get killed off in basic training."

Ramona was chilled to see that nobody batted an eye at the idea—but she had to admit it made sense, from what they knew about the Kilrathi.

Harcourt turned to Ramona. "Any ideas about how they think?"

"The Psych boys have come up with a lot," Ramona said slowly, "but no evidence of outright insanity yet. Of course, they wouldn't, if their maniacs never get off the ground, just get locked up in hospitals."

"Oh. The Kilrathi do let them live?" Flip asked, plainly skeptical.

"I didn't say that," Ramona admitted. "Neither did Psych. They suspect the ones who really can't function just get killed off in the natural course of things."

"So even in a stolen ship, we still get shot down," Harcourt summarized. "Still, it gives us a better chance than we've got so far. As we are now, we wouldn't get within a planetary diameter of Vukar Tag."

"A *big* planet," Lorraine said.

"As we are?" Coriander looked up. "Maybe we could change that—weld on some sheet metal cutouts that give us their silhouette. Save us the trouble of trying to capture one of them."

"It would take time . . ." Harcourt began.

"Or . . . *Wait*!" Coriander snapped her fingers, both arms out, like a traffic cop. "If we're going to talk about add-ons, let's use asteroids! We've got plenty of 'em! One day, and I could weld on enough so that we'd look like just one big piece of space junk!"

"Good, as far as it goes," Harcourt said judiciously. "We could get a lot closer—but they'd still shoot us down."

"Not if we got close enough to the planet, they wouldn't! They'd be worried about meteorites falling and kicking up so much dust that they'd have a desert in the sky instead of on the ground—so much that it would mask the sun and cut off their heat source, not to mention light for whatever few plants they manage to grow!"

"A good thought," Harcourt said. "That one has possibilities. Let's keep it in the file and see what we can add to it. Who's next?"

Barney was, then Lorraine, then Coriander again, and finally, Ramona managed to come up with an option herself. "We could stuff a large asteroid with explosives and launch it out toward Vukar Tag with a time fuse," she suggested. "While they're busy checking it out, we could zip in and steal a few quick pix." But she knew it was dumb even as she said it. "No. They'd only send a *few* ships, wouldn't they? And there would be plenty more to jump us."

"Still, the idea of a distraction is good," Harcourt said. "Anybody got any other diversions that would get *all* of them?"

They did, but none of them were really very good. They all foundered on the rock of Kilrathi fanaticism—if something even looked as though it might come near the planet, the Kilrathi would be apt to blow it to smithereens first and try to figure out where it came from later.

After an hour, Harcourt saw the first faint signs of frustration and mental fatigue. "End of session for now." He stretched. "My turn to get the coffee. Everyone take half an hour, then meet for dinner—and no talking over the situation until after dessert!"

But by the time they were done with dessert, he still hadn't come up with a better idea. He wasn't looking forward to the next skull session, as he tailed onto the line past the disposer to shove his tray in.

They filed past, then into the little lounge at the end of the wardroom. Harcourt sank into a recliner and looked around. "Anybody come up with anything new?"

They all shook their heads.

Anger burned within Ramona. She felt hopelessly inadequate, because she hadn't been able to come up with anything but one very weak idea, while her shipmates had come up with a dozen. "Well, we have to do *something*," she blurted.

"Yes, we do," Harcourt sighed. "The longer we sit and wait, the better the chances that some random scan will find us. Since we haven't thought of anything better, we'll try Chief Coriander's idea, and go in dressed up as an asteroid. Six hours shut-eye, folks. Then we start catching rocks and welding them. Billy, you have first watch."

Breakfast the next morning was pretty tense, but it showed as much in bad jokes and too much laughter, as in snarling. Right after, Grounder caught Harcourt and Ramona both trying to suit up, and read them the riot act about their responsibilities to the ship, crew, and mission. Instead, Coriander, Harry, and Flip suited up to go out with, surprisingly enough, a very large butterfly net made of steel cables; Coriander had whipped it up before breakfast. Out they went, to start catching rocks.

They filed out through the small EVA hatch, onto the hull of the ship, fastening their safety lines to ringbolts, magnetic boots clamping firm. The four stood looking out at the surrounding night, admiring the view of shifting stars for a minute, before they got down to work.

Then Coriander stiffened. "What the hell is *that*?"

They were all silent, staring.

"Well, what is it?" Harcourt's voice crackled on the

headphones. "We can't see anything in here that doesn't give off a signal. What have you spotted?"

"It gave off a signal once," Coriander said slowly, "lots of them. It's a Venture-class corvette."

The intercom was very silent for a moment.

Then Harcourt said, "You mean a Kilrathi Kamekh, don't you?"

"No," Coriander said. "I know my silhouettes, Captain—and this is more than a silhouette. It's close enough so we can see a three-quarter profile. It's a Confederation corvette, and the name on the bow is in Roman letters."

Inside, the bridge was frozen. Then Harcourt asked, "What's the name?"

"The *John Bunyan*," Coriander answered.

"*Pilgrim's Progress*," Ramona whispered.

"This pilgrim did make some progress, all right," Harcourt said, "but not enough. What kind of shape is she in, Coriander?"

"She's a wreck, Captain. Half of the tail is shot away, holes in it big enough to dock a Ferret . . . . I can't see from here, but I think the vision port is gone; at least, it's not reflecting any light. She's dead, Captain. And she died hard. Probably fled this far, and hid in here to lick her wounds."

Harcourt could envision it—a lone Confederation ship, its panicked crew holding onto composure and sanity by their fingernails, space suits closed against vacuum, hoping, waiting frantically for a rescue, while around the asteroid belt, dozens of Kilrathi fighters hovered, waiting for them to come back out.

They never had.

Harcourt pushed himself away from his console. "This time I *am* going out—with a rocket pack!"

"Captain, you can't!" Grounder cried.

"Don't worry, I'll wear a very, very long fishline."

"Then why don't you let me do it?" Harry's voice

asked over the intercom. "I'm all suited up already. Just give me the booster pack and the fishline, and I'll shoot over, attach it to the wreck. Then all you have to do is reel us in."

Harcourt hesitated, remembering his responsibilities. He sighed. "You guys get all the fun. Okay, Harry, go catch me a fish." He turned to Grounder. "See if you can find anything in the data stores about a corvette named *John Bunyan*."

Harry's boots thudded against the hull. He looked around. "There have to be eyebolts here, same as there are on our ship, Captain, for clipping onto when you go EVA."

"Yeah, there have to be," Harcourt's voice said in his earphones. The signal was coming over the wire rope, to maintain radio silence. "But after you clip it onto the ship, Harry, make sure you hold onto that cable until you're inside the hatch! Got it?"

"Oh, don't worry, Captain. I brought along an EVA cable of my own." Harry unwound it from around his waist. "And here's an eyebolt." He clipped his cable onto the eye, then made sure it was fast to his belt. He unclipped the "fishing line" and snapped it into the eyebolt, too. "It's in the eyebolt, Captain. I'm going in through the hatch now."

"As long as it's the hatch . . ."

Harry punched the entry patch and waited. When it had been too long, he frowned, and punched it again. Nothing happened.

"There's no power on board that ship," Coriander told him, "no power at all. Deader'n a duck at a shotgun convention, Captain."

"Yeah, I guess so." Harry frowned. "I could go in through one of the blast holes. . . ."

"Be *real* careful, okay, Harry?" Harcourt said. "The

broken edges on that metal might be sharp as knives. I'd rather not have you drinking vacuum."

Harry eyed one of the dark holes with a leery glance. "If it's all the same to you, Captain, I think I'd rather stay out here."

"Good." Harcourt nodded vigorously. "We'll wait until the docking's over. Just make sure your cable stays fastened on both ends, okay?"

"Will do, Captain."

Back on the bridge, Harcourt turned to Grounder. "Can I get my suit on now, Mommy?"

She gave him a look of exasperation. "Well, I suppose I can hold things together, if you're within shouting range."

Ramona turned away, so they wouldn't see her roll up her eyes in despair.

Coriander knew right where to find the external power input that the repair crews used in dry dock. After all, the *John Bunyan* was exactly like her own ship. The airlock opened; Harcourt and Ramona stepped in; the lock hatch closed.

Inside, the emergency lights gave a feeble glow. The green patch lit; the lock had cycled in record time—of course. No problem matching pressures, when there was none on either side of the door. The inner hatch swung open and the two stepped in, their helmet lamps lending harsh accents to the eldritch gloom of the emergencies.

Harcourt went first to the nearest blast hole, stuck an arm through, being careful not to touch any of the jagged edges, and felt the connector Harry pushed into his hand. "Thanks," he said, so Harry would know he could let go, then pulled, turning away. The computer cable came in behind him—a coil floating free between the two ships, connected at its far end to the brain of the *Johnny Greene*.

They went through corridors that were eerily familiar, copies of the ones on their own ship, with the computer cable snaking behind them. They stepped into the bridge just as . . .

The ship accumulated enough power, and lit all the instruments.

The familiar, warm darkness was lightened by the battle display—but only a grid of curving lines, as theirs had been not very long ago. The individual screens glowed to life. The work lights spotlighted the consoles at each position—and the crewmen slumped over them.

Harcourt was intensely grateful that the space suits, and especially the helmets, prevented him from seeing the mummies within.

Ramona paced beside him, completely silent. Harcourt wasn't feeling all that talkative himself, but he said, by way of apology, "We have to know what happened," and stepped up to the captain's console.

The captain sat slumped over the slanted surface, helmet on gauntlets. Harcourt was glad he didn't have to push the corpse aside; the cable receptacle was low on the console's side, and clear. He pushed it in, made sure the two connectors meshed, then said, "Okay, Chief. Drain the memory."

"Yes, sir," Coriander's voice said in his earphones. "Just a straight file transfer, or do you want an audio analog while it's going?"

"Just the straight file. Let me know when the dump is finished, so we can come home."

"Yes, sir."

There was no sound, of course—they hadn't called for audio analog—but Harcourt saw the green jewel come on.

He turned away, looking out over the bridge, trying to avoid staring at the bodies. He noticed the gaping hole in the roof, the crewman lying prone on the floor with a long, brown-stained gash in his pressure suit, the two who sat side by side, arms about one another, slumped in death. . . .

"Dump finished, Captain," Coriander reported in his ears.

"Gotcha, Chief." Harcourt turned back to Ramona. "Anything else we need to see?"

Ramona glanced at him with haunted eyes. Then her gaze roved around the rest of the bridge. She shook her head. "Nothing, Captain." She turned and went out.

Harcourt unplugged the cable and followed her, rolling it as he went.

They cycled through the airlock, hauled themselves across the linking cable to their own ship, and cycled through again, blessing the hiss of air as it jetted into the lock. The patch glowed green; the hatch opened, and they stepped through. Ramona gave her helmet a half-twist and tilted it back with a grateful sigh. "Those poor bastards," she said. "Those poor, brave bastards."

Harcourt nodded, thinking that "lambs" might have been a better term—sacrificial lambs.

No. Not lambs. They had died fighting—or trying to. "We have to bury them," he said. "We owe them that much."

"Why?" Ramona countered. "They've got the perfect coffin as it is."

Her face was very bleak. Glancing at her, Harcourt felt a chill. What was going on in that mind of hers?

"Captain to the bridge!"

"Coming." Harcourt hurried away, unfastening his pressure suit. He came into the bridge with his helmet still under his arm. "What did you get, Chief?"

"The whole ship's log," Coriander said, "at least for this mission, from the time they were asked to volunteer up until they died." Her face paled as she watched the screen.

Harcourt was tempted to ask for an audio analog. Instead, he said, "Give me the digest."

"The *John Bunyan* was ordered to run a reconnaissance mission past Vukar Tag," she said, "six months ago. They tried to get close to the planet, but fighters swarmed up to defend, and they had to run for the asteroid belt. They were Swiss cheese by the time they got here, but they had taken out seven Kilrathi ships on the way. The only atmosphere left was in the pressure bottles on their suits. They stayed in the asteroid belt, hoping the Kilrathi would give up and go away so they could make a run for the jump point—but the Cats stayed. They hung around for eight hours, twelve hours . . . The captain recorded the last entry just before he blacked out from lack of oxygen." She paused, then said, "The computer made one final automatic entry, noting that the fusion plant had been hit by a parting shot, a random Kilrathi missile. Then the reserve battery ran out, and the computer couldn't do anything more, either."

Harcourt turned to Ramona. "Did you know there had been a ship assigned to this mission before us?"

Ramona stared, frozen. Then she gave a quick, jerky nod. "Yes, Captain. They didn't tell you, huh?"

"Not a word." Harcourt's lips thinned. He had a nasty, sneaking suspicion that Ramona had known the information had not been included in his briefing—but maybe he was being paranoid. After all, it *had* sounded like a good deal, at the time . . .

As long as they weren't told the whole truth.

"Captain," Billy called.

"What is it?" Harcourt knew that tone in Billy's voice. His tension increased.

Billy was pointing out the vision port. "Silhouette. Just coming out from behind that big rock."

Harcourt stared. Then he said, "Can you get that on your screen?"

"Electron telescope." Billy jabbed at his panel a few times, and another screen lit. "There it is, Captain. Full magnification?"

Harcourt nodded.

Billy twisted something, the image expanded . . .

Into the silhouette of a Venture-class corvette. Badly damaged, missing a lot of pieces, but a Confederation corvette nonetheless.

"So," Harcourt breathed, "we're Number Three." He turned to Ramona. "Or is it Number Four? Or Five? Or Six?"

She shook her head, ghostly pale. "They didn't tell you this, Captain? They really didn't tell you any of it?"

Harcourt forced his voice to be gentle. "No, Commander. None."

"We're Number Three," she said, "and the Admiralty's really upset that the first two missions disappeared."

"I'll just bet they are!"

Ramona shrugged helplessly. "They're afraid all this spying will attract the Kilrathi's attention."

Harcourt just stared at her.

Then he said, in a very soft voice, "Oh, are they really, now?"

He turned back to look at the hulk on the screen. "I'd say they attracted attention, Commander. Yes, I think you could say that."

Ramona was silent.

After a minute, Harcourt turned back to her. Her eyes had hardened, but they were still fixed on the wrecked silhouette on the screen. "You know," she said, "if you didn't captain a corvette yourself, you might never recognize that shape, it's been chewed up so badly."

"Yes, you might not." Harcourt felt as though a

gust of cold air had blown through him. What was she thinking?

He found out soon enough.

"We need to talk in private, Captain."

He looked in her eyes and said, "Yes. Of course. The wardroom." He turned to the staring eyes all about them. "No one interrupt." Then he rose and went out the door.

Ramona followed.

In the wardroom, Ramona toggled off the intercom and locked it. Then she told him what she had in mind.

"No! It's sure suicide! I won't hear of it!"

"It's the only way." Ramona paced the wardroom. "We need a ruse, right? Well, this is it—better than going in disguised as an asteroid, even. A dead hulk, no emissions of any kind, so badly shot up that its silhouette isn't even recognizable any more! I get aboard that wreck, you tow me up to cruising velocity, then disengage and let me go. Vukar Tag grabs me into orbit, but I'm going so fast that the planet can't hold me. I swing around it once, get my pictures, shoot off toward the asteroid belt again—and voila! Mission accomplished!"

"Impossible!" Harcourt snapped. "If we're off by one degree on the calculations, you'll get sucked into Vukar Tag's gravity well and crash!"

Ramona shrugged. "That's the chance I take, that everyone in the Fleet takes whenever they go into battle. What's the matter? Don't trust your own computer? Or Ensign Barnes?"

"Barney is a damn fine astrogator!" Harcourt barked.

"Yes, I know—so crashing is the least of my worries." She came back, leaned over him. "Look, I volunteered for an extremely dangerous mission. I knew I might not come back alive."

"Yeah, but at least you could accomplish something by your death! This way, you might still get shot down before you get close enough for a single frame! When the Kilrathi see a bogey coming in to Vukar Tag, they're apt to hit it with everything they've got, just to be on the safe side!"

"No, they won't," Ramona said, "because they'll be too busy chasing after you."

Harcourt didn't move, but he went rigid. "Oh, will they?"

"Sure. A diversion, distraction, just as you were talking about with your crew during the brainstorm session."

Harcourt leaned back, eyeing her very warily. "Just what kind of distraction did you have in mind?"

"Act like a Viking," she said. "Private enterprise. A privateer, Free Trader—call it what you want. You attack one of their supply ships."

Harcourt just stared at her in disbelief.

Then the idea sank in, and he went loose. "Yes. That would distract their attention, wouldn't it?"

"You bet it would! They'll come swarming up to stop you! As soon as you see they're on their way, you take off and head for the jump point."

"And leave you behind? Not a chance!"

"Simmer down, Captain—I'm not talking about suicide." Ramona held up a hand. "Remember how we talked about using the planet as a slingshot, tractoring a chunk of atmosphere, ending up with us heading right toward the jump point? Well, instead, you have *me* come out heading toward the asteroid belt. Then you loop around, attack one of their fighters, exchange a few shots, then cut off all exterior emissions. They'll think you're dead, and won't worry too much when you 'crash' into the asteroid belt and don't come back out. Once you're in there, you can maneuver on thrusters and pick me up."

Harcourt sat glowering at her, trying to find a flaw in the plan.

He found it.

"Fine," he said, "but how do we get home?"

"You won't really be damaged, won't be losing air the way the *John Bunyan* was." Ramona knew she was talking more from hope than from logic. "But you'll pretend to be, so they'll think you are—and they'll wait a few days, maybe a week, then go away. But your life-support systems will be intact, and you have rations enough for a couple of months. So when they decide you're dead, and go away back to their bases . . ."

"*If* they decide we're dead and go away."

Ramona shrugged. "They did with the *John Bunyan*. Why shouldn't they do it with you?"

Harcourt glared at her, trying to think of an answer again—but this time, he couldn't. It was a lousy plan, one that was almost guaranteed to get her killed, without the information she'd come to get . . . "What if you *are* shot down in the middle of it? And the chances are very good that you will be. The pictures don't get back to us, the mission fails, you're dead—for nothing!"

"Of course I get the pictures back to you," she said scornfully. "I beam them by microwave. There will be plenty of time, before you turn to fake that attack on the fighter. Even if I do crash or get shot down, you'll have all the pictures I shot up until then."

A chill enveloped Harcourt's back.

She saw it in his eyes and nodded. "Yes, Captain. Once you have that information, you have to forget about me, if that's the only way to escape and get the data back to the Admiralty."

"No," Harcourt whispered. "I won't abandon one of my crew."

"I'm *not* one of your crew," she countered. "I'm in

charge of the mission—and I rank you. Especially when I'm no longer aboard your own ship."

Harcourt said nothing. He couldn't. Not just because she had finally hit the point at which she could legitimately give him orders—but because she was right.

There are times when you have to take the only course of action that's open to you, no matter how much you dislike it. This was one of them.

Oh, Harcourt could have commanded them all to turn the ship around, leap through the jump point, go home, and report that the mission was impossible. He would also have been stripped of rank or, at the very least, given up hope of all promotion. But his crew would have been alive, and so would Ramona.

She, however, seemed to have a death wish—and she *was* in charge of the mission. He couldn't go back without disobeying orders—technically, mutiny, even though it was his own ship.

Harry and Flip volunteered for the grisly task of moving all the bodies back to the wardroom of the *John Bunyan*. If Ramona's scheme worked, if she came out alive, they would take her aboard the *Johnny Greene* and Harcourt would read the Service for the Dead over the derelict, then leave it as a floating coffin in the asteroid belt forever.

If it didn't work, there wouldn't be anything left to bury.

Ramona moved into the bridge of the *John Bunyan*. All her mysterious cases came open. She set up her arcane gear, replaced the dead nose camera with something that looked like the grandmother of all gadgets, then pressed Coriander into helping her install some very sophisticated cameras of her own. The Chief mounted the microwave dish for her and hooked up a little computer programmed to keep it always aimed at the jump point and therefore toward the *Johnny Greene*. Then they substituted a magnetic grapple for the towing hook . . .

And sat. And waited. And waited.

Finally, Billy called out, "Transport! Just in from the jump point!"

"Battle stations!" Harcourt snapped, and Grounder hit the klaxon.

The crew scrambled to stations, Lorraine fired up their two original engines, and they burst out of the asteroid belt as though they had the Wild Hunt right behind. They accelerated up to cruising velocity, aiming the *John Bunyan* exactly right, and let it go. The hulk sped away from them on a trajectory that should loop it around Vukar Tag in a hyperbolic orbit, spinning it out faster than it came in.

Harcourt triggered one short transmission: "Good luck, Commander. We'll be waiting."

He hoped.

"That," said Billy, "is one gutsy lady."

"I really feel badly now, about having been such a shrew to her," Grounder said.

Harcourt shook his head. "You had orders to follow, Lieutenant."

"Yes," said Barney, "but we could have tried to warm up to her."

"I did," Coriander said. "She wasn't having any."

Harcourt nodded heavily. "I think someone must have told her about 'the loneliness of command' at a very impressionable age—so she decided that if she was a commander, she should always be lonely." Then he shook himself. "Enough. We could have been warmer, we should have been, but she didn't exactly encourage it. She's got a job to do, we've got a job to do—and if we want her to have a hope in Hades of living through it, we'd better get busy with our end. Turn and aim for that transport. How long till we catch it, Number One?"

"Two hours, Captain."

"Close enough."

"Fighters coming up off the moon like popcorn without a lid!" Billy reported.

But a stern chase is a long chase, and the *Johnny Greene* was already up to cruising velocity. When it turned, levelling off toward the transport, Harcourt ordered, "All engines full."

Now they did what Ramona had commanded at the wrong time—kicked in their two captured Kilrathi engines. On all four, they ran up to the maximum velocity for any Confederation corvette, and past it.

Way past it.

The supply ship swelled in their screen, bigger and bigger.

"They're coming up off the gas giant's orbital station!" Billy snapped.

On the battle display, the *Johnny Green* was a bright green circle at the center. Above it, near the top, was the yellow oblong of the supply ship. Below, there was an arc of red arrowheads—Kilrathi fighters.

Now more little red arrowheads came swooping in from ten o'clock.

"You wanted attention? We got it!" Harry howled. "When can I start shooting, Captain?"

"You've got ranging computers again," Harcourt answered. "When they register enemy, you can start shooting."

Jolie gave a whoop of joy.

A minute, five minutes, ten . . .

"Range!" Billy snapped.

Jolie howled.

Her gun was in tune now—there was no *Whumpf!* echoing through the hull—but dots of blue sprang up in the space between the red arrowheads and the green dot.

Even Harcourt felt the satisfaction of being back in battle, the relief now that the shooting had started. Fear hollowed him, but a terrible excitement seethed up to fill that emptiness. He knew he very well might not live through this one—but he felt more intensely alive than he ever had.

How was Ramona feeling, he wondered? His gaze strayed toward the rim of the screen at eight o'clock, where the fat yellow arc that was Vukar Tag loomed. There was no blue dot near it—she was flying a dead ship, after all. Harcourt ached to send out a scan, but knew they couldn't spare it; ached to know how she was doing, what she was seeing . . .

Coriander had charged all the batteries on the *John Bunyan*, and Ramona had brought plenty of her own, so she could watch the screen to see what her cameras saw as they recorded the fly-by. Of course, she couldn't activate them until they were near the planet, but the ship's batteries were enough to show her what the passive sensors saw—not on the huge battle display, of course; it would have taken a major dry dock to repair that. Coriander had revived the lookout's screen, though, and Ramona watched, her heart in her throat, a pool of icy fear in her stomach sending out rivulets all through her body. She saw the little red arrowheads darting up from Vukar Tag, darting toward her; they had to be levelling their guns on her . . .

Then they were swinging away, passing her by. She heaved a huge sigh of relief. She was only a piece of floating space junk to them, after all—an asteroid about to become a meteor, to be burned up as it flashed through the atmosphere, on its way toward becoming dust. Nothing to worry about; it certainly was nothing that was going so fast that they couldn't come back and finish it, if they had to.

But the active blip, the "Free Trader" that was pouncing on their transport—that was something they had to eliminate. What impelled them to send what must be every ship in the system against one lone corsair, though? The logical conclusion sank within her like lead: they couldn't let any Confederation ship get away with news of Vukar Tag.

What the hell was on there, anyway?

Well, she would find out in a few minutes. The planet loomed beyond the vision port, hovering over her, ready to fall on her . . . .

She pressed the "record" patch, and her camera's viewfinder lit up.

Then, suddenly, Vukar Tag was beneath her, and she was skimming over it.

There was nothing to hear from her cameras, of course—everything was recorded in solid memory with automatic backups in a redundant system. None of the archaic frustrations of a transport system, of spinning wheels and fragile tape that could snap or stretch, nor any danger of a crash from a magnetic or laser head hovering over a spinning surface. The data went straight into memory, with an anti-erase lock.

The lenses were electronic, able to show her a drinking mug on the surface in fine detail—but just in case they failed, there was one optical zoom lens, only a foot long, but capable of the same amazing magnification as the electron-telescope.

What did she see?

Sand.

She was zoomed out as wide as she could be—she had to cover a whole hemisphere, since she could only be sure of the one orbit (and not even that, really). The boys back home could expand anything they saw that might be worth expanding. For herself, out of idle curiosity, she could isolate any one feature of the surface, hold it in a buffer memory, and expand it to full view.

She intended to. If she was going to give her life for this look, she meant to have it.

She tested the buffer on a faint line that she thought might be a mountain range. Sure enough, there they were, rounded humps swelling up toward her—old mountains, worn down by wind. Not water, though—there was too little of it on this planet . . .

She cancelled the view, hovering over her instruments, the enemy forgotten in the thrill of fulfilling her mission, of seeing the closely guarded secret, whatever it may have been.

The miles unrolled beneath her. The pole shifted slowly, a tiny ice cap moving from the top of the screen to the center, then to the bottom, and the southern ice cap began to come into view. . . .

All of a sudden, she remembered the Kilrathi fighters. She stepped back over to the lookout's screen. There they were, red sawteeth chasing a green dot, thousands of kilometers away.

But what was this? A larger triangle, a bomber at least, perhaps a small ship, spurring away from a cruiser, chasing after her!

Her heart leaped into her throat again. She poised, ready to leap to her recording equipment, ready to hit the patch that would activate the burst transmission of all the data gathered so far . . .

And saw a tiny oblong in the center of the Southern hemisphere, halfway down her screen. It was too regular to be a natural formation.

Triumph flamed through her veins as she punched to isolate the oblong into the buffer, then swelled it to fill the screen . . .

It was a fairy-tale castle.

It was a bird's-eye view of a fairy-tale castle, all

turrets and alabaster and sapphire, glowing in the sunset as though it were all made of jewels.

All about it lay only desert, empty rock, empty sand . . .

The words leaped unbidden into her head:

"My name is Ozymandias, king of kings.
Look on my works, ye Mighty, and despair!"
Nothing beside remains. Round the decay
Of that colossal wreck, boundless and bare
The lone and level sands stretch far away.

This was it. She didn't know how or why she knew it, didn't know what it was or why it was important—but this was it. This was why Vukar Tag was so heavily guarded, why it was crucial. Some ancient treasure of the Kilrathi, some source of racial pride, an emotional anchor, a ceremonial site—whatever it was, it was vital to them, drastically important.

A beep came from the sentry screen. She turned, staring at it, saw the red triangle closing on the green dot in the center of the screen that was her own hulk.

She leaped, and hit the "Transmit" button.

Above her, atop the hulk, the microwave dish sent a half-second burst of encoded data spinning after the *Johnny Greene* at a hundred times its speed . . .

Ramona felt the final, surging euphoria of victory. She stood next to her recording equipment, watching the empty sand unroll before her, feeling the singing victory, but with the horrible dread coming up beneath it, the certainty of doom.

There was nothing she could do. The ship had no engines, no thrusters, no way to steer or run at all. She could only wait, only trust to blind luck, only hope that she would live to see the completion of her orbit, to once more see the *Joh—*

* * *

Aboard the *Johnny Greene*, Billy saw the flash and let out a high, keening wail.

"They got her." Grounder sat rigid.

"Annihilated!" Billy mourned. "Nothing left but atoms! Brave woman! Valiant warrior!"

"Did she die for nothing?" Coriander barked.

"No," Billy said. "I got her burst transmission five seconds before the flash. Stored on crystal, and I just backed it up. Heaven only knows what it was!" His voice sank low, tragic in tone. "Lord, I hope it was worth her life!"

Grounder stared at him, amazed, realizing Ramona had made far more of an impact on Billy than any of them had known—including him. He had a thing for her. Shrew though she was, he had it bad.

"I hope it's worth *our* lives!" Harcourt's voice snapped them out of it. "No point in going back for her now. You're sure she's dead, Billy? Not the slightest chance?"

Billy shook his head, already deep in grief. "When a blue dot turns yellow and takes up that much space on the screen, Captain, there's nothing left but ions. I don't know what they hit her with, but it did a real thorough job."

"Then the hell with Vukar Tag, and the hell with their asteroid belt," Harcourt snapped. "We can make her death worth something, by getting that data back to the Admiralty."

The ship began to shudder, ever so slightly.

"How much longer can we take the stress of full thrust, Chief?" Harcourt snapped.

"Half an hour sure, forty-five minutes maybe." Coriander watched the battle display, transfixed.

"How far to the jump point at this velocity, Barney?" Harcourt demanded.

"Twenty-five minutes, if those fighters from the gas giant don't get us first," Barney answered.

"Range!" Billy shouted, his face suddenly savage. "Tear 'em apart, gunners!"

"Fire," Harcourt said quickly, so that Billy wouldn't have been giving an order beyond his rank.

Harry's whoop echoed through the intercom, with Flip's warbling yell right behind it. The guns were in phase, so they felt nothing, they heard nothing—but the battle display showed dots of blue breaking out all along the line of red arrowheads. Blue met red; they turned yellow, expanding.

But something big was coming up behind them—a destroyer.

"Missiles!" Harcourt snapped. "Fire One! Two!"

Larger blue dots shot away from the *Johnny Greene*, through the red arrowheads—but the arrowheads converged on them like bees on a bear. One blue circle turned yellow with the dozen arrowheads that had beset it—but the other broke through.

Some of the red arrowheads were past the little blue dots.

"Hit 'em, Harry!" Harcourt yelled,

Harry answered with a cowboy's holler, and the blue dots peppered the red arrowheads. One went up in a yellow flash, another, another . . .

The last spat a red dot of its own.

The *Johnny Greene* rocked, the sound of the explosion echoing through its hull.

"Harry!" Harcourt snapped.

"Oh, I'm fine," Harry growled, disgusted. "There! And there!"

The red arrowhead turned yellow, expanding.

"Jump point ahead!" Grounder snapped.

"Three Cats astern!" Billy cried.

Jolie whooped over the intercom.

On the battle display, another field of blue dots sprang out behind the *Johnny Greene*.

"Got any use for a dead Cat?" Jolie shrilled. "I'll get you a few!"

On the screen, one of the arrowheads turned into a yellow flash, expanding—but the other lanced through the arc of blue dots, closing on the green circle that was their ship, closing, closing . . .

The ship bucked, as though it were a schooner that had just plowed over a submerged sandbank, then kept on. The stars in the viewscreen shifted drastically, to a totally different sky.

Harcourt went limp. So did the bridge crew—except for Billy. "Jump completed!" he called out. "No bogeys in evidence, no hostiles at all!"

"We're clear," Grounder whispered.

"Only for the moment." Harcourt knew he had to keep them moving. They didn't dare let up—not for long. "Barney, plot the course for the next jump point. They could be right on our tails."

"Course plotted and feeding!"

"I might've known. Chief! Damage?"

"None from the jump." Coriander scanned her board. "Just from that one shot that got through—a leak amidships."

"Patched," Lorraine's voice said over the intercom. "But it won't last long."

"It doesn't need to." Coriander picked up her tool kit. "I'm on my way."

She had recovered amazingly quickly, Harcourt thought as he watched her slim figure dart out the hatch, a figure that was more remembered than seen. "Keep scanning, Billy. No real reason to expect them to have stationed an intercept out here, but you never know."

"They will from now on, I betcha." Billy kept his eyes on the screen.

"You don't really think they will, do you, Captain?" Grounder asked.

Harcourt shrugged. "You always assume your enemy will do the worst—and the most unexpected, Lieutenant. You know that."

More to the point, though, he needed to keep their minds off the gallant woman who had died doing her duty, to whom they really should have shown much more kindness . . .

He felt the guilt sinking within him, fought it, knowing he had only done his duty. It was up to him, though, to make sure she had not died in vain. Whatever it was on Vukar Tag that the Cats guarded so closely, the Admiralty would find some way to use it against them.

Kipling's lines echoed in his head:

If there should follow a thousand swords
To carry my bones away,
Belike the price of a jackal's meal
Were more than a thief could pay.

Oh, the Kilrathi were thieves, all right—very vicious, but very competent, thieves—and the revenge for Ramona would follow.

Oh, yes, the revenge would follow.

PART II

END RUN

by William R. Forstchen

• CHAPTER I

Cleared for landing, Lieutenant Commander Jason "Bear" Bondarevsky turned his Ferret in on final approach. The carrier off his port quarter was the newest addition to the fleet, emblazoned upon its armored bow the proud name *CVE-8 Tarawa*—and the sight of her did not impress him in the slightest.

His idea of a carrier was more on the lines of the *Concordia* where, after the mutiny incident on the old *Gettysburg*, Admiral Tolwyn had taken him in for a tour of duty. With the casualties of the last two campaigns, promotion had been rapid, and he had never dreamed that at the ripe old age of twenty-five he would actually be in charge of an entire wing aboard a carrier . . . but what a carrier. He shook his head with disdain.

Maniac had roared with sardonic delight when he had heard about the promotion and transfer to this new ship.

"A carrier, you're kidding aren't you? Its a damned transport scow and a death trap," Maniac announced, and Jason could not help but agree.

The CVE class had been a source of intense debate back in the *Concordia*'s pilot ready room. This new class of ships was a rush job to try and plug the gaps after the heavy losses of the last campaign. Nine transport ships, already three quarters completed, were pulled out of the transport assembly stations and converted into escort carriers; and a single look at her convinced Jason of the folly of the whole damn thing.

There was only a single landing and launch deck, no backup if they should ever take a hit. That was a tactic the Kilrathi were most fond of, and he remembered the surprise strike on the *Concordia*, which had shut down both launch bays and almost finished the ship off, except for some last minute help from Phoenix and his wingmate, scrambling up from a nearby base. New design doctrine was calling for three, even four launch bays, and now some idiot desk jockey back in headquarters had come out with this.

As he cleared the forward bow he spared a quick look from his approach vector readout to look at the forward defense. A heavy quad-barreled neutron gun was mounted on the bow, obviously cobbled on to the transport's frame and held together with a little spit and glue. To either side of the approach deck were two mass driver cannons, medium caliber at least. As he came in on approach he had seen two more beam weapons and several launch racks for missiles along the bottom of the ship. He could only hope that at least the missiles had the new gatling launch system that could pop out a spread of ten of the new anti-torpedo rounds in under two seconds.

Jason nudged reverse thrust and kicked in a little lateral move to starboard. The damn entry port was as narrow as a needle's eye and he felt embarrassed by the necessity of this last minute adjustment. Landing on fleet carriers had spoiled him; there wasn't the slightest room for error here.

It wasn't the type of landing the new wing commander should put on in his first approach. He felt a flash of anger with himself, he had violated his own cardinal rule—a mission isn't over till it's over so don't think of anything else till the job's done.

He cleared the energy field airlock and felt the slowing resistance of air on his wings. There was barely thirty meters of maneuver room inside the hangar and the deck was packed. To his port side was a squadron of F-54C Rapiers. On the starboard side was the squadron of strike fighter/bombers, F-57B Sabres, with the new upgrade of a copilot in a cramped backseat to handle the weapons launch while the pilot continued to fly. He still wasn't sure if he liked this hybrid design, created specifically for the CVE class, when it was realized that there simply wasn't enough hangar space for the battle-tested Broadswords. A pilot and flight officer crammed into a space originally designed for one was going to be a tight fit. He wondered if the design boys had thought this one out all the way. That was something that always bothered him—an instrument located in the wrong place might mean that a valuable bit of information was overlooked—or while wasting a second to take a look you don't see the shot coming straight into your face.

It was far too tight a deck to take a last squirt off the reverse thrusters and Jason punched down hard on the deck, gritting his teeth at the screeching of the landing skids. From the corner of his eye he saw deck personnel step back to avoid the shower of sparks. He slid down the deck, the nose of his ship jerking to a stop just inches shy of the emergency barrier nets. Cursing, he leaned back in his seat and quickly ran through his checkout, ignoring the bump of the ladder and the shadow of a crew chief scrambling up to wait outside the cockpit.

Shutting down the engine pumps, Jason double-checked that all weapons were on secured safety, and then leaned over to toggle the eject safety. After making sure everything was secure he finally toggled off the main engine and shielding circuits. More than one pilot had smeared himself on a hangar deck ceiling by not double-checking the eject safety before shutting down, since a full power failure and shield cut off would automatically initiate ejection unless overridden within five seconds. The design manual said that such an event was not supposed to happen if the ship was shut down in a pressurized environment, but more than one pilot had learned that sometimes the manual just didn't get it quite right. He hit the canopy switch and it flipped open.

"Welcome aboard, sir!"

"Well damn me if it isn't Sparks."

The crew chief was looking down at him and grinning broadly.

"So they got you on this bucket too," Jason said, glad to see the familiar and attractive face of the finest crew chief he had ever worked with.

"You'll find quite a few of the old crowd here," Sparks said, "we're the only experienced hands on this ship. The admiral scrapped up a couple of dozen of us to help this ship along. The rest are all new, straight out of the training schools."

He sighed and shook his head.

"I wonder whose nest we took a dump on to get this assignment," he sighed.

"Oh, she doesn't seem to be that bad a ship," Sparks replied, and Jason could detect the false sincerity in her voice.

"I wish I could believe you, Sparks."

"The Captain's waiting for you, sir, so I guess you should get moving."

"How is he?"

"I'll leave that for you to decide, sir," she replied, showing the age old diplomacy of a non-commissioned officer who didn't want to tell an upper rank just how she really felt.

Jason unsnapped his harness and stood up to look around. He could sense that all eyes on the deck were focused on him. After all, he was the new commander of all the ships flying off the *Tarawa*. He ignored their stares, his attention for the moment focused solely on the gleaming row of fighter craft under his command. They all looked new at least; that was an advantage, and a curse, since there were always some bugs to be worked out in the first couple of hundred hours of flying. The squadron of Ferret scout and recon ships were crammed in behind the Sabres. That would have to be changed at once. Moving the heavier craft could waste several precious minutes if the crunch was on and they needed a quick recon launch.

He was tempted to pass a comment on to Sparks but let it pass. He'd find out who the launch deck officer was later on and get it taken care of.

Sparks scrambled down the ladder and he followed. As he hit the deck a shrill piping cut the air that sent a corkscrew shiver down his back. Damn, with the new promotion he now rated the ritual of a formal greeting for his first reporting aboard.

He turned away from his Ferret and saw half a dozen deck crew lined up in shining dress blues, all at attention. Coming to attention himself, he saluted the Confederation flag which hung from the bulkhead wall and then saluted the young ensign commanding the detail.

"Permission to come aboard," Jason snapped, trying not to sound too peeved by the pomp and circumstance.

"Permission granted, sir," and her voice cracked, coming out like a high-pitched squeak.

He stood for several seconds, not sure what to do next and then he saw a towering dark form lumbering through the main doorway onto the hangar deck.

The fighter pilot approaching him came to attention and then with his usual, almost languid air, that seemed to drip with depression and futility, Doomsday saluted.

"The captain's waiting to see you, sir."

Jason grinned as he returned the salute and quickly fell in beside his old comrade. The two left the deck, heading down a narrow corridor.

"So my request came through," Jason said, barely able to keep from smiling.

"What request?"

"When Admiral Tolwyn laid the promotion of lieutenant commander on me and then sent me off to this bucket he said I could pick my squadron commanders."

"So you're the damn jerk who got me pulled from R&R and sent back out here?" Doomsday groaned, looking over at Jason.

"I needed somebody I could count on, and I wanted you to handle the fighter bomber squadron."

"Something in my bones told me I'd wind up dying soon, and you're making sure it comes true."

"Hey, I got you the extra stripe, what more do you want?"

Doomsday allowed the slightest flicker of a smile.

"Thanks, at least it'll mean a bigger pension for my family after you're done killing me."

"How's the captain?"

"I'll let you decide," Doomsday said, and pointed towards the wardroom door. "He's waiting in there for you, Jason."

Without offering to come along Doomsday turned and disappeared back down the corridor.

Jason went up to the door and knocked.

There was a long pause and he was tempted to knock again when he heard a soft, almost distant voice.

"Come."

He opened the door and stepped into the room.

The captain of the ship was standing with his back to the door, his attention focused on a 3-D holo map of the sector. The captain stood, shoulders slightly hunched, as if deeply absorbed in thought, all his attention concentrated on the map, as if attempting to divinate out some hidden meaning.

Jason felt uncomfortable with the pose, his discomfort magnified when he noticed that the leather of the captain's empty chair was gradually shifting outward, a sign that the commanding officer had been sitting, and then got up and turned to the map before calling for Jason to come in.

The captain studied the map for a long moment as if Jason were not even in the room. Finally he turned around, moving slowly, first looking at Jason over his shoulder. The man's face was lined with deep set wrinkles as if the skin was gradually losing its hold on his skull. His eyes were dark, intense. He was balding on top, his hair combed over from one side as if to cover up the loss. His nose was bulbous, heavily veined and dark red. A drinker's nose, Jason realized.

"Lieutenant Commander Jason Bondarevsky?"

Jason saluted.

The captain studied him for a long moment before finally saluting in return.

"I watched your landing on the screen, seemed a bit shaky, yes indeed, a bit shaky it was."

Jason said nothing. Not a great landing, he had to agree, but it had nothing to do with shakiness. However he was not going to blurt out a defensive response.

The captain looked at him, his features set, and then finally the corners of the mouth creased upward.

"How is my good friend Admiral Tolwyn?"

"In fine health when I left him, sir."

The captain nodded gravely, as if this was the most important news in the universe.

"I've looked at your file, Bondarevsky. You were part of that *Gettysburg* mutiny affair a year or so back."

"I was, sir." Jason replied quietly, not wanting to sound defensive.

"Dirty business that, a nasty dirty business."

"How so?" Jason asked cautiously.

The official court of inquiry had fully cleared him of the situation, acknowledging the criminal actions of his old captain, and agreeing with the crew's decision to remove him from command. Jason had come out of it not only with a full exoneration but a decoration and the confidence of Admiral Tolwyn.

"Just that, Bonevsky, a dirty business."

"It's Bondarevsky," Jason said.

"Yes, of course."

He walked back to the map and turned his back on Jason for a moment, posing as if caught up in some deep and profound decision. He finally turned, a smile creasing his features.

"I'm Commodore Thaddeus O'Brian, welcome aboard."

Jason took his hand, noticing that the grip was weak, the palms clammy. He found he was forming an instant dislike and he fought it down. He knew too many people who made snap decisions about what they thought of others, a trait that he didn't quite approve of. Also, this was his first real command, and it just wouldn't work to have yet another conflict with a superior officer.

"Your first time aboard a CVE?"

"Yes, sir."

"Well, what do you think of her?"

The captain looked up at him almost as if seeking some approval.

"I haven't had a chance to form an opinion yet, sir, I just came aboard."

"Well, let's go have a look at my ship then."

Going to the back of his office, Thaddeus opened another door and motioned for Jason to follow as they started down a short corridor.

"Had a hand in the design of her, I did," O'Brian announced, his pride evident.

"Oh really, sir?"

"Yes indeed, I was with transport ship design and helped in the change over of this model to light escort carrier configuration. Since I knew transports inside and out, the Admiralty office decided to give this one to me."

"Transport ship design?"

"Not much excitement, oh no," O'Brian said, his voice suddenly cold. "Captained transports for twenty years before being sent into the office back at Earth. But without us, you fly-boy heroes wouldn't have been able to get past the airlock. We're the ones who kept you going with weapons, food, everything that a fleet needs and little thanks we got, precious little thanks."

Jason noticed the tone of bitterness in O'Brian's voice. The rivalry between those who were at the cutting edge of the war and those in the rear was nothing new to him; he knew it was as old as war itself and he had experienced it often enough while on leave. At times it could get so intense that those at the front and those at the rear could hate each other even more than the common enemy.

"Here's our bridge," O'Brian announced, leading Jason into the semi-darkened room.

It was located near the topside of the ship, just forward of the jump drive room. A small crew of deck officers and non-coms manned the various banks of displays and instruments.

"They're almost all new people, a bit slow, but

someday they'll get the hang of it," O'Brian announced.

Jason looked around and saw more than one of the crew members hunch over with the captain's sarcastic words.

"When Admiralty finalized the design concept for the light escort carrier they saw four roles," O'Brian announced.

"The mission design calls for it to serve as a transport for fighter, recon, and bomber spacecraft to keep the heavy carriers freshly stocked. We haul them out, and then they fly straight in to their new homes ready for action."

"We were running short more than once," Jason replied, "it's a good idea, better than having to uncrate them from the transports and spend several hundred man-hours of work with reassembly and testing."

"Why? Did you have a problem with how our transports delivered them to you?"

Jason looked around the room and saw several of the watch officers look over at him curiously, as if wondering how he would respond.

"No, sir, it was just a question of time, that's all."

O'Brian smiled expansively.

"Come on, let's see the rest of the ship."

Leaving the bridge, they headed down to the lower level and moved to the stern. Jason stopped for a moment to check one of the particle cannon firing ports. The firing system and targeting unit were located inside the ship, rather than projected out on a hull nacelle. The positioning limited the ability of the gun to fire on a line flush with the hull. If a Kilrathi fighter should ever realize that, he could come in close and hug the ship, protected by the blind spot.

He was disappointed as well not to see one of the

new gatling missile mounts, finding instead the standard single tube launch array. He was tempted to comment, but from the way his captain bubbled on about the design he realized it was best to say nothing.

"I think I was telling you about the potential missions for this class of ship, wasn't I?"

Jason nodded, realizing that O'Brian had been jumping from one topic to the next and that it was getting increasingly difficult to get a fix on what the man was leading to from one moment to the next.

"Did I mention the part about serving as a transport?"

"You did, sir," Jason replied quietly.

"Oh yes indeed, I suppose I did. So many things to remember, don't you know."

Jason said nothing.

"We're also to serve on convoy duty, which is the mission we're hooking up to now, covering nine marine transport ships as they move up to the Uruk Sector for a planet assault training exercise. We've been losing too many ships to the occasional Kilrathi raider, pirates and such. There's no sense in tying up one of our precious fleet carriers for such an operation, and the one or two exterior mounted fighters that we were strapping on to the transports took forever to launch and recover."

Jason found that he had to agree with that point. There was a constant and annoying wastage of transports to such raids. They had tried the idea of simply strapping a fighter to the outside of a ship and launching when needed. It was a nightmare and a suicide job. A pilot had to suit up, go EVA along with his launch crew. If they were in the middle of a fight and the transport did any maneuver while they were outside, they were dumped off and lost.

"Next we're to serve as ground support for secondary

operations and landings, hence the names of the ships in this class, all for amphibious operations."

"Any chance for that type of action?" Jason asked, feeling a quick tug of hope for himself, tempered by anxiety for his squadrons. He'd been in on several such operations, and the transition from space flight, to atmosphere combat, and then back to space was challenging stuff, and deadly on new pilots without the experience.

"You fly boys are always eager for blood, aren't you?"

"We're trained to do a job, if that's what you mean, sir," Jason replied coldly.

"Well, I doubt it," O'Brian said, "we've just got orders to guard the convoy and nothing else. It'll be milk runs for this ship and nothing more. I got the inside word on that one, so trust me on it," and Jason detected a note of relief in O'Brian's voice.

Reaching the stern of the ship O'Brian led the way into the engine core area. At the moment they were coasting along at a leisurely one hundred KPS and the drag scoops were raking in the stray atoms of hydrogen found out in deep space which would then serve as fuel. Jason quickly scanned the engine controls and nodded.

"Well, I'll be damned, a Gilgamesh class engine system," he said.

A ship's engineer turned to look at Jason and smiled.

"Top grade design this engine is, sir," and she came to attention and saluted.

"Ship's propulsion engineer, Mashumi."

"You've got a good-looking system here, Mashumi."

"We pulled the Mark 33 transport engines out and put one of these hot machines in," Mashumi announced. "We've been able to click her up to just over 247KPS, with scoops full open. Shut the scoops down, get her to streamlined configuration and we can crank up a ten gee acceleration and have you up to over ten thousand KPS in thirty minutes."

"Well, I'll be damned, something is looking good here after all," Jason said, and instantly he cursed himself. It was a trait that had gotten him into hot water more than once—not thinking about who was listening before he spoke.

O'Brian, who had not even bothered to look at Mashumi, turned to Jason.

"The Mark 33 served well enough."

"Sir, if we get into any tight spots, this engine can double what a transport ship's engine can kick up. The way I see it we can get in fast, and if need be get out fast. We can even give a Ralatha-class destroyer a run for its money."

"Where we're going, and what we're doing, I doubt we'll ever see such a ship," O'Brian replied tartly. "Our main job is convoy patrol and I can't see any sense in putting in an engine that cost almost as much as all the rest of the ship. Financial responsibility son, you fighter boys don't think about that, but financial responsibility is important."

"If we ever get in a jam, sir, you'll see what I mean and thank God we have this Gilgamesh power plant on board."

"You're referring to the fourth mission concept for the CVE, is that it?" O'Brian said, his voice now betraying a clear anxiety.

Jason looked over at O'Brian.

"I did study up on the ship in the few hours I had between getting this assignment and leaving."

Jason looked over at Mashumi and the others in the engine room. There was no sense in worrying them about it all and he didn't want O'Brian to bring the subject up in front of the crew. The concept was obvious. The CVE was cheap and quick to build. It was, above all else, designed to be expendable, unlike the precious heavy and medium carriers of the main fleet. It was therefore ideally suited for high-risk deep penetration raids into the Empire, or to serve as a decoy, or even as a sacrifice delaying force to cover the retreat of far more valuable ships. It was made to be thrown away if the need should ever arise.

"They won't send us out on any suicide runs, Bonevisky. Not on my watch," O'Brian said, his eyes shifting back and forth uneasily, his words spilling out hurriedly as if trying to reassure himself. "I've got friends and contacts in the right offices back home. It'll never happen while I'm around."

Jason looked over at Mashumi, suddenly embarrassed by the captain's shaky display.

"I'd better go and meet my pilots, sir," Jason announced, his tone indicating that it was best to end the conversation.

"Oh yes, indeed, but of course. How thoughtless of me," O'Brian said. "Perhaps dinner tonight? I managed to get one of my old cooks assigned here, he makes a wonderful cherry tart and his other pastries are magnificent. I think we can even dig up a little claret, some fine stock which I managed to pack along."

Such suggestions were of course orders, though he would have preferred to have spent the time with Doomsday going over the fitness reports of his pilots, flight deck officers, and crew chiefs.

"I'd be glad to, sir."

"Fine then," and O'Brian turned and left the engine room.

Jason looked over at Mashumi, who gave a curious smile of resignation before turning back to checking her engines.

Jason strode into the pilot ready room and he could not help but allow himself a slight thrill of satisfaction as the pilots snapped to attention. He was now the commander of all flight operations aboard ship, answerable only to the Captain. He had served under some damned fine men and women, he had also served under more than one fool—but now he was the one in charge.

He walked briskly to the front of the room, stopping in front of the holo briefing map.

"At ease, be seated," he snapped and the men and women who were now his command settled down. He looked around the room. Doomsday and Janice "Starlight" Parker were the only two familiar faces. He had first met Janice when they were going through flight school together and then had gone their separate ways to hook back up again on *Concordia*. She was the ideal choice for running his recon squadron, a damned fine pilot, quick, aggressive, and a master with fighting a Ferret. He looked over at her and she flashed him a wink and sly grin. It was hard not to smile. He knew that she had always had a bit of "a thing," for him, but it had never gone beyond that, especially because of Svetlana, her roommate at school. He pushed that thought aside.

All the rest looked far too young and had that open innocent look. After a tour of combat that would change. You could look into a pilot's eyes and know in an instant whether he had been there or not. Fighting for your life, where a split second decision would decide whether you were still here or splattered across several hundred cubic kilometers of space, tended to change you rather quickly. That, and watching friends die, then at night lying quietly in your sweat-soaked bed, waiting for the next mission—it slowly ate you up and these young pilots had yet to stare into the maw of the killing machine.

"I only have a couple of things to say to you," he began, realizing that they were watching him nervously.

They were most likely scared half to death. The instructors back at the flight academies had drilled the same line into him so many years ago—within a month after reaching the front you're either a veteran or dead, with the odds staked high for the less pleasant of alternatives.

At least, he realized, they'd have a chance if the *Tarawa* stayed on the back roads of the bigger show; it'd give him time to teach them every trick he knew.

"Some of you might think you are very hot stuff right now, after all you're wearing a brand new set of shiny wings. If that's the way you feel, believe me you're bound for a very short life. Those of you who are scared, that's half good. Stay scared. I'm scared every time I climb into the cockpit. That's what keeps me on my toes and kept me, and Doomsday, and Starlight alive when facing down some of the best the Kilrathi Empire can offer. But if you ever let your fear take complete control, it'll kill you, your wingman, and maybe your entire squadron.

"Starting first watch tomorrow, we're going on a full schedule of training. I'm taking you back to square one with basic formation flying, touch down, turn around, combat landings, standard tactical maneuvers, and when I think you're ready we'll move up to advanced unit tactics. We're going to drill, drill, drill, and then drill some more. You're going to get more flying in over the next few weeks than you've had in the last six months. I want you ready for whatever comes and we're going to run this wing as if we're on the cutting edge of the front.

"I understand you had an easy ride out here from Earth; well, the party's over."

He looked around the room. Their expressions were fixed, betraying no feelings of either approval or disagreement. They were being cautious and he approved.

"Doomsday will be squadron commander for the Sabre fighter bombers, Starlight will be in charge of the recon and patrol Ferrets. I'm taking personal charge of the Rapier squadron. Are there any questions?"

The room was silent.

"Sir, we've heard that this here CVE will never even get to the front."

Jason looked around the room.

"When someone has a comment, stand and deliver it."

A tall lanky pilot stood up, his red hair pushing the edge of a regulation cut. He had a superior, almost disdainful air about him, as if this meeting was nothing more than a bore that was interrupting other pleasures.

"Your name, lieutenant?"

"Kevin Tolwyn," and he paused for a moment, "sir."

Shocked, Jason took a second to recover. The resemblance seemed to be there, the sharp eyes, the aquiline nose.

"Yes, sir, the admiral is my uncle," Kevin finally added.

Jason could not help but shoot a quick glance at Doomsday. Little was known of the admiral's personal life, other than the fact that his wife and three sons had all died in a Kilrathi raid very early in the war.

"The way you say that, you seem to expect something," Jason finally snapped.

"Oh, I don't expect anything from you, or this ship, sir. Though I should add we're all very impressed by your record on the *Gettysburg*."

There was a stunned silence in the room and all turned to look at Kevin and then back to Jason.

"Listen hard, mister, real hard," Jason snapped. "What's the rear line today could be overrun tomorrow.

The war hasn't been going well. I don't know what bull they've been handing to you and the civilians back home, but we're hanging on by our fingernails. We lost a third of our carriers in the last three months standard, half of our fleet in the last nine months. I know that's classified information, but you might as well know the truth now. That's three carriers in just the last two actions, with full compliment of five hundred spacecraft, six hundred pilots, and ten thousand crew. The Kilrathi got the edge and they're pushing it straight into our guts. So damn it, listen up. I don't care if you're the nephew of God himself, but aboard this ship, and in my command you're going to run your butt off or I'll kick it from here all the way back to your uncle's office and it'll be years before they put you back together again. Do you read me, mister?"

Kevin's features flushed with rage. He opened his mouth as if to speak but a pilot sitting next to him reached up and pulled him back down to his seat.

"All right then. Get some sleep. I want all of you in the hangar deck at 0400 tomorrow and expect all your craft to be preflighted and ready for launch by 0445. Dismissed."

The pilots stood up and started to file out and from the corner of his eye Jason saw O'Brian standing in the open doorway, as if he had been eavesdropping on the talk.

As the pilots left the room he saw O'Brian fall in by Kevin's side, the two exchanging quick salutes and then a friendly handshake.

"So the captain knows where the bread is buttered."

Jason turned around to see Janice by his side.

"I've heard he's been sucking up to that Tolwyn brat ever since they left Earth orbit. Made him acting wing commander until Doomsday and I checked on board yesterday. Doomsday has some real scuttlebutt on that captain," Janice said.

"I don't want to hear it, Janice," Jason said wearily.

"All right then. But he's a political climber like we haven't seen in a long time. Never had a combat command. Right after he graduated from the Academy he dinged a destroyer in a docking maneuver and they pulled him off to transport command where he's been ever since. The bastard pulled this assignment thinking it's a quick tour of duty, he gets his ticket punched, a red combat tab in his file and then he runs back to fleet headquarters and continues the climb."

"I said I don't want to hear it."

"All right then Bear, all right," she said with a smile. "But if the fur starts to fly, it's gonna be real interesting to see how he acts."

"If the fur starts to fly, we'll be far more worried about keeping our new pups alive without getting killed ourselves," Doomsday said, coming up to join the group, bringing along a mug of coffee, thick, black, and with four sugars the way Jason liked it.

Doomsday took a look sip of his own drink, and sighing leaned against the bulkhead.

"Average pilot here's got less than three hundred hours, some were sent up with only two hundred and fifty of combat training flight time."

Jason nodded. Fleet training was forced to cut corners, the pressure was so heavy to get replacements up. But it was a trade-off: less training, they got here quicker, and died quicker, destroying their precious spacecraft at the same time.

"How do their records look?"

"Oh the usual," Janice said. "All the right check marks, but precious little real information to go on."

"Well, we'll find out tomorrow morning then," Jason said quietly.

• CHAPTER II

"Clear flight deck for combat launching sequence. Repeat, clear flight deck . . ."

Jason stood to one side taking in every detail. Lyford Beverage, the flight deck officer who looked like he showed real promise, ran down the length of the deck, shouting out orders. The young lieutenant was most likely exhausted. Jason had simply mentioned his wish to have the recon ships positioned in front of the fighter bombers and Lyford had stayed up through the night to get the job done right. There still seemed to be a lot of unnecessary movement going on, missing was the calm, almost dancelike choreography of launching, that he was used to aboard the *Concordia*.

His pilots were already in their cockpits. At least for this first time out he gave them that advantage. For safety's sake he wanted to first see how they flew, before taking them up to a full emergency scramble, going from asleep in their bunks to launch in under four minutes.

Janice was first to go. Beverage gained the flight deck control room, located on an elevated platform facing the airlock door, took a final scan of the deck, and then raised his hand in a thumbs-up gesture to the launch and recovery officer, thus signaling that all was ready. The launch and recovery officer was now in control of the deck and for that matter the entire ship, since the captain of the ship had to clear any course or speed changes with him first.

Above the airlock door a green light snapped on. The exhaust deflector shielding snapped up behind Janice's ship, she powered up, and snapped off the thumbs-up that all systems were go. The launch chief petty officer down on the deck gave a thumbs-up, saluted, and crouched down low, pointing forward. The launch officer back in the control room hit the catapult button. Janice's ship snapped out of the bay and she broke hard right as soon as she was in space.

The ground crew hurried the next recon ship into place and Jason looked down at his watch. Nearly a minute passed before the green light signaled again and the second ship launched, this one breaking left off the port side in a wobbly turn that was using far too much control and thrust.

"Damn, its going to be a long day," he sighed, and Doomsday nodded in agreement.

One after the other the ships went out, after the sixth recon the first three Rapier fighters, and then the second six recon Ferrets. Next went six more Rapier fighters to form the close-in combat air patrol, and by this time nearly a half hour had passed, exacerbated by the abort of two launches, one with an overheating engine, the other with a full power shutdown, made worse by several seconds of panic on the part of the pilot when he wasn't sure if he had toggled the eject system back on, or had secured it to full off.

Both craft had to be towed off the launch line and Doomsday groaned with despair.

"*Concordia* would have launched eighty craft by now. If the furballs jump us, we're cooked."

"We're going to have to go with four recon ships out at all times," Jason said. "I want forward warning round the clock. A stealth could jump in, and before our ship tracking system found it, we'd be finished."

"Should keep a Sabre on the hot line loaded with a dogfighting and anti-torpedo array ready to go in under a minute's warning," Doomsday added, and Jason nodded an agreement. It'd mean that Janice's people would be flying eight hours a day, while every bomber pilot, copilot, and gunner would be sitting in their cockpits for two and a half hours a day on the hot line. The training at least would be good for them but he could well imagine how the captain would howl when he heard how much engine time the Ferrets would be burning up.

The launch cycle continued and dictating in some last minute notes on his wrist-mounted memo pad Jason turned away from Doomsday, went over to his Rapier, and climbed into the cockpit.

"I've checked them all out myself," Sparks said, climbing up on the wing to help Jason in. "This one's the best of the lot so I made sure she was assigned to you, sir."

"Thanks, Sparks."

"The kids will learn, just give them some time, sir."

"Let's hope we get that time."

She climbed off the wing, and hand signaled for the ground crew to clear. The tiny tow tractor hooked on to the nose wheel and started to pull him up to the launch ramp. The ship in front of him, a Sabre, slashed out through the airlock, kicking on full afterburners as it cleared the side of the *Tarawa*. The pilot looked good, perhaps showing off by wanting to peel a little paint, but it revealed a certain cockiness that was healthy.

He revved his engines up and ran through the final check on his instruments, everything running in the green. Jason felt the nudge of the catapult arm hooking into his nose wheel. He looked down at the launch chief and gave the thumbs-up. The launch chief returned the thumbs-up, saluted, then crouched down low, point forward. The catapult slammed him back into the seat. He felt the slight shudder of clearing the airlock force field and then he was in space, kicking on afterburners and pulling straight up. A full combat launch was a kick that he loved almost as much as the flying, far more exciting than the leisurely stand down launch which was nothing more than a ship gliding out under its own power at a couple of meters a second.

It was a glorious morning. Three hundred million clicks off his port bow was the boiling red giant of the Oberan System, the sun filling a good ten degrees of the heavens. As he pulled through his looping turn he saw the Caldargar globular cluster hanging in space like a handful of diamonds and around him were his charges, circling the *Tarawa* fifty kilometers out, scattered across space in every direction.

"All right people, Blue Leader to Blue, Red, and Green squadrons. Time for the chicks to come to the rooster. Set your nav system on me and form up in standard V by squadrons."

The drill began. He knew it was bad form to yell at a pilot over the comm link for everyone to hear, but within the first hour he felt as if he would explode. If this was what the Academies and Officer flight training schools were calling combat-ready pilots, then the Confederation was in a hell of a fix.

Several of the fighter pilots had a pretty good hang of keeping formation and could follow him through the basic stuff of Immelmanns, wing overs, afterburner skid turns, and diamond breaks against rear attacks. A young pilot named Chamberlain, with the call sign of Round Top, and another sporting the call sign Mongol seemed to have a natural flair. Tolwyn, who was using the call sign "Lone Wolf," appeared to have the knack as well. But the others left him shaking his head with despair. One of them broke to port and dropped while all the others broke to starboard and climbed, because she had been flying upside down relative to the rest of the squadron, and as a result almost killed herself and two others.

Three hours into the practice, Jason took Mongol and Chamberlain with him, broke out on afterburners to ten thousand clicks and then came around to simulate an attack run. One attempt at this convinced him to hold off on such maneuvers for several days: all hell broke loose and three ships came within meters of colliding.

As for Tolwyn, Jason couldn't get a read. He sensed there might be a hell of a pilot in the young man, but there was a defiance evident in following through on the basic maneuvers. He knew the type, the pilot who wanted to fly the way Maniac or some of the other lone gun hotshots fought.

"All right people," Jason finally announced. "Starlight, detail off four of your pilots for continued patrol. We should be hooking up with the transport ships on the far side of this star within the next hour. Chamberlain, you have combat air patrol; close in on *Tarawa*, keep a circle two hundred clicks out. The rest of you in sequence start your combat landing approaches and make them sharp. I'll go in first."

Lining up on the *Tarawa* he called in for landing permission and then alerted the flight deck officer to prepare for a full wing landing. He could imagine the mad scramble down there as they prepared to take in forty-two craft at thirty-second intervals. One screw-up, which he fully expected would happen, and it could delay return of all ships for hours.

Ignoring the sight-seeing tour he had indulged in the last time, Jason lined up on the narrow flight approach and came in smartly, giving a last burst of reverse thruster just forward of the *Tarawa's* bow, drifting in sharply and skidding to a stop a dozen meters shy of the safety net.

Sparks led the ground crew up at the run, hooking on the electric tow cart which pulled him off the flight ramp. Looking into his rear mirror he saw the next fighter come in hard, sliding down the deck and stopping with its nose just touching the net. Not too bad, he was forced to admit, still embarrassed about his own landing of yesterday.

Canopy up, he climbed out of the fighter.

"Prep her up for another run," Jason shouted, and he jumped off the ladder, trotting down the length of the deck to join the launch and recovery officer. He felt a cold shudder when he saw O'Brian standing in the control room. He had to remind himself that this was where a captain should be during launch and recovery though he would have preferred him back on the main bridge.

The last of the fighters came in and then the Sabres lined up, Doomsday coming in first for a perfect touchdown.

The third bomber was somewhat shaky, slamming into the safety net, causing the next bomber in line to drop out of its approach for a go-around. The deck crew struggled to free the Sabre, causing yet more delay and another wave off of the bomber, whose pilot called in that his starboard engine was overheating, forcing him to shut the engine down.

"Green three," Jason said, patching in on the landing officer's comm line. "Do you wish to declare an emergency?"

"Negative on that Blue Leader."

"Who is this?"

"Rodriquez, sir."

"Landing that baby's hard enough on this small

ship, bring her in slow and easy, non combat. We're cancelling the combat landings till you're aboard."

"Copy that Blue Leader, no problem."

Green three circled in, and Jason watched him on the holo screen. The ship was dropping low, the red dot of the laser guide beam now a dozen meters above the ship. Jason kept his mouth shut. Only one person was supposed to talk at a time like this and that was the landing officer.

"Bring her up son, bring her up. This is not a combat landing son, so don't push it."

Jason watched, tensing. The kid was trying to show off, to prove himself in front of the old man.

"Abort, abort," Jason snapped, breaking in on the landing officer.

"I've got it, I've got it. I've . . ."

The Sabre started to pull up hard, and then yo-yoed back down. Jason watched, horrified when he saw the ship start to yaw, Rodriquez slamming in power at the last second of panic when he finally decided to abort, forgetting that one engine was already shut down.

The Sabre pivoted, the nose of the ship slamming against the side of the airlock port, sheering off just in front of the cockpit.

The deck safety officer standing behind Jason slammed down on the crash alarm, the klaxon roaring to life, the fire retardant nozzles in the bay ceiling kicking on, spraying down on the deck. The ship spun down the flightline, the emergency safety nets detonating out from the deck floor like a spider web, ground crews diving towards the emergency safety bunkers.

Jason held his breath. If the fuel storage pods should rupture, the deck would be swept by an inferno. The ship came to a rest and within seconds a crash cart was alongside, spraying out a curtain of foam. Jason watched the safety and rescue crews with open admiration. While everyone else was running, it was their job to rush into the thick of it. Ignoring procedures, he pulled open the door from the control room and started to run down the flight deck, nearly losing his footing on the slippery foam. The safety crew was up on the ship and in the confusion of spray and smoke he saw a bright flicker of flame from inside the cockpit and then he heard the screaming. Sickened, he stood riveted, knowing there was nothing he could do.

The crew worked frantically, one of them finally taking a laser cutter to slash the cockpit open. The cockpit canopy blew back, flame exploding upward, the crew sticking a hose straight in, a crew member climbing in, ignoring the risk from the fire and a possible cook off of the ejector. He pulled a blackened, struggling form out, shrieks echoing across the flight deck. Another body was dragged out, and horrified Jason looked away; fortunately that one was already dead. A look at the rear turret, crushed beneath the collapsed landing gear, made it clear that there was no survivor in there either.

He turned away and O'Brian was standing before him, hands on hips.

"Satisfied, Commander?" O'Brian snarled.

"Just what the hell do you mean, sir?"

"You pushed them too hard. You pushed them too hard the first day out and you killed a crew, smashed up a Sabre worth tens of millions and damn near blew out this entire ship. Now just how the hell do you think this is going to look on my report?"

"Sir, perhaps you've forgotten we're at war," Jason replied coldly, "and people get killed. That boy screwed it, then disobeyed my orders, and he died. It's tragic, but damn it, sir, it happens. These kids have got to learn how to fly in combat, and some of them might die in the learning, but better now than when it's the real thing."

"You coldhearted son of a bitch." O'Brian snapped, his voice almost breaking.

Jason could not even reply, realizing that the exchange was being observed by everyone on the deck.

"Is that all, sir?" Jason asked, the rage in his voice barely under control.

"No mister, that's not all. Oh, I'm going to file a report on you. I never did care for you hotshot fly boy types and now I see why."

"Then may I ask, sir, if you don't like pilots why are you in command of a carrier?"

O'Brian's features flushed and he raised a threatening finger, pointing it in Jason's face.

"I'll make sure you get taken care of," he finally cried, and then he stormed off.

"The kid screwed up, not you."

Jason turned to look at the landing and recovery officer.

"I didn't ask for your input mister," Jason snapped and turned away.

"All right people, I want you to take a long hard look."

Jason stood before the wrecked Sabre, hands on his hips, glaring at the assembled pilots. There was a distinct smell heavy in the air, cutting through the stench of scorched wiring, burned metal, and fire retardant. One of the recon pilots suddenly ran to the corner of the flight deck and rather noisily threw up. Jason tried to ignore the sound of retching and the cloying scent of burned flesh.

"Rodriquez is dead, gunnery sergeant Singh is dead and his copilot Emilia died an hour ago. I want all of you to take a damned hard look at their ship. If you don't make mistakes you just might outlive this war; if you do make mistakes you'll end up like they did. I ordered Rodriquez to abort the landing but he thought he knew better, and now he's dead. Now get this straight, people. When I or the landing control officer says break, then damn it, break and the hell with your pride.

"In two hours we're going out again so get yourselves ready, but before you do I want each one of you to go up to what's left of Rodriquez's ship and take a damned hard look inside. Dismissed."

He turned and walked off.

"Coldhearted son of a bitch."

The words were just barely audible but he recognized Tolwyn's voice. He kept on going and retreated into his office.

Pulling up a chair, he settled down. After a long minute he finally opened his desk and pulled out a pad of notepaper and a pen. It was an old-fashioned gesture, but it was a long-standing tradition with the fleet. He took the pen up, feeling a bit clumsy, and started to print out the words.

My Dear Mrs. Rodriquez . . . I had the honor of serving with your gallant son as his commanding officer . . .

He paused. Did I kill her boy, he wondered? God help me, did I kill her boy? What could I have done better? He felt a flicker of doubt, a feeling that he knew could be fatal if allowed to take permanent hold. God, my first command and am I screwing it up?

He looked down at the paper, a painful memory rushing back to the day when his mother had opened a similar letter that told her about her now dead husband. It was a week after that day when he had forged a birth certificate form that he stole from the town clerk's office, went down to the recruiter, and signed up at the age of sixteen. Four years later his mother received another letter, this time for his brother, killed in the defense of Khosan. He could imagine Rodriquez's mother standing in the doorway of her home, hands shaking, reading what he was now attempting to write, the gold star hanging in her window now replaced by a blue star.

"God damn this war," Jason sighed.

• CHAPTER III

Doomsday came into Jason's office, carrying three cups of syrupy coffee and he placed one down on Jason's desk and then passed the other to Janice.

"I think they're showing some improvement," Doomsday said. "Noragami scored twenty out of twenty-one today on the simulated missile strike, the best score yet."

"Same here," Janice interjected, "I'm marking three of my people down as still unsatisfactory, but that's better than all fourteen of them on the list three weeks ago."

Jason nodded, leaning back in his chair, aware that the back of his neck was still stiff from putting in nearly ten hours of flight time in the last twenty-four. There were three weeks into their run, another week to go till the nine marine transport ships they were escorting docked at Khartoum Station and then deployed for the ground assault exercises. Moving some of the best marine regiments of the fleet to a quiet sector for this training run just didn't seem right, and Jason couldn't shake the feeling that the so-called "exercises" were a cover for something else. It was stretching the number of assault regiments up on the front far too thin to suddenly turn around and pull a reinforced division off the line. The run itself was uneventful, except for the fact that their last two jumps seemed to be curving them fairly close up to where the action was. But their ultimate destination, whatever it was, didn't concern Jason at the moment. Whether it was cover for a combat operation or not, the training time this milk run had allowed him had become his sole focus, that and the running feud with O'Brian.

"Still a long way to go before they're combat ready," Jason said, as he picked up the coffee mug and took another long sip, glad that the caffeine was kicking in.

"Or for that matter this entire ship," Doomsday replied. "Morale is lower than a snake's ass in a mud hole."

"I wish someone would space that damned jerk up on the bridge," Janice snapped.

"All right people, enough," Jason snarled.

It was hard to be in command; only weeks before he would have gladly joined in their gripe session about the captain. The man showed a maddening inconsistency, one minute almost too friendly with his subordinates, the next minute climbing up on a high horse to lecture and shout. It was obvious he knew nothing about the running of flight operations, and on one occasion even attempted to usurp the launch and recovery officer's job in the middle of a high-speed combat recovery simulating a full bomber return, refit, and relaunch. The launch officer demanded that the captain leave the launch control room, an action which was within his right, and now the man was up on court-martial charges. There was the other dark rumor as well, that on several occasions O'Brian appeared on the bridge smelling a little too strongly of his precious claret. Fleet policies about alcohol were strict and demanding. The only drinking allowed aboard ship was in the observation lounge.

Personnel had to be off duty, the ship in a code green stand down situation. Liquor was allowed into private quarters only if it was prescribed by the medical officer as a "bracer" after a particularly rough go of things, or at the captain's table for a formal meal. It had yet to interfere with O'Brian's performance but Jason worried about it. Drinking had been one of the symptoms of trouble with his *Gettysburg* commander as well. Briefly he wondered what he had done in a past life to get saddled with two such in a row.

He was also a nightmare for paperwork, demanding lengthily written reports to be fed into his command computer every twelve hours, returning the reports with sarcastic notations about grammatical errors. For Jason, English, the language of the fleet, was not his native tongue. Though his mother was Australian, his father was Russian and he had been raised in a Russian colony on Alpha Centauri. Jason found himself reduced to dictating his reports while out on maneuvers and it was slowly driving him mad, something he knew O'Brian took delight in. Worse, however, was O'Brian's open playing up to Kevin Tolwyn, inviting him to the wardroom for dinner, currying favor, and also pumping him for information.

Janice finished her coffee, went to the side table, and poured herself another cup.

"Oh, by the way, I heard the Marine First Commando battalion, the old Cat Killers, are in this little convoy," Janice announced casually, and as she spoke she looked over at Jason from the corner of her eye.

"So what," Doomsday interjected, "those planet jumpers are all crazy; they live even shorter lives than pilots. At least we get clean sheets to sleep on and when we die a decent body bag if they can find our pieces; they're buried in a hundred thousand unmarked graves on a hundred planets whose names we barely even remember."

"Cheerful advantage," Janice replied. "I never looked at it that way before."

"So why the interest in First Commando?" Doomsday asked.

"Oh, just an old friend is with them, that's all," Janice replied.

Doomsday, seeing that Janice was looking at Jason, turned around and saw the look on Jason's face.

"What's with this First Commando unit, Jason?"

Jason felt as if he had been kicked in the gut and was tempted to haul off and chew Janice out, even as she stood before him with a smug expression.

"I really needed to hear that Janice, thanks a lot."

"Oh, no problem at all boss."

She settled back into her chair and looked at him, just waiting, not saying a word.

"I'm missing something here," Doomsday said.

"Just an old friend from when Jason and I were in flight school."

"I take it a female friend from that 'punched-between-the-eyes look,'" Doomsday said, looking back at Jason.

Jason only nodded, still saying nothing.

"Do you think she knows I'm with the convoy?" Jason finally asked.

"How should I know?" Janice replied innocently.

"Some woman you're trying to steer clear of?" Doomsday asked.

Jason felt his face go red. It was over, it'd been over ever since she flunked a lousy ground school exam and run off in a fit of hurt pride to join the Marines. She had refused to pull an assignment on board *Gettysburg* with him, where they could have been together, perhaps even gotten married. Damn it, it was over, and even as he tried to argue that point with himself he could still feel the hurt.

Doomsday chuckled softly.

"Remember that girl I told you about that I met on my last R&R? Gloria, that was her name. Gloria with the glorious . . ."

"Shut the hell up," Jason snapped, "it wasn't like that at all."

"You know you could drop over for a friendly chat. You need an afternoon off," Janice said coyly. "Her unit's on the *Bangor*. Doomsday and I will stand watch. Take one of the Ferrets."

"She'd most likely break my arm, or something else for that matter."

"I doubt it," Janice said with a smile.

"Bear, you are cleared for external dock."

"Thank you *Bangor*, initiating clamp-down now."

Hovering above the top side docking bay, Jason gave a nudge to his down thruster and felt his Ferret scrape up on the deck of the transport ship. There was a quick groaning snap as the *Bangor*'s external docking locks clamped around the landing skids of his ship.

Shutting down his ship, he bled off the cabin air until it was vacuum, and then popped the canopy hatch. Slowly standing up he looked out across the open vista of space. A glorious binary was off to port, a red giant with a tiny white dwarf above it, a trail of incandescent fire spiraling up from the red giant's surface into the glowing white dwarf. The Milky Way spanned the heavens with a hundred million jewels of light and he paused for a moment to admire the view. It was hard to imagine that there was really a war on. The silence of space was all encompassing, an eternity to be explored, and he again felt that wonder of it all, and the sense of irony about the fact that even out here, humankind could not escape the bitterness of war.

He realized as well that he was stalling. Cautiously

taking hold of the side of the canopy he pulled himself out of his cockpit, turning a somersault while still holding on to his ship. If he didn't lock to the deck of the *Bangor*, and should let go now, it'd be most embarrassing to call for a rescue party to come out and reel him back in. He always hated external dockings for that reason. *Bangor*, as did all marine landing transports, had a launch bay, but they were just large enough to hold the assault landing craft, without an inch to spare for anything else.

His feet hit the hull of the *Bangor* and he felt the magnetic lock snap his shoes down. Moving slowly he walked across the deck and reached the airlock door, punching it open and then stepping inside. The door shut, and he felt the ship's gravity take hold, slapping him from weightlessness to one standard gravity as a flood of air washed around him. Seconds later the interior door opened, and a marine corporal in dress blues was before him, standing at rigid attention.

"Permission to come aboard," Jason said.

The guard saluted him, Jason returned the salute and then saluted the ship's colors painted on the far side of the corridor wall.

He stepped into the corridor and instantly felt a difference between this ship and the one he had just left. Marine transport vessels were a compromise between minimal comfort and the ability to haul as many marines and their equipment as possible. The corridor was narrow, painted standard fleet green, and lined down its entire length with crates of supplies.

"Looking for headquarters company, First Commando battalion," Jason said.

The corporal gave directions and Jason set off, weaving his way down corridors, ducking low through emergency airlocks. There was a slightly gamey smell to the ship and it made him realize just how luxurious a pilot's life was with three cooked meals a day rather than ship standard rations, and the luxury of luxuries, a hot shower as often as you wanted one, rather than the one allowed per week aboard military transports.

He lost his way more than once, stumbling into an exercise room, where a company of a hundred marines were working out in hand-to-hand combat drill. It struck him as an anachronism, the thought of killing an opponent by hand. It was rare that he even thought of his opponent in the other ship; rather it was a machine that was trying to kill him and he had to destroy it first.

The marines were tough, far beyond what he was used to seeing. They seemed to possess a cat-like grace, their bodies lean, hardened, more than one scarred by laser rifle burns. He asked directions, most of the group stopping to look at him, until a sergeant barked out a few choice words and the drill continued. He realized that he must be a rare curiosity, still wearing his combat survival suit, his helmet tucked under his arm.

He reached the ship's lower deck and above an airlock he saw the insignia of the First Commando, crossed knives above a Kilrathi skull, "Cat Killers," emblazoned in Gothic letters beneath it.

He went through the open lock. The corridor was packed with gear, marines sitting about, talking, laughing, playing cards, arguing, cleaning and checking their weapons, one of them looking up with a cold grin while continuing to sharpen a durasteel knife.

"I'm looking for Captain Svetlana Ivanova."

"You'll find the Talker down the end of the corridor, third door to your right."

He continued on, trying not to feel uncomfortable with the realization that all conversation in the corridor had come to a dead stop.

He reached the door, and had the sudden desire to forget about it and get the hell off the ship as quickly as possible. He started to turn around and then realized that every marine in the hall was watching him.

He knocked on the door.

"Come."

He pushed the open button and stepped in.

"Be with you in a moment."

Her back was turned and she was leaning over a holo screen, studying a map, tracing out what Jason realized were air strike runs on a ground target

Even from the back he instantly recognized her. Her hair was cropped short to marine regulation, still golden with a slight streaking of strawberry to it. The neck was thin, tanned, and the rest of her—though well conditioned, the female side of Svetlana was still very much in evidence.

"What do you want?"

"Hello, Svetlana."

Her back stiffened and there was a long silence. She turned slowly and looked up at him.

"Jason?"

He smiled nervously and felt his heart skip over. Her blue eyes were wide with wonder. Her lips parted slightly in shock. She had aged; seven years of war did that. There were the beginnings of crinkled lines around the edge of her eyes, and a thin scar creasing back from her temple to behind her right ear. But she still looked much the same, and all he could see for a moment was the Svetlana of so many years ago—the Svetlana from back home, two years older than himself, who had gone off to join the fleet.

For years he had suffered with an insane crush on her, believing her off limits since she was, after all, "an older woman." His older brother Joshua had tried for her, but her nickname of Ice Princess came from the hard experience of more than one starry-eyed boy whom she had shot down. And then by wonderful chance they had met again at the officer's candidate flight school, he had been eighteen, and she, twenty. It had simply gone from there; both were first drawn to each other as friends from home, but the relationship had quickly blossomed into far more.

"It is you," she whispered.

"It's me."

She nodded, and for a moment he thought she was going to fill up, her eyes suddenly sparkling. She lowered her head then looked back up.

"You damned son of a bitch, so what brings you back now?"

"Svetlana."

"Don't Svetlana me you rotten bum. I haven't seen you, heard from you in years, then you show up like a piece of bad luck and expect that damn smile of yours and little boy charm will get you right back in to my heart again, is that it?"

As she spoke she stood up and came towards him like a tiger ready to pounce. She came up close, pointing a finger into his face.

"Now wait a minute, damn it," Jason snapped. "I couldn't help it that you flunked that test. It sure as hell wasn't my fault. I'm not the one that gets my stupid butt transferred to the marines and then goes disappearing. So don't blame it all on me!"

"Blame it on me then, is that it?" she shouted. "Why don't you get assigned to the fleet, maybe we'll get married someday once the war's over you said. Bull. This war will never be over. If I couldn't fly, I wanted to be where the action was, and not go following you around as your bat boy, your second fiddle, stuck on the ground while you grab all the glory."

She turned away and he felt a brief instant of relief, half fearing that she was actually building up to hauling off and decking him. He half suspected that with the condition she was in, and the training of a commando, she could kill him with her bare hands and not even work up a sweat doing it.

"Fleet policy would have allowed us to get married and assigned to the same ship," Jason said quietly.

"But not as pilots," she said, her back still turned to him, her voice thick with emotion. "You just never got it. I wanted to fly more than anything. Your dad was a pilot, so was mine. There was no way I was going home after that, to sit in the kitchen and wait for a letter to come in from your commander telling me how bravely you died."

Her voice started to crack and she looked away for a moment.

"You were the one who ran amok with your pride," Jason shouted in reply. "You were the one who transferred to the marines and said 'stay in touch baby,' I'd be damned if I was going to wait around for you to finish your first five-year tour of duty."

She looked back at him.

"I wanted a piece of the action, too," she replied. "You're not the only one this damned war has screwed, at least your mother and brother didn't buy it the way half my family did."

"Joshua died defending Khosan," Jason said quietly.

"Oh God, Jason, I'm sorry," she whispered and the anger dropped away, and she stepped closer, putting a hand on his arm.

"You didn't know," he sighed. "It's all right."

"And your mom, how is she?"

"All right I guess, I thought I'd see her on leave but I got pulled to take over as wing commander for the *Tarawa*."

"You're on the *Tarawa*?"

"That's how I got here. Janice is with me too, by the way, she's one of my squadron commanders."

"You're a wing commander?"

Jason nodded, almost afraid to admit it since she might interpret it as boasting. He remembered her in school, before she had run afoul of the dreaded advanced spaceflight and jump point physics course. Before that course everyone thought she'd be another hotshot ace once she got up to the front. He knew the desire to prove something came from what happened to her father. That was a tragedy Jason never had the courage to ask her about, for his own father had told him how Svetlana's dad had panicked in one of the early engagements of the war, killing himself and causing the loss of his carrier. He often wondered if Svetlana really knew the truth, which had been covered up for reasons of public morale.

"How is Janice?" Svetlana asked, and there was a note of affection in her voice.

"Same Janice as always. Thirty-two kills to her credit and a squadron commander."

"She still have that crush on you?"

"I don't think so."

"Liar."

"Well, nothing's ever come of it."

"I bet," and he detected the jealously in her voice.

She went back to her desk and sat down, motioning for Jason to sit on her bunk.

He settled down, putting his helmet and gloves down and loosening his survival suit collar.

"Something to drink?"

"I'm flying again shortly. I've got to be back aboard ship before the next jump."

She nodded, and then reached into her desk draw, pulled out a small silver flask. She poured out a cap full, downed it in a single gulp, and then put the flask away. The action shocked him a bit, the Svetlana he remembered would never touch a drink.

"Why did you have to come back into my life now?"

"Janice told me your unit was with this convoy. I

couldn't stay away. Last I heard you were way the hell out past the Niven Section."

"We got pulled from the front."

"To go with this convoy to practice exercises in the rear?"

"You're fishing for information, Jason," she said, and a smile brightened her features.

He felt a quick tug, her smile could always melt him.

"Well it does seem a bit strange, Svetlana. Nine regiments of marines and a commando battalion getting pulled for landing exercises. Hell, your division had five combat jumps in the last year alone. Last thing you marines need is a milk run practice landing."

"So you've been following our record have you?" and she looked over at him curiously.

"Who hasn't?" and he realized he had fumbled it yet again. "And besides," he quickly added, "I knew you were with the unit."

"Yeah sure, and all filled with concern."

He lowered his head.

"Anyhow, it does seem a bit strange to be pulling vets off the line, especially with all that talk of another Kilrathi offensive in the works."

She hesitated for a moment.

"That's bull. It's just a security cover."

She hesitated again.

"There have been too many security leaks. I heard they had some major problems with that on the *Concordia*."

"That traitor damned near killed everyone on board. It was before I got transferred there, but they're still talking about it."

"By the way, I heard how you handled things on *Gettysburg*. It took a lot of guts to rebel like that."

"I wasn't about to kill unarmed civilians asking for sanctuary, even if they are Kilrathi."

"They sure as hell did it on Khosan and a hundred other worlds, Jason. I've seen the results."

"Just because we're fighting in the gutter doesn't mean we have to get down and wallow in it the way the cats do."

She smiled sadly and nodded as if he were a child who had yet to grow up.

"I guess I can tell you," she finally said, her voice dropping to a near whisper. "Your captain's most likely getting briefed right now by the convoy commandant. Colonel Merritt, my CO, and I just got out of briefing an hour ago. Next jump has been changed. We're turning about, and doing a high-speed run back through the sector. In three days standard we're going to jump into Vukar Tag and take the planet."

"Vukar Tag? Never heard of it."

"Take a look." She turned back to her desk and punched up a holo map display of the sector.

Jason watched as she first scrolled through a strategic map and then focused in on the planet, data about the planet's size and defenses flashing up on the screen.

"I don't get it," Jason said softly, "no strategic materials, no juncture point for major jumps, it's a backwater rock floating in the middle of nowhere."

"Yeah, I know. It's a worthless rock in a worthless corner of the Kilrathi Empire, but something's cooking. We're taking the planet with a full ground assault and with orders to smash everything on it. Our units received a special assignment to blow a palace complex, though why they need to send us in to do the job when we could smash it from the air is beyond me. The place isn't fortified and shielding is minimal."

"Resistance?"

"We've been briefed that they're at least two

regiments of Kilrathi Imperial Guard from their 23rd Claw division garrisoned there."

"Imperial Guard. What the hell for? The planet looks like a crap hole and not worth the cost of a single life."

"Got me, Jason, but that's the scoop."

Janice punched a key and the holo map image dissolved to be replaced by the strike map she had been working on. Jason leaned over and studied the map intently.

"Yeah, I'm still doing air-to-ground strike coordination for the battalion."

"It must hurt," he said quietly.

"They figured that with my flight background I was the best one for the job and I've been the Talker, the air-to-ground coordinator for the commando battalion, ever since I joined. For this operation I'm working with the Commandant for the entire show, since he's going in with us."

She hesitated.

"I'd have made a good pilot. It kills me to watch you hotshots come in and make your runs, me talking you through."

"I'm sorry."

"Nothing to be sorry for. I do my job well. I save a hell of a lot of grunts from getting fried, and I get my strikes in where they're needed. I guess I'll be your liaison for ground support. You people will be flying combat cover for our sector in the landing. We're coming straight in on the Imperial Guard barracks area next to the palace."

"So we're going with you?"

"That's the plan."

"Damn. I barely got my pups flying right in space. Now you're telling me they'll be flying atmosphere and doing ground strikes?"

"We're hooking up with another CVE at jump

through but as far as I know *Tarawa*'s crew has the ground-pounding work."

"I guess I'd better get back," Jason said, softly.

"I guess you'd better."

He stood up, not sure of what to do. She stood up as well, and the two looked at each other awkwardly.

"If only you'd stayed with the fleet, or simply gotten out, I'd have married you," Jason said. "But there was no sense to it. It'd have been years before we saw each other again."

"And it has been years," she sighed.

He stepped forward, ready to take her up in his arms but she backed away.

"It's over, Jason."

"Someone else then?" he asked, his voice suddenly cold.

"None of your damned business. And what about you, Jason? With that little boy smile I bet more than one ensign has melted for the chance to claim a fighter pilot."

"None of your damned business, either."

She looked at him coldly.

"Get the hell out of my room and don't come back."

• CHAPTER IV

"That's the mission then, any questions?"

Jason looked around the room, feeling a deep sense of uneasiness. His pilots were of course displaying the expected level of excitement, this was after all the virgin mission for everyone in this room except for Doomsday, Janice, and himself—and that was exactly why he was worried. He would have preferred another month or two of training first, several more quiet convoy runs to polish their skills, but that, quite simply, was not going to be the case. There never seemed enough time to get ready when a war was on.

Svetlana was right on the mark. Less than an hour after he had returned to the *Tarawa*, O'Brian called a staff meeting to brief them on the reassignment. The captain could barely conceal his displeasure, and made more than one passing reference to half-baked, last-minute ideas, but Jason instantly picked up as well that O'Brian was miffed that he had been kept in the dark that the story of a training mission was nothing more than a security cover for this mission.

They had pulled the three jumps into the edge of the Kilrathi sector without detection, and the next jump was slated for initiation in just under eight hours.

Eight hours. He looked around the room. His pilots

were projecting what they expected to be the proper model of someone about to go forth and meet the enemy—a casual indifference, or open expressions of eagerness, but he knew better. It was almost hard now to remember his own first combat flight, and the humiliation of throwing up in the head only minutes before reporting to the flight line.

"All right then. Stand down, try to grab a quick nap if you can. Report to the flight line at 0415. The moment jump-through into the Vukar Tag system is completed we launch."

"Jump initiation sequence is at full automatic and counting at ten, nine . . ."

Jason leaned back in the cockpit of his Rapier and closed his eyes. No matter how many hundreds of times he jumped, it still left a bit of a twinge in his stomach.

"Three, two, one . . ."

Space on the other side of the airlock suddenly flashed. There was a momentary sparkle effect, and the faint sensation that he was falling and then another flash. It was as if a holo screen channel had been switched and a view of one sector instantly replaced with another.

There was a momentary pause, an expectant hush as the *Tarawa*'s auto nav system locked on to the target stars in the new system, checking to see that they had arrived at where they were supposed to arrive. It was never a 100 percent sure thing with a jump. A transit point could have shifted, maybe even shut down, or the nav officer in charge might have screwed up. There was also the slim chance that two ships would jump into the same place, at exactly the same instant, but if that ever happened, Jason realized, there would not even be a split second of understanding before the total destruction of the ships in an incandescent flash.

"*Tarawa* nav confirms location," a computerized voice whispered in his headset. He looked down at his fighter's nav screen and a second later saw the navigational information being fed into his fighter's computer.

Jason clicked on his comm link.

"Wing launch is go."

He looked up and saw Janice's ship slam out through the airlock, followed thirty seconds later by a second recon ship. The tractor hooked to the front of Jason's Rapier started forward, pulling him up to the launch ramp, while the third Ferret went out and then the fourth. He was rolled into place and locked into the catapult. Check out completed, he gave the thumbs-up, leaned back, and two seconds later was in space, afterburners screaming into life as he roared straight ahead.

Twenty kilometers to starboard he saw CVE-4 *Sevastopol* and heard the chatter of her pilots on the other carrier's channel. The ship had jumped through five minutes ahead of them and most of their fighter squadron was out.

"Tar Blue Leader, do you copy? This is Pol Wing Command."

"Tar Blue Leader here," Jason replied.

"We've got negative on Kilrathi combat patrol. Repeat, no bogeys yet."

"Good news on that Pol. My people are forming for strike, keep me posted, Blue Leader out."

There was a flicker of light to port and Jason looked over as the first of the Marine transports materialized into the sector. Ten seconds later a second ship appeared, and within another minute all nine were in, kicking up to full speed. From their forward bays the first assault landing craft emerged.

Thirty million clicks ahead the dirty brown and red crescent of Vukar Tag was barely visible. He could imagine that all hell was breaking loose down there as the Kilrathi planet defense system picked up the unexpected visitors. It was going to be a three hour run down to the planet, escorting the landing craft in with Pol's fighters providing the forward sweep and then Combat Air Patrol for the fleet and backup. By the time Pol's fighters got there, they'd be ready.

He settled back, circling the *Tarawa* at ten kilometers out, waiting for his pups to form.

"Tar Blue Leader, this is Pol Wing Command, starting forward sweep, will keep advised."

Jason settled back, listening to the *Sevastopol's* air command channel as the recon and fighter sweep went in to check out the planet's defenses. Space was rapidly getting crowded as each marine transport disgorged twenty landing craft, each ladened down with a company of a hundred grunts, followed by the heavy weapons support craft. *Sevastopol*'s first squadron continued on in, its second forming a close-in combat patrol around the fleet, while *Tarawa*'s attack force formed up to go in with the assault.

"Tar Blue Leader this is White Knight, marine air-ground support control."

He swallowed hard at the sound of Svetlana's voice.

"Go ahead White Knight."

"All landing craft are away, beginning assault."

Jason looked down at his watch. Twenty-seven minutes; damn, they were good. He toggled back to the *Tarawa* and quietly groaned when he found out that six fighters and three bombers were still waiting to get up. They'd have to catch up, the assault couldn't wait.

"Go ahead White Knight, we're with you."

The assault landing craft, spread out across a thousand cubic kilometers of space started in, Jason keeping his formation forward of the landing force. The three-hour run in was almost too quiet, a lone Drakhi recon ship, quickly dispatched by *Sevastopol's* forward sweep the only encounter. The planet soon filled most of space before him and they crossed the orbit of Vukar Tag's only moon.

The Kilrathi finally responded. From the barren and airless surface of the moon a full spread of missiles suddenly snapped loose, the high-pitched whine of their tracking systems ringing in Jason's headphones.

"Tar Blue Leader, to Blue Squadron, here's our first job. Follow me."

He broke hard right, kicking on afterburners into a skidding turn and rolling over to drop beneath the marine landing craft. Target acquisition sorted through the mad scramble of data and showed fifty outbound missiles, accelerating up and aimed into the heart of the assault.

"Break and pick your targets."

He heard a high pitched shout of glee from one of his pilots and tried to mark down who it was for a later chewing out. Pushing in hard, he aimed straight at the missile spread, locked on with laser cannons, and snapped off a volley, detonating his first target. Exploding missiles snapped in silent death. A missile guidance system, overriding its initial programming to go for the landing craft, swung about, cutting in behind Jason. He toggled off a chaff pod, cutting a tight roll. The missile, momentarily confused by the chaff, regained lock.

It continued to close.

"I'm on him, sir."

It was Chamberlain and Jason looked up to his rear projection mirror to see a flash of light a dozen clicks astern as the missile detonated.

"Thanks, Round Top."

He continued in towards the planet, and his combat information computer, analyzing the trajectories of the missiles traced them back to their source. Jason fed the information over to Doomsday who detailed off a strike bomber to go down and nail the concealed enemy base. Less than a minute later he saw the flash of an explosion on the planet's surface, followed an instant later by a ripple of secondaries. The bomber, with load expended, pulled up and away and started back for rearming to *Tarawa*, which was following in behind the assault.

"Three broke through to transports, Blue Leader."

"We're on them, White Knight."

Jason did a quick scan of his squadron. They were scattered out across several hundred cubic kilometers, locking on to their targets, nailing them, and then chasing the next. His people were too spread out.

The landing craft laser guns and mass driver mini cannons kicked into point defense even as he turned back in towards the marine ships. Space was criss-crossed with flashes of lights and exploding warheads, and then there was nothing but darkness.

"White Knight, what's the tally?"

"One ship damaged, she'll still make landing though, a handful of casualties. Thanks for the cover, Blue Leader."

"It's our job, White Knight."

He found it hard to believe that Svetlana was on the other end of the conversation. She was now so coldly professional, her voice calm, almost disembodied.

"Blue Leader, initiate Plan Bravo."

"Initiating Plan Bravo," and he passed the command up to his Rapiers and to Doomsday's Sabres, while Starlight pulled her recon Ferrets back to act as point defense for the landing craft if anything went wrong.

"Form up, you know your targets."

He took a deep breath, and dived straight in at the planet, following the track of his auto nav system which was programmed with the target, a Kilrathi landing field and barracks area, believed to be the center of planetary defense, which the First and Fifth Marines, augmented by the commando battalion were planning to seize. It was going to be a tough run.

The squadrons dove towards the planet's surface. Planetary defenses were up, an orbital station already engaged by *Sevastapol*'s fighter bombers, ground defenses kicking on their jamming and attempting to gain lock on the incoming Confederation ships. He did a quick switch over to a Kilrathi channel and through the shifting hum of the encoding system Jason could still pick up the angry chatter and shouted commands. He barked off a quick curse, not sure of the exact Kilrathi pronunciation for a rather impossible anatomical act, and laughing, switched back to his main comm channel.

"All right Tar squadrons, don't hit that atmosphere too hard, or you'll regret it."

He hated atmosphere fighting, where anything much beyond a click a second was far too much. He bled off speed, watching the nav screen which was plotting out his trajectory, a thin blue line on the bottom of the screen showing the edge of the atmosphere. He felt the controls go mushy, the Rapier's computer automatically switching from thrusters to wing control surfaces. Fuel was now going to be a constant concern; flying inside the atmosphere, the hydrogen scoops would simply create too much drag. He closed the scoops and soared in.

Behind him the rest of the Rapier and Sabre squadrons were following. Doomsday peeled off, taking two craft with him to hit a suspected communication and control sector several hundred clicks from the landing areas, other fighters and bombers turning off seconds later to hit their assigned targets.

A light cloud cover was ahead, high in the atmosphere. He punched through and below him, clear in the shimmering desert heat, was his target, the base clearly visible in the middle of a high plateau. The planet was a scorched ball of desert with atmospheric density nearly a third higher than Earth standard, and gravity .2 above that of Earth's. The only habitable places were on high plateaus and mountain peaks, where the air was thinner, and the temperature a tolerable hundred degrees Fahrenheit.

He saw a flicker of lights—point defense of lasers and the flash snap of ground-to-air missile batteries. He went into a dive, aiming for a canyon cut into the side of the plateau. Just as he entered the canyon a missile streaked by straight overhead and slammed into the far side of the crevice, the concussion rattling his ship. He wove down the canyon for half a dozen kilometers, mentally calculating the moment, and then popped back up and turned straight in at the base. He released a missile which streaked away and several seconds later was broken into half a hundred sub munitions, each of the small arm-length bolts locking on to individual radar and comm link targets and tracking them in. The Kilrathi ground defense array shut down, but it was already too late; missiles had their locks. Skimming in low, less than fifty feet off the ground, Jason watched as the volley of shots leaped ahead. Several seconds later the first round hit, the matter/antimatter explosive heads mushrooming out. The entire top of the plateau suddenly seemed to lift into the air as all fifty warheads found their marks and cut loose. He pulled up, rolled over, and then started into a dive, lacing what appeared to be a barracks area with a blast from his neutron cannons, the rounds striking with such force that the buildings were ripped apart by the massive release of energy.

Listening in on the commlink, he heard the chatter of his pilots, their shouts of excitement and fear, the reports coming in of successful strikes. One of them called that he was hit and pulled out and away, and Jason keyed over to Starlight, telling her to send in three of the recon ships to finish the target up with their Ferrets' mass driver cannons.

"Blue Leader this is White Knight, how goes it?"

"Primary landing area is suppressed, will fly cover, bring the boys in."

"Good work, Blue Leader."

Pulling up to an altitude of twenty kilometers, he kept a steady eye on his main screen, waiting for the first flicker of an enemy radar. But their system appeared to be either totally destroyed, or shut down for self preservation. Far over the horizon, where Doomsday and two of his Sabres were working over a well dug-in defense which three marine regiments were supposed to take, there was still a flurry of activity, half a dozen missiles gaining space, only to be knocked out by the back up of Ferrets which were flying in with the landing craft.

Jason switched to his main screen for an instant and followed the main assault wave. The screen was alive with blue blips breaking through the atmosphere. Off to his right he saw a brilliant flash, and looked up towards space. A flare as bright as the hot yellow sun above the world snapped up, casting a second line of shadows on the planetary surface below. On the main link he heard the triumphal report of the Pol's wing leader, announcing that the main reactor of the Kilrathi space defense platform had detonated, either from a hit or in a final suicide act by the defenders to avoid capture.

The first marine landing craft shot past, an instant

later over forty more came in, their laser cannons firing a spread of shots into the flaming wreckage of the Kilrathi base. A volley of area bombardment missiles snapped out from the undercarriage of each ship, winging down, and seconds later the entire plateau was turned into a cauldron of fire. Jason watched, mesmerized by the total destruction that a marine landing wrought when it unleashed a suppressive bombardment from its ships.

He rolled over and dived in, following the landing down.

Five red blips appeared on his screen.

"Get 'em down White Knight, we've got company!" Jason shouted.

He rolled his ship again, looking for a visual and saw them, four Sartha and a lone Krant, launching out from a concealed base on a mountain peak overlooking the plateau. The Kilrathi had kept low, waiting for the landing craft to come in.

"Mongol and Round Top, vector down here on the double!"

Jason kicked up his afterburners, feeling the controls in his hands start to shudder as he tore through the heavy atmosphere, realizing that his wingtips would most likely be glowing from the friction.

He lined up on the lead Sartha, and nailed it with his guns, the ship detonating in a flaring ball of flame. The marine landing craft went into evasive, but they were like sitting ducks against the agile light fighters. The Kilrathi pressed straight in, ignoring Jason's onset, going instead to knock out part of the landing force. He pulled in hard and in an offhanded deflection shot dropped a second Sartha and then lined up the Krant, which pulled up and over and came in head-on.

The two ships traded shots, the range closing at several kilometers a second. He wanted to close his eyes as the two played the game of chicken to see who would break first. A snap of electrical shorting burst through his cabin from a direct hit to his forward shielding, which glowed hot white in the atmosphere. He switched to an IFF missile, the only weapon he dare discharge with so many marine landing craft about and let it tear. The Kilrathi, not worried about such concerns, fired a spread of two missiles in return and Jason rolled ninety degrees at the last instant, presenting a vertical silhoutte. The missiles streaked past and detonated, while his own tracked in and slammed into the enemy's port side. The ship spun over and then atmospheric drag took over. The enemy pilot might have been good in space, Jason realized, he certainly was gutsy enough, but when you're knocked for a spin in atmosphere you usually were on a one way ride. The pilot overcompensated on the controls, went into a high-speed stall and spiraled down to the planet's surface, the ship detonating in a dirty plume of oily smoke.

Jason pulled around to chase the other two Sartha and he felt his heart sink. Two marine landing craft were going down, trailing fire, breaking apart, and for a brief instant he saw the bodies tumbling out of the ships just before impact. Two other craft, both badly damaged, were going down as well, struggling to at least make controlled landings.

"Blue Leader, we're on them."

He saw the two blips of Mongol and Round Top streaking in. They were flying heavy-handed, over controlling for atmosphere and Jason held his breath when it appeared as if Mongol would go straight into the side of a mountain while chasing his prey. The Sartha's pilot was damn good as well, and Jason realized that the Kilrathi had pulled the diving maneuver with the hope of leading his pursuer into the ground. Chamberlain, flying above Mongol, cut the Kilrathi off as he tried to pull straight up. His first volley missed, but the second one nailed the ship right in the cockpit. The ship rolled over and dived into the ground.

The last Sartha was gone, diving down off the plateau and disappearing into the rabbit warren of canyons. Jason called up to a recon Ferret positioned above the landing at the edge of the atmosphere, acting as look down radar, called for a track and several seconds later he got the fix.

"Mongol and Round Top, cover this sector, I'm going for the Sartha."

Following the guidance from the Ferret, Jason kicked in his afterburners and skimmed across the plateau into the jumble of mountains and crevices.

"Blue Leader, he's off your starboard bow, bearing to you forty three degrees, heading sixty eight degrees."

"On him."

"Now turning, bearing zero three degrees, heading three two eight degrees."

Jason followed the directions, which changed every few seconds. He caught a flurry of dust and boulders kicking off a mountain side and realized it must have been triggered by the close passage of the Sartha. He set out, turning into the narrow valley, following it, hugging the sinewy passage, the G force of the accelerated turns pressing him into his seat, causing the world to go gray. The Sartha was far more maneuverable, and that was the payoff in this type of flying through a needle slit of mountains and crevices.

"You're gaining on him, Blue Leader," the Ferret announced.

He was tempted to pull up out of the canyon and skim overhead, but feared he might lose his quarry, whose passage was now evident by the eddies of dust and tumbling boulders kicked loose by the supersonic passage. He pulled tightly around a hairpin turn and for a brief instant saw the tail of the enemy ship.

He pressed the throttle up, feeling his palms go sweaty as he raced down the canyon, banking through the turn so tightly that the compensator began to overload and he thought he'd black out. Again a glimpse, almost the same distance. The Kilrathi was good, and his craft better designed for this type of work. Jason toggled up his one remaining missile, a dumb fire bolt, and waited. He pulled through the next turn, a shudder joggling his ship as his shielding struggled to repel him away from the canyon wall. There he was. He fired the missile off and it leaped forward, racing down the canyon, passing straight over the top of the Sartha.

The missile slammed into the next turn of the canyon wall just as the Sartha reached the turn point. A shower of rocks detonated outward and then there was nothing but fire and smoke. Jason pulled up out of the canyon, the shock wave of the blast buffeting his ship.

"Red blip gone, Blue Leader," the Ferret watching from overhead announced.

Jason throttled back as he approached the turn, banking over it from several hundred meters higher up. The side of the canyon was an ugly red smear of fire and wreckage. The missile had done its work, sending back a spray of rocks and debris that smashed the Kilrathi ship down.

"Confirmed kill," Jason announced as he turned back around and headed for the main action.

"Good shooting, sir."

"Good work recon, keep it up."

"Thank you, sir," and as the pilot spoke Jason realized it was a pilot whom Starlight had put on the unsatisfactory list and decided to keep out of the main action. The woman had done a good job after all.

He pulled up to a hundred meters above the plateau and swept over it. Mongol and Chamberlain were lower down, weaving S turns back and forth, waiting for targets to crop up. In the dust and confusion he saw the grunts clambering out of their ships, racing through the wreckage, ground fighting vehicles pouring out the forward hatches, hovering up, and then skimming away. The heavy weapons landers touched down, disgorging their massive "walkers" which could traverse any terrain and carried as much armaments as a light corvette. There was a flurry of laser rifle fire, more secondary explosions, one of the landing craft, now serving as a medevac, already taking off and heading back out to space.

"White Knight, what's the situation?" He held his breath, still not sure if Svetlana's ship might have been one of the casualties in the assault.

"Blue Leader?"

"The same," and he quietly breathed a sigh of relief.

"LZ is secured. You sure didn't leave much down here for us to mop up."

"That's what we're paid for."

"I know," and he could hear the touch of irony in her voice.

"We'll keep air patrol over you till *Tarawa* catches up and we return for reload."

"Roger on that Blue Leader. Commando battalion now deploying to strike primary ground target, will keep you advised if we need assistance."

"Take care, Knight, and give us a whistle if you have any jobs left."

He skimmed down lower, streaking across the ground at a quarter of a click a second, taking in the show, grunts looking up at him as he streaked past, raising triumphal clenched fists in the air. A pocket of resistance near a Kilrathi bunker complex required some work and Jason called in one of Doomsday's craft, which had been loitering out in space after completing its primary mission, to unleash a load which cratered several dozen acres of ground. The attack swept forward and Jason joined in, punching out a Kilrathi medium assault tank with his neutron guns.

Svetlana's unit was called in for backup, and with Mongol flying wing, Jason weaved through the smoke darkened plateau, reaching the target area within a minute. The objective caught him by surprise. The building was beautiful, almost like a fairy-tale medieval fortress of polished limestone, complete to minareted towers. Its military significance seemed doubtful but from the chatter on the ground link it was obvious that the entire commando battalion was committed to taking it. He hovered above the palace for nearly an hour, slashing out neutron rounds, suppressing pockets of resistance, and taking half a dozen nasty hits from ground cannons that just about knocked out his bottom shielding. The strength of the commando battalion was overwhelming, however, and through the ground command channel he heard the announcement that the palace had been secured. Now that they had it Jason wondered just what was so important about the ancient building, which could have just as easily been flattened from the air with a matter/antimatter warhead.

Svetlana's voice suddenly cut into his thoughts.

"Blue Leader, clear the area, repeat, clear the area by at least three clicks."

Jason pulled back, not quite sure of the logic of the command. From out of the front of the building he saw hundreds of commandos emerging, race to their ground assault vehicles. The vehicles revved to life, hovered up and skimmed away.

The palace suddenly disappeared in the hot white flash of a matter/antimatter detonation, that sent a tower of smoke and rubble thousands of meters into the air, the explosion spreading out into an ugly mushroom-shaped cloud, streaked with lightning.

The destruction left him with a curious feeling. There was, after all, the almost childlike joy of destruction, especially when one was destroying the property of an enemy that deserved to be hated, but on the other side he watched the explosion with a vague sense of loss. The building appeared to be ancient, a treasure that should have been preserved, its military significance a mystery.

Seconds later he picked up an encoded Kilrathi burst signal. It was on for only a second, then shut down and his ship's targeting system picked up on it and secured a lock. He turned his Rapier around to go after the source of the transmission.

"Blue Leader, this is White Knight."

"Blue Leader here. Going after a transmission source coming from a mountain twenty clicks from here, back shortly."

"Belay that attack Blue Leader, repeat, belay that attack, your people are not to hit that source till ordered to."

"What gives White Knight? It's a threat, it could be calling in counter strike information. I'm going for it."

"Blue Leader, that is a direct order from Big Duke One."

"Acknowledge," Jason replied, now thoroughly confused. Big Duke One was the marine commandant in charge of the entire assault. So the commandant decided to go in with the commando battalion and lead from the ground. It was just like him, Jason realized. But was there a reason why he was at that now ruined palace, and just why the hell did they want a Kilrathi station broadcasting in the middle of a damned invasion?

His fuel nearly expended, Jason finally pulled back up, calling Mongol and Round Top in as well to head back to *Tarawa* for a rearm and refuel.

He switched through the comm link channels, checking on his other pups, calling for them to signal in their status reports, checking his screen to see what damage they had sustained. Most of his people were dangerously low on fuel, several of them with barely enough to return to space, and he ordered his squadrons back up, leaving Doomsday and Janice to hover above the landing areas for support, requesting that a section of *Sevastopol*'s fighters act as backup for ground support, now that space based defenses had been suppressed.

"I'm hit, I'm hit, losing power."

It took him a second to lock on the signal. It was a Sabre, flying suppression above the one Kilrathi city on the planet. The port engine of the ship had taken a small heat seeker and it appeared as if all shielding was gone.

"Head for space, Green four," Jason commanded, and then checked his nav screen for an escort.

"Blue five acknowledge."

"Lone Wolf here,"

"Kevin, escort Green four back to the *Tarawa*. He's lost all shielding and an engine; he'll need cover if anything shows up."

"Acknowledge."

Jason watched his screen as Tolwyn maneuvered in behind the damaged Sabre. The crippled ship cleared the atmosphere and he breathed a sigh of relief. Even if it lost all power now, they could still tractor beam the craft back to *Tarawa* for repairs.

"This is *Tarawa* combat information, we've got bogeys coming up off the moon's surface."

"Damn!"

Jason looked at his fuel supply, it was barely enough

to get back to *Tarawa*, and there might be a fight brewing out there.

"We're tracking one lone Sartha, vectoring in on Green four and Blue five."

"Kevin did you copy that?"

"Got him on lock Blue Leader," Kevin cried, his voice edged with excitement, his signal scratchy and breaking up.

"He'll try and take out the Sabre. Stay close to that cripple and provide cover."

There was no reply, and Jason felt a quick stab of anxiety.

"Blue Leader, Blue Leader, Lone Wolf is breaking off in pursuit of the Sartha, it's heading back towards the moon."

"Lone Wolf acknowledge!" Jason snapped.

There was no reply.

Jason punched in afterburners, calling for Mongol and Round Top to follow as he raced towards the crippled Sabre, which then announced that it was shutting down its remaining engine.

Mongol was finally forced to drop out, his afterburner fuel expended, reduced to coasting back towards *Tarawa*.

The comm link to *Tarawa* kicked on again. "We've got three, repeat three inbound bogeys, moving on Green four."

"Blue Leader, we're sitting ducks, we're going to get cooked!" The pilot sounded on the edge of panic.

Jason could well imagine the fear building up, sitting damned near motionless, watching as the red blips closed in for the kill.

The range was still ten thousand clicks off. He rammed his throttle to maximum, racing forward. Ahead his vision-enhanced screen showed the three Kilrathi ships closing in for the kill. A volley of shots raked the crippled Sabre.

"Eject, get out, get out now!" Jason screamed.

The Sabre detonated silently, a brief flair in the darkness of space. He closed the range, the first Kilrathi ship, an old style Salthi starting into its turn to make good his escape. Jason punched in one last shot of afterburner, lined up on the ship's bottom rear and fired off a quick succession of salvos. The enemy ship disintegrated, Round Top swinging about to make his second kill of the day, the third ship racing away to disappear around the far side of the moon.

"Break off attack," Jason called, then signalling over to *Sevastopol* with an angry gibe about not having suppressed all space based activity.

He swung back towards the still expanding wreckage of the Sabre, and detected two rescue transponders and called in the location.

Seething with barely suppressed rage, Jason lined up on the *Tarawa* and came in to land.

The flight deck was in near chaos as the ground crews raced to refuel and rearm the incoming ships for another sortie. Pulled off the launch ramp, Jason leaned back in his seat as Sparks ran the ladder up alongside the cockpit. She scrambled up and tossed him a towel to wipe the sweat from his face. Standing up he stretched and then climbed down from his craft and strode over to the ready room. As he came in the pilots looked over at him expectantly.

He took a deep breath.

"Not bad, not bad at all," he finally said, and there was a circle of grins.

He walked over to the mission board and then looked back at the situation map which was projecting a tactical image of the action on the ground. He listened to the situation report as it came in over the commlink and then turned back to the pilots.

"Third section of Blue squadron, scramble back out. Mongol, you're in charge of the section, report in to White Knight on the ground link channel, she'll give you your assignments."

"Thank you, sir!" Mongol grinned and he raced out of the room, followed by three other pilots.

Round Top came in to the room and Jason went up to him and shook his hand.

"Damned fine work, Round Top, another couple of missions and you'll be an ace."

"I was scared to death the whole time," Round Top said sheepishly.

"Good, stay scared, and just keep shooting straight."

Jason turned away, barely noticing the cup of coffee that one of the pilots put in his hand as he punched up the situation board on the holo screen to check on the status of each spacecraft. Three fighters, one recon, and one Sabre fighter/bomber were down for repairs and off the mission list.

Doomsday came into the room and angrily threw his helmet on a chair.

"They're picking up Griffin and his tail gunner right now. The kid sounded badly shaken."

"Hell it took a week to stop the shakes after my first eject," Jason said.

"His co, Jim Conklin, is dead."

Jason nodded, he had assumed that one of the crew was gone.

"That little spoiled jerk screwed it."

Jason said nothing, looking back at the status board. Kevin was on final approach for landing.

Jason walked out of the room and back out on to the flight deck. Tolwyn's fighter was pulled off the flight line and came to a stop. The canopy popped open and an exuberant pilot stood up and climbed out of his ship, joyfully slapping his ground crew chief on the back.

"I got one, I got a Drakhri," Kevin announced, coming towards Jason.

Jason said nothing, looking at Kevin coldly.

"Didn't you hear me, sir? I got a Drakhri."

"First off it was a Sartha, so get your plane recognition straight."

"I'm sorry, sir. I guess I'm just excited."

"That Sabre you were supposed to cover," Jason started, his voice cold.

"That Sartha was coming straight in on us," Kevin interrupted, "I snapped a thousand clicks ahead to meet him and the furball turned and ran back towards the moon's surface. I figured if I didn't nail him right there he'd be back up for more trouble, maybe hit some of the medevac's coming back up. So I went down and got him."

Jason said nothing in reply.

"The Sabre got back all right?" Kevin asked, his voice suddenly nervous.

"You fell for the oldest trick in the book. Lure away the escorts and then jump the bombers. Three Kilrathi sortied as soon as you were clear. They got the ship."

Kevin looked at the deck.

"The crew?"

"Remember Jim Conklin?"

"Yeah."

"Well remember him, he's dead."

"What about Griffin and Tarku?" he whispered, his head lowered.

"Rescue is picking them up."

Kevin stood silent.

"You killed Jim Conklin because you were out after glory. You wanted a kill and you disobeyed my order to stay with the cripple."

"But sir—"

"Don't 'but sir' me," Jason said softly, his voice barely raised, ground crews not twenty feet away not even aware that a major chewing out was in progress.

"I didn't get the order," Kevin said quietly.

"Let me guess, your radio was on the blink."

Kevin nodded.

"I got scorched a bit down on the planet, it was drifting in and out."

"That's bull. That line's been out there since pilots first flew and wanted to ignore an order. So don't hand that crap to me, mister."

Kevin looked at him defiantly.

"I thought I was doing the right thing."

"You're grounded, mister. I'm giving your ship to Nova, her ship got shot up."

"She can't fly worth a damn."

"I don't give a damn if she couldn't fly through the middle of the Ring Nebula with her eyes open. I'd rather have her on my wing than you," Jason snarled, raising his voice for the first time. "You're confined to quarters."

Kevin turned and stalked off, his face pale, and Jason returned to the ready room.

Doomsday came over to Jason's side.

"So what are you going to do with Tolwyn?"

"I grounded him for the duration of this mission."

"Grounded him? That damned spoiled brat should have his wings permanently clipped. We lost a Sabre because of him and a damned promising copilot."

Jason nodded.

He noticed Sparks standing to one side.

"What the hell is it now, Sparks?"

"Sir, Lone Wolf's crew chief just told me that the kid's entire bottom shielding is gone, his durasteel armor down to just twenty millimeters. He was scorching it close."

"And his radio?"

"Blown out, sir."

"Thanks Sparks, and sorry I barked."

"It's all right, sir," and again she flashed her radiant smile and went back to overseeing her crews.

Jason sighed and looked back at Doomsday.

"I think he made a judgement call, and figured that it was best to dump that Kilrathi before he got away. It's just that he guessed wrong. He disobeyed standard operating procedures in leaving a crippled plane. If nothing had happened I'd have chewed him out a little and then sent him on his way. As to the radio? Maybe it did blink out before the Sabre was lost, maybe it didn't, but you know we've all used that excuse when we were out after a kill we just didn't want to get away."

Doomsday chuckled and nodded.

"I think his killer instinct took over," Jason continued. "It's what makes us fighter pilots rather than jockeying some damned transport ship back in the rear, or teaching ground school to a bunch of pimply kids. He's got the killer instinct, and we need more like him. We've just got to break him first, rub that snobby upper crust crap out of his hide, teach him the ropes, and teach him to think with his head, rather than fly like another Maniac."

"What about Conklin?"

"War kills people," Jason said quietly. "It's another letter for me to write. But we got off light for a bunch of amateur kids. I was expecting five times as many casualties."

"I still think that kid is a spoiled brat and a royal pain in the ass."

"Oh, I fully agree," Jason replied, "but someday he just might make a damned fine fighter pilot."

"My lord Thrakhath."

He turned his chair to look at the messenger. Something was wrong; it was evident by the young warrior's face. This one could not conceal his emotions, not a good thing for a staff officer. Even in the worst of times he expected absolute calm.

"Go on then."

"We've just received this communication from Imperial Fleet Command."

The messenger placed a sheet of folded paper on Thrakhath's desk, the top cover of the sheet bearing the red triangle denoting that the message was top secret.

"Have you read the message?"

"I was the one who transcribed it, sire, as it came through the coding system."

"Now tell me this, Jamuka," Thrakhath said quietly, looking up at the messenger. "Did you walk or run from the communications center?"

"I walked, sire."

"You lie, you are breathing heavily."

The messenger was unable to reply.

"Consider what is now occurring aboard my ship. You are seen running, your expression one of agitation, something is therefore wrong. In your hand is a message bearing a top secret code stamp, and I am willing to venture that you carried it with the code marking face outward because you wanted others to see just how important you were, bearing a secret communication to my office. Am I not right?"

The messenger hesitated.

"Am I not right?" Thrakhath snarled.

"You are right, my lord."

"Fine. Do you now realize what is happening aboard this vessel? Already a rumor is flying that something has gone wrong, that I have received a top secret message and it bears bad news. Before this watch is finished that word will have spread to all two thousand of this crew. Rumors will become fact, speculation of what disaster has befallen our Empire will gain embellishment, morale will decline, fighting efficiency will drop."

He paused for a moment, looking down at the message.

"All because of your agitated, childlike stupidity."

Ashamed, the messenger lowered his head.

"What does the message say?"

"Perhaps you should read it, sire."

"You know its contents. I am willing to venture that the moment you leave my quarters you will be bombarded with requests concerning the contents. You will show your anxiety and, I am willing to venture, will whisper what is written on this scrap of paper to show off your importance, especially to impress some female that you wish to mate with."

"I have never spoken a word of what I transcribe," the messenger said indignantly.

"You don't need to speak; your face reveals it," Thrakhath replied, his voice cold. "Now tell me."

"Sire. A burst transmission was picked up from the planet Vukar Tag. Nine Confederation troop ships attacked the planet, escorted by two light carriers of a new design."

Thrakhath felt a cold chill but revealed nothing, his features set.

"Go on."

"The scum landed on the planet with a full strike force and destroyed the ancestral home of the Emperor's Dowager Mother. A holo image of the attack was transmitted with the message and is attached to the memo."

Thrakhath was silent, looking at the messenger.

"You have disgraced yourself by your agitated demeanor. You are to leave my presence, speak to no one, and retire to your cabin. I think you know the only alternative you now have in order to redeem your honor. Now leave me."

The messenger's eyes grew wide with astonishment and fear at what he had just been commanded to do.

"But sire—"

"You know what you need to do," Thrakhath said coldly.

"But sire, my family, I am the only son . . ." and his voice trailed away.

"Then don't disgrace the ending of your line by groveling," Thrakhath snapped, turning away as if the messenger no longer existed.

The young messenger attempted to compose his features and he bowed low. Walking slowly he left the room.

Thrakhath took the message and opened it. A small hologram disk was attached to the paper and he inserted it into his computer. The image was blurred, a problem with burst transmission which compressed a large amount of data into one extremely short signal in the hope of thus avoiding detection when the message was sent.

The camera operator, shooting from long distance, focused in on the ancestral home. Thrakhath felt a quick tug of pain, remembering a time so long ago, when he had gone there to visit his great-grandmother, who though already ancient in years was still spry and so full of life. She had taken him hunting in the canyons and there he had made his first kill of an Urgaka flying serpent. He smiled for an instant with the happy memory of her glowing pride in his accomplishment.

At least she was safely back at the Imperial Palace. With the start of the war her son, the Emperor, had insisted that she be moved from what might become a front line area.

He watched the image flickering on the screen. It was obvious what the damned humans were after. It was an assassination attempt, an attempt not on a warrior, but rather a cowardly attack on an old woman. They could have destroyed it all from the air and he studied the strike attack of the enemy fighters and bombers, none of which closed in on the palace. No, they wanted to do this one by hand, to desecrate and to truly make sure she was dead.

The human assault troops went in. He froze the image and enhanced the view of one of the ground assault vehicles. The crossed daggers and skull were clearly emblazoned upon the side. They had sent their best, the First Marine commando. Good troops, even a match for Imperial Guard. So they had sent their best for this defilement and he felt his anger build as he contemplated their foul smelling presence trampling through Imperial property. He unfroze the image and then stopped it again seconds later. He placed a cross hair marker on one of the humans, telling his computer to enhance the image and then cross check it against the human personnel file. Seconds later a small picture snapped on the screen with an intelligence bio briefing underneath. So their best division commander of the human assault marines was there as well. They had definitely sent their elite in, the commander taking personal charge. He unfroze the image letting it play out, watching as the commander stood with hands on hips and then appeared to laugh as the first commandos came back out, carrying their loot. The commander then walked up to the smashed gates of the palace. Prince Thrakhath watched with unbelieving horror as the filthy human relieved himself against the side of the building, the other males laughing, cheering, joining in to do the same.

"Lowborn bastards," the Prince snarled angrily.

They fled the building, most of them carrying loot, sacred family relics, ancient works of art—the filthy bastard scum—piling into their vehicles, pulling back; and then there was the flash of light.

Thrakhath lowered his head for a moment, his heart sick with rage. He struggled for control, wishing to strike out somehow. No, he had to keep control. This was done as an insult, a deliberate attempt at murder and vengeance, this was no longer war.

He looked down again at the report. Nine transports and two carriers. The report did not specify. A modification of the *Concordia* design perhaps? No, there would have been more air support. Smaller carriers. He'd need more data, more information before formulating a plan, they'd have to contact the hidden surveillance base and get a close-up sweep of the enemy ships. But this had to be answered. Vukar Tag had to be retaken, the trick was not just to retake it, but also to gain a bloody and fitting revenge for this act of defilement.

He breathed deeply, closing his eyes, reaching inward for calm rational thought to help guide his plan.

There was a knock on the door.

He closed the report and switched off the holo screen.

"Enter."

Another messenger stood in the doorway, features fixed with an appearance of cold detachment.

"Sire."

"What is it?"

"Jamuka was just found in his quarters."

"And?"

"He's cut his own throat. He's dead sire."

"I know."

The messenger looked puzzled and then the detached look returned.

"Bring our ship about, send an order to the entire home fleet to rendezvous at once at the Ujarka Sector.

I will have detailed orders for the rendezvous within the hour. Also, I want a secured channel opened to the Imperial Palace. I wish to speak at once to my grandfather."

The messenger, never displaying a flicker of emotion, bowed and closed the door.

• CHAPTER V

"Jump initiation sequence is on full automatic and counting at ten, nine . . ."

Jason looked over at the holo screen in his office as it showed a forward projection from the bow of the *Tarawa*. The jump hit and the screen took a second to refocus. He felt a sudden tug at his heart as they came into the Niven Sector. He didn't need a computer nav check to tell him he was back in a sector in which he had flown for hundreds of hours. A minute later the marine transport *Bangor* flashed into the sector several dozen clicks behind them and they both set course for the rendezvous point.

A flight of four Rapiers standing sentry at the jump point pulled a perfect fly by, breaking into a diamond pattern and rolling as they shot past *Tarawa*.

"Only one group of pilots can fly that well," Janice said, coming up to sit by Jason's side to watch the show.

He nodded, saying nothing.

"Any guess as to what's going on?"

Jason looked over at her, tempted to imply that he was in the know, but couldn't.

"Your guess is as good as mine."

"Kind of strange. We get diverted to pull a surprise landing. The battle is still being fought and less than twelve hours after the assault they pull their top commando unit out, us along with 'em, and ship us out here, straight to our main battle task force."

"Think O'Brian knows?" Janice asked.

"Doubt it. He seemed in a real stew over it all at staff meeting, that guy is like a Centauri bear with a feather rammed up its snout when he's been kept in the dark for security reasons; acts like it's a personal affront to his dignity.

"There she is," Doomsday said quietly, and nodded back to the holoscreen, having remained silent throughout his comrades' bout of speculation.

Jason sighed as he looked at the screen. Smack in the middle was *Wolfhound*, sister ship of the long gone *Tiger's Claw*, and flagship of the Confederation's main task force under the command of Admiral Banbridge. But he paid it scant notice, for off the starboard beam of *Wolfhound* were two of his old homes—*Gettysburg* and *Concordia*. *Concordia* appeared to have picked up a few more wounds, the blast scorching dead amidships seemed like a recent addition. The ship was like an old slashed-up boxer, covered from one end to the other with scars. It'd been a long time since she had seen dry dock for repairs and a new paint job. In a lot of areas the bare durasteel was exposed to space.

"Damn, the whole fleet's here," Janice announced, and she pointed out CVA *Trafalgar*, cruising astern of the flagship, the four carriers surrounded by a swarm of corvettes, destroyers, cruisers, supply ships, minesweeps, and light battle frigates.

"A balloon is definitely going up," Doomsday said quietly. "There hasn't been a fleet gathering like this in half a dozen years. There's gonna be a whole hell of a lot of killing."

"And somebody's called *Tarawa* in for the show."

"Time to go folks," Jason said, and his two comrades looked at him enviously.

"Give my regards to the old crew," Doomsday said, "tell 'em that contrary to all my predictions I'm still alive out here."

Jason left his friends and headed out to the flight deck.

Repairs were still under way for the craft damaged in the assault on Vukar Tag. He saw Chamberlain under his Rapier, covered in soot, helping out his crew chief. It was the type of spirit he liked in a pilot. A crew chief, more than anyone else alive, knew all the ins and outs of a fighter, and helping on the repairs could teach a pilot a hell of a lot. The rest of the pilots were standing down, some of them sleeping, the ones who thought they knew it all, the others were in the flight simulators, or studying the gun camera holos of their strikes to try and figure out how to do things better. They had a hell of a long way to go, but with only one gunner and one copilot lost and two injured while covering a major landing, he had to admit that their record was a damned sight better than average, though he would never tell them that.

He walked down the flight line, scanning each ship as if trying to sense if everything was right. At last he reached the Sabre that would serve today as a shuttle. O'Brian was waiting.

"You're three minutes late, mister."

Jason, unable to contain his growing dislike, made a show of checking his watch and then nodded an apology.

"We can't keep the admirals waiting, mister."

"After you, sir."

O'Brian climbed up the ladder into the cockpit of the fighter-bomber and settled into the front seat.

"Ah sir, that's the pilot's seat," Jason said quietly.

O'Brian looked up at him coldly, climbed back out

and then moved to the backseat. Jason followed him in, sat down, and snapped his harness in place. He looked back at O'Brian, who was fumbling with the straps.

"Need help, sir?"

O'Brian looked at him, and Jason felt a flash of sympathy for the man. He was completely out of his league, not only in the cockpit of this plane, but on the bridge of an escort carrier as well. He looked at O'Brian with a friendly smile, as if willing to offer far more than just advice on how to strap into a cockpit. Damn, if only this man would get off his high horse for a moment, quietly admit his shortcomings and try to learn from the handful of combat veterans aboard ship. It was a lesson he had learned when still a second class flight deck mate on his first cruise and he never forgot it—listen to the old hands no matter what their rank.

"I can do it myself, mister," O'Brian snapped in reply.

"Sir, if you connect that part of the harness up that way, when you eject you'll get kicked out of the chair and have your legs ripped off on the way out.

"Don't you think I know that?"

"Sir, honestly," and he forced a friendly smile again, "I don't think you do know, but that's OK. There's nothing wrong with that."

"When I need your advice I'll ask for it."

"Have it your way, sir," Jason said quietly, his features flushing with embarrassment. He found that he was actually feeling sorry for the man.

"One thing though, sir. If something goes wrong, and I shout eject three times, all you have to do is reach down between your legs, grab hold of the D ring, and yank."

O'Brian looked at him wide eyed.

"That's not going to happen?"

"Of course not, sir, but standard procedure requires that I make sure you're aware of how that works."

O'Brian was quiet, and he nervously reached down to touch the ring.

"And just make sure your suit is fully pressurized, sir, before we launch."

Without waiting for a reply Jason pulled his helmet visor down, ran through a final check and then looked over at the deck launch officer giving the thumbs-up.

Since it was not a combat launch he simply nudged his throttle and the ship slowly drifted down the launch ramp and poked through the airlock barrier at a stately two meters a second. He provided a touch of vertical lift and rose up off of the *Tarawa*. When safely cleared he couldn't resist the temptation.

"Hang on, sir."

He slammed on full throttle and then kicked in the afterburners for good measure.

"Damn it, Jason."

"Sir, you said we were three minutes late. I'm making the time up."

He knew it was cruel, but damn it all, he just couldn't help himself. Tapping his stick over he quickly snapped the Sabre through a 720-degree spin, pulled a sharp wing over, then banked up hard, snap rolling again to level out on *Concordia*, calling in for clearance. The flight was over in less than three minutes and as they taxied to a stop and he pulled his helmet visor back up he detected a rather unpleasant sourish smell in the cockpit. For the sake of a captain's dignity he felt it best not to look back.

"We're on time now," Jason said quietly, as he stood up. He climbed out of the Sabre and looked around the flight deck. It was like coming home. After weeks aboard the *Tarawa* it was damned good to be on a real flight deck again, spacious, plenty of landing, hangar and work room, everyone moving about with an air of calm efficiency. Other fighters and shuttle craft were coming in, a steady stream of brass dismounting, moving purposefully across the flight deck.

O'Brian, his knees wobbly, came down on to the deck and looked over at Jason.

"Was that deliberate?"

"Oh, no, sir. I had to check the engine and controls out on the run over; the ship's regular pilot said that the throttle and stick were mushy. It's standard procedure to do that, sir, I assure you."

"Oh."

"I think you need to freshen up a bit sir. The head is over against that far bulkhead; I'll meet you in the briefing room."

Glad to be rid of the rather foul smelling O'Brian, Jason set off, knowing the way so that he could do it blindfolded. Everywhere there were familiar faces and he felt a warm tug of nostalgia at each greeting. He had never known much of a home life before the military, his older brother and he fending for themselves most of the time while their mother worked. Lying about one's age to join at sixteen, and then working up through the ranks, leaping from 2nd class flight deck hand to a wing commander in eight years was no mean feat. But almost all that time had been aboard either the *Gettysburg* or the *Concordia* and he felt like a kid coming back home who had finally made good.

He hit the main deck and reached the briefing room. He hesitated for a moment; it was crawling with brass and he suddenly felt very junior indeed at the sight of so many captain's stars, and the gold insignias of commodores and rear admirals. He took a deep breath and plunged in.

"Jason."

"Admiral Tolwyn, sir."

He came to attention and the Admiral, smiling, motioned for him to be at ease.

"You're part of the brass at this little briefing, so relax, son."

"Thank you, sir."

"How do you like being in command?"

"A challenge, sir."

"I knew you were the right officer for the job. *Tarawa*'s crew is young, mostly fresh scrubbed kids out for their first look at the madness. I thought it best that they have a young fellow like you running them and from what I've picked up, I was right. So what do you think of the *Tarawa*?"

"It's a fine ship, sir."

Tolwyn smiled.

"Listen, son. First commands sometimes turn out to be like your first really true love. Not the infatuation with a beautiful young girl type of thing, I mean the first really true love of your life. In the beginning you can never understand what anyone might see in her, she's not flashy or anything, and then one day you get hit over the head, and for the rest of your life you'll never forget her. I think you'll feel that way about the *Tarawa* if things work out."

He hesitated, as if he had suddenly said too much.

"I'll be talking to you later, son. Admiral Banbridge is coming in now."

"Banbridge?"

The call for attention swept the room, and Jason stood rigid, a bit surprised at the sight of Admiral Tolwyn standing as stiffly as everyone else.

The Admiral was old, balding, his remaining hair long since gone to white. But his carriage was trim, still spry and erect as he strode down the length of the room. As he gained the podium he smiled.

"All right folks, stand at ease and be seated."

His voice was pleasant, holding a touch of an

American southern accent, but filled with a certain determination.

He walked over to the holo screen and held up a small hand controller and pointed it. The screen snapped to life, and Jason looked at it with surprise. It was the Vukar Tag Sector.

"Gentlemen, this is Vukar Tag," Banbridge began. "Three days ago, nine regiments of marines, supported by two of our new escort carriers, stormed the planet and seized it.

"This, gentlemen, is the opening move in Operation Back Lash."

So something bigger was afoot. Jason looked around the room and saw Big Duke One, the marine commandant, and by his side were Svetlana and Colonel Jim Merritt, commander of the First Marine Commando battalion. So Big Duke had come back with the *Bangor*. If he was leaving the mop-up operation on the planet, it meant that there was definitely some larger plan at work. He settled back and listened as Banbridge ran through a brief review of the assault, swelling a bit with pride when mention was made of the ground support provided by *Tarawa*. From the corner of his eye he saw Tolwyn look over at him and nod his head with approval.

"I should now clarify something here. Our objective was not, and never was, to seize this planet. As a jump point into the Kilrathi Empire it is but a secondary approach, a single line of jump points with no branch-offs. To approach this way would be a slugging match and we simply don't have the resources. Our main objective was this."

He turned back to the holo screen and the image shifted to the ancient palace which was destroyed in the assault.

"Eight months ago intelligence ascertained that this building was the ancestral home of the Emperor's mother, the Dowager Empress Graknala. Our Kilrathi Psychological and Societal Profile Sector reported that such sites are considered to be sacred and out of bounds in time of war. The Kilrathi Empire has been wreaked by numerous civil wars down through its history, but never have such historic sites been violated. We have changed that approach."

He clicked the screen again and the ancient home disappeared in a fireball flash.

"We allowed a Kilrathi comm center to stay in operation throughout the assault and we are certain that this same image, of the Empress's home going up in flames, has already been viewed by the Emperor himself.

"We knew that the Empress was back on her home world of Kilrah at the Imperial Palace, but the Kilrathi don't know that we are aware of this. They can only assume that we came to destroy that sacred place, and perhaps to seize or kill the Empress as well."

He paused for a moment.

"Needless to say, we can assume that the Emperor is now rather thoroughly pissed off."

"We'll make his palace a low-rent district as well before we're done," a rear admiral growled from the back of the room, and there was a chorus of cheers at his comment.

Banbridge smiled and nodded.

"Our action has caused a tremendous loss of face for the Imperial family and has undoubtably struck at a raw nerve. It is a defilement undreamed of. Our Psych Profile people have assured my staff and me that the only response possible will be a sortie of the entire home fleet, a crushing display of force to retake the planet as quickly as possible and to slaughter any and all humans who dared to step foot on the planet. We've noticed a standard profile that when a deep insult has been offered, the only response possible is a crushing retaliation; to do otherwise is to show a lack of strength and resolve.

"Deep space drone surveillance has already detected a threefold increase in sub space transmissions on their fleet channels. Gentlemen, the Kilrathi fleet will move and it will come straight here,"

He paused and pointed back at the holo screen, "straight in to Vukar Tag."

He smiled softly.

"And we shall be there to meet them with this entire task force."

There was a nervous shifting of chairs, a low hum of whispers.

"We have spent half a year planning this campaign, making sure ever piece was in place. Here at this rendezvous point we have assembled the largest task force in nearly a decade, four major carriers and over seventy other ships. We will position ourselves one jump point back from Vukar Tag. A number of drones and several corvettes are already being vectored over to the Enigma Sector to establish a heavy pattern of false transmissions, to lead the Kilrathi into believing that our fleet is weeks away from Vukar.

"They'll strike with everything they have. The marine regiments will be down there, and well dug in. We will be sending in a number of supply ships with heavy ground armor, and a construction battalion to help with the fortifications and to create the impression that we plan to stay and convert the planet into a main base. We want the Kilrathi to think that we are there to stay and that a counterstrike must hit as quickly as possible. The mission for the marines now is simply to hold out against a concentrated and deadly assault from the finest ships and troops the Empire can throw at them.

"Let the bastards come, Wayne," the marine commandant snapped. "Hell, even without your fleet we'll kick their butts. In fifteen days we'll be dug in so deep it'd take ten legions of Imperial Guards to even make a dent."

"Believe me, they'll come, Duke," Banbridge said, "but this fight's going to be shared out to us blue suits. We want their fleet in the bag as well. Just as the Kilrathi start to launch their own ground assault, with what we expect to be a fair portion of their Imperial legions, this entire task force will jump into the sector, move at flank speed, and engage the enemy at close range in a battle of annihilation. It will be an attack dependent on total surprise. If all goes right we'll catch them with their fighters and bombers committed and configured for ground assault, their attention focused in on the planet.

"Gentlemen, I expect to tear the guts out of the Kilrathi Home Fleet, smash their carriers, and shatter their ground assault legions in their transports or while trapped in their landing assault craft."

He stopped and looked around the room.

Jason settled back, stunned by the audacity of the plan. The Confederation was just barely holding on, losses had been horrific over the last year and now Banbridge was talking about wagering most of the remaining fleet in an all or nothing throw of the dice.

"How many carriers will we be facing?" a rear admiral, the commander of the *Trafalgar*, asked.

"Intelligence estimates eight, possibly as many as ten."

"Damn," a voice whispered from the back of the room.

Jason settled back, his stomach in a knot. The *Tarawa* in such a fight would be dead meat. He listened quietly, sensing that though the assembled officers were game for the mission, they had their doubts that any of them would survive. It was a desperate long shot, but the way the war was going, a desperate long shot was what they needed.

At the end of the hour briefing, Banbridge called for any final questions. The room was silent.

"All right then, gentlemen. We'll break for section briefings by ship's class. This assault must go like clockwork; one slipup and we're all cooked. This fleet will be positioned for action in exactly six days and eight hours standard time. We've got a lot of work ahead of us. Good luck, and good hunting."

He strode down from the podium and everyone came to attention. Jason looked around, not quite sure of where to go next. Ship's captains were heading off to their separate briefing rooms but there were no other wing officers present. Suddenly he found himself wondering just why in hell he had been invited to attend in the first place.

"Lieutenant Commander Bondarevsky?"

Jason turned around to face an attractive young staff officer.

"Yes."

"I'm with Admiral Banbridge's staff. You are requested to follow me."

"What's it all about, Ensign?"

"Sir," and now her voice was all seriousness, "just follow me please."

Jason did as he was told and followed the young ensign, trying not to notice the rather provocative sway to her walk. He suddenly felt as if he was being watched in turn, and looked back over his shoulder to see Svetlana following him.

Damn, she must have known I was checking the ensign out and he felt his features flush with embarrassment.

They weaved their way through the ship and entered a section guarded by a detachment of marines. The ensign stopped at a door blocked by a lean muscular marine, armed with a laser rifle and wearing full body armor. She showed her identification.

"Your ID card, sir," the marine asked, his voice firm and direct. Jason handed him the card. The marine checked a printout list, then held the card up, looked at it closely, then looked at Jason, studying his features for several seconds.

"Your mother's maiden name, sir."

"Houston."

The marine looked back at the list and then stepped away from the door.

"Pass sir."

Jason took his card back. The door slapped open and then slammed shut behind him with a metallic clang. He took a deep breath. Banbridge and Tolwyn were in the room, which was nothing more than a bare unpainted cubical. He noticed a voice distorter attached to a wall, which would pick up every word spoken in this room, and send out a vibration that exactly countered the sound. If anyone was attempting to listen in from an adjacent room with a laser vibration detector they would get an absolute flat line. This had to be major to go through such extreme precautions.

The door slammed open again, and Svetlana entered. Next came two ship commanders, one of whom Jason smiled at, remembering him as a destroyer commander who had picked him up several years back after he was forced to eject. The commander, recognizing Jason, smiled in return.

"Congratulations on your promotion, Bear."

"Thanks, sir, I wouldn't have been here to get it if you hadn't risked your neck to reel me in."

"Know this lad, Grierson?" Tolwyn asked.

"Let's just say we shared a little fun with a tractor

beam while a couple of Kilrathi destroyers were on our tail."

The commando battalion commander and finally O'Brian entered the room, O'Brian looking around nervously.

"Gentlemen," Banbridge said, his voice flat, "from the security procedure instituted here, I don't think it is necessary to tell you that this little meeting of ours has an A-level security assigned to it. Any violation of this security is deemed to be a capital offense in time of war. Do we understand each other?"

Jason saw O'Brian's features, already pale, go even whiter.

"You all heard the briefing and before we continue I want to know what you think of the plan."

The room was silent. Jason looked around and though realizing that caution on the part of junior officers was a basic tenet of survival he decided to speak up anyhow.

"A gutsy move, Admiral."

Banbridge smiled.

"Thank you, Commander."

"But frankly, sir, I think you're going to get your butt kicked."

Banbridge looked at Jason and there was a flicker of emotion. Tolwyn smiled and turned slightly so Banbridge couldn't see his reaction.

"You're out of line, mister," O'Brian growled. "Admiral, I want to apologize—"

"Go on," Banbridge said, cutting O'Brian off, "Bondarevsky, isn't it?"

"Sir, you said eight, possibly ten, carriers will be in the Kilrathi home fleet that comes out to take Vukar. These won't be second-rate fliers, the home guard variety who are rusty and wear gold-plated armor. These will be their elite forces. Home fleet assignment in the Kilrathi Empire goes only to veterans and is considered an honor, since they are under the direct eye of the Emperor himself. It's also a Kilrathi tradition to keep the best in reserve to protect the Imperial throne, not only from external enemies but also internal. It's part and parcel of their political system. If you don't keep the best fliers in your vest pocket, one of your potential rivals might have them in his."

"Are you saying that our pilots aren't a match for them?"

"Admiral Tolwyn can answer that better than I can, sir. The *Concordia*'s met Imperial Guard and kicked their butts, and I've done my share of kicking. But, sir, you are talking about odds of up to two and a half to one. If they cripple but one of our carriers, the odds instantly jump to over three to one. We could take down five of their ships and they'd still be ahead of us."

He hesitated for a moment.

"I don't know what production is like back home, but I never did trust the promises of all those new ships we kept hearing about. Sir, as far as I know we simply don't have any more reserves. We've lost half our fleet carriers in the last year. We lose four more in a single action and those furballs will be at Earth's front door."

"The best defense is a good offense," Banbridge said quietly.

"I agree, sir. That's why I said it was a gutsy move, but you wanted an opinion and I guess I just gave it to you."

Banbridge looked at Jason closely and Jason found himself wondering if he had just sunk his career and would be working a security patrol base at the far end of the confederation until his teeth and hair finally fell out.

O'Brian looked over at Jason with barely concealed rage.

"Mr. Bondarevsky," Banbridge finally replied, "four weeks ago I took part in a series of full-scale computer-holo simulations of the battle we are planning at Vukar. That simulation confirmed exactly what you just said. If the Kilrathi arrive with ten carriers, we will most likely kill three, perhaps as many as five in the first strike. But that will leave five left over, and half our strike fighters and bombers already out of the fight due to damage or depletion."

Jason felt his blood chill at the term depletion. What it meant was that more than one of his friends would be floating through space, torn into tiny chunks of frozen, flame-scorched meat.

"After our first strike they will reorganize, pursue, and most likely destroy our carriers in turn, perhaps losing two or three more of their ships in the process if we should decide to strip our own defensive combat patrol and sortie them straight in for another offensive strike. We replayed that simulation from every angle possible and it came out the same.

"Quite frankly, and quite coldly, it'd be worth the trade-off if we were outproducing them in capital ships and trained pilots, but we are not. We're just barely hanging on. You are right, if we lose four more fleet carriers, half of all we've got left, the war is lost."

Banbridge sighed and leaned back in his chair. Jason wanted to ask him why he was then going to pursue the attack anyhow but knew he was going to get the answer, and had said too much already.

"Out of that simulation came a plan. What we have to do is to divert three, better yet four of the enemy carriers. If we're facing six or seven rather than nine or ten, we just might clean their clocks. What we have to do is get them to split their fleet."

Jason looked around the room.

"And I guess that's where we come in," Captain Grierson said quietly.

The Admiral nodded.

"As of this moment *Tarawa* and the escort ships *Intrepid* and *Kagimasha* are hereby designated Strike Force Valkyrie. The First Marine Battalion is hereby reassigned for transport aboard the *Tarawa* with ten landing craft. Captain O'Brian, you are hereby promoted to acting commodore of this strike force."

O'Brian puffed up visibly and smiled.

"And your mission is this, gentlemen."

Banbridge reached into a briefcase and pulled out a small portable computer and holo projector and opened it. A three-dimensional image of a sector of space suddenly appeared to float in the middle of the room over the desk.

"Holy mother," Jason whispered and Banbridge smiled.

"Your mission is to drive straight into the heart of the Kilrathi Empire and to launch a strike on their home system."

O'Brian's features instantly deflated and a look of near panic filled his eyes. Jason looked over at him, expecting the man to instantly break down. O'Brian lowered his head.

"If anything will split off the home fleet it will be this action. We've traced out a route into the Empire which will follow back trade lanes, using a recently discovered jump point that will take you across a dozen sectors in a single leap. From there, you'll be down into the bottom side of the Empire nearly five hundred parsecs from here and just four jumps from their home world of Kilrah. You'll then drive straight up, relying on speed and stealth. The key point, however, is that you will let the Kilrathi know you're coming."

"Know we're coming?" O'Brian asked, his voice a barely controlled whisper.

"Precisely, that's the heart of the plan. We expect

that once you've completed that long jump, the Kilrathi home fleet will be over halfway out here to Vukar and then, suddenly, you push the backdoor alarm bell. They'll be between a rock and a hard place. They won't know about the trap waiting at Vukar, but they will know about you. We expect that interior defenses will be damn near stripped for their offensive. Ignore you, and the home planet gets a hell of a shaking up. Abandon the offensive and race back home and honor is lost for not immediately retaking Vukar.

"So they'll split off several of their carriers to come back in and take care of us, while the rest of the fleet presses on to avenge the honor of the Dowager Empress," Svetlana said quietly.

"Precisely," Banbridge said, his features grim, as if the battle was already joined. "They'll walk into the trap with part of their fleet missing and we'll smash it to pieces. If it works, it just might trigger a political crisis that could bring down the Emperor himself and at the very least we'll have bagged half a dozen of their finest capital ships."

"It's a hell of a plan," Grierson said, "but frankly sir, what about us? I mean, I was sort of counting on being in on the victory parade and telling my grandkids how I helped win the great Kilrathi War."

Banbridge nodded and looked over at Tolwyn as if expecting him to speak. Tolwyn remained silent and Jason sensed that all was not right between the two.

"You're on your own," Banbridge said quietly. "I expect your task force to reach the home system of the Kilrathi. Do as much damage as you can, though I should add that for political reasons, the Emperor's residence is off-limits for right now. We have information that the outer moon orbiting Kilrah is a major military construction base and naval yard and I would suggest that as your primary target. We could bomb their capital for propaganda purposes but I want hard results that are going to help us out here on the front line."

"Damn, I wanted to see the Emperor fry," Jason snapped out angrily. "If we're going to be that close, why not go for the head furball and waste him?"

"We're trying to trigger a civil war here, not a holy war of revenge, so he is strictly off limits. If we hit him the entire Empire will bury its differences, unite under Prince Thrakhath, and go absolutely berserk," Banbridge said coldly.

"The second moon of the home planet is nothing but one giant military base and carrier construction center; it's an ideal target worth hitting and the one I'd recommend, but our surveillance is sketchy so that is not a hard and fast order.

"You are to stay in the area until the Kilrathi fleet jumps back in after you. Once that happens, we expect to already be engaged at Vukar. We've traced out several escape and evasion routes; get out, and make a run for it."

There were a million things Jason wanted to say but knew that there was no sense to it now. He looked at the map, tracing out the lines of approach and suggested retreat. He knew as well that they'd never come back. The *Tarawa* was not a fleet carrier, it simply didn't have the punch to cut a way through.

It was a ship designed to be expendable.

Banbridge looked around the room, his eyes fixed as if he wanted to say more but couldn't.

"A team of security people will report to your ships in exactly ninety minutes to load the flight plan into your ship's navigation computers, along with our latest intelligence regarding jump point positions and routes within the Kilrathi Empire. That is highly classified information and this will be the first time the Kilrathi find out just how much we know. A lot of good people died getting the intelligence data for Vukar Tag and on their internal defenses. We're blowing a lot of highly classified information on this raid, gentlemen, so I expect you to make it worth something. Your nav centers will be guarded until your departure which is slated for exactly seven and one half hours from now. Your crews are not to know the full extent of this mission until you are inside Kilrathi territory and have revealed your position.

"Colonel Merritt, Lieutenant Commander Bondarevsky, and Captain Ivanova, a special team will brief you on potential landing sites and air-to-ground strike targets, based upon what little intelligence we have, and I want a strike plan profile from the three of you before you depart."

Jason realized that if they were lost no information would ever come back as to what they accomplished. Banbridge wanted the strike plan before departure so that a rough assessment might be made later of what happened if they did get through to the target.

"Colonel Merritt, you are to move your battalion on board the *Tarawa*. New landing craft, fully loaded with combat supplies will come over from the 12th Marine transport ship *Weisbaden*. Those craft will pick up your battalion, move them to *Tarawa*, and your people will travel aboard that ship."

"Sir, our flight deck is already crammed to the gills," Jason said.

"Then it'll be even more crowded," Banbridge replied.

Jason looked over at O'Brian as if expecting some backup, but the captain was still in shock, sitting silently, hands folded.

Banbridge looked around the room one last time.

"Good luck, God's speed, and good hunting," he said, his voice suddenly husky. He stood up and strode out of the room, Tolwyn following.

"Into the valley of death rode the six hundred," Merritt whispered.

"Well, I'd better go check on my life insurance policy, see if I have time to double it," Grierson sighed, as he stood up and walked out of the room.

Jason looked over at Svetlana who sat back calmly, forcing a weak smile. Her commander got up and she followed him out, along with the other two escort ship commanders.

"We're all going to die," O'Brian whispered, looking up at Jason.

"Sir, you've got to pull yourself together."

"We're all going to die."

"I know that, sir. We're in the hole, but for God's sake, sir, you've got to lead us."

O'Brian sat silently.

"However I can help, sir, let me do it."

O'Brian looked up at him.

"I knew it all along. You're out after my job, but I'll be damned if you ever get it."

Startled, Jason stepped back as O'Brian stood up.

"There's a plan within a plan, I tell you that. I know the right people. They'll send someone in to get us out; they just can't tell us for security reasons. They wouldn't leave me out there to die."

He smiled.

"Yes, that's it, and we'll all come back heroes. That's it."

He walked out of the room.

Not sure if he was more shaken by O'Brian or by the briefing, Jason slowly followed after him.

"Bear."

Jason looked up to see Tolwyn standing in a side corridor motioning for him to follow.

Jason walked down the hallway and followed Tolwyn into a small wardroom, the Admiral closing the door behind them.

"Have a seat, son."

"I've got to get my captain back to the ship."

"It'll wait."

Tolwyn went over to a side cabinet, pulled out a small bottle, and poured himself a drink. He looked over at Jason.

"Sorry, bad manners, you've got to fly."

"It's all right, sir, I'll have a good stiff one once I'm back on *Tarawa*."

"It's a hell of a mess I got you, Starlight, and Doomsday into," Tolwyn said quietly. "I had no idea about the *Tarawa*'s mission when I was asked to pick out my best people for a new command. I thought I was doing you a favor."

"It's all right, sir," Jason said quietly.

"No, damn it, it's not all right," Tolwyn snapped. "The military lives and dies by its oaths and promises. You pledge to serve and obey. For some countries, in some wars, that's as far as the deal goes. If you, her warriors, get lost, or taken prisoner, and it's expedient for a bunch of lousy politicians to turn their backs on you and forget you, well that's all right. But a country that does that to its soldiers is nothing better than a whore and its leaders should be dragged out and shot."

"I wouldn't say that in public if I were you, Admiral."

Tolwyn smiled. "But I can still think it. A system worth fighting for makes the pledge go both ways. You fight for us, but by God we'll sacrifice everything we have to get you back. If you're willing to risk your life to protect us, then we're willing to risk all our treasures, our careers, everything to bring you back. No one gets left behind, ever. A country that abandons its soldiers and does nothing to save them isn't worth a pinch of owl dung."

Jason was quiet, realizing yet again why he would not hesitate to lay down his life for this man.

"I feel like hell over this deal, Jason. The Confederation is in desperate straits. A year ago it looked like we were finally getting the edge, but you know as well as I that the last year's been a disaster. If we don't turn things around, and damned fast, the Kilrathi will be dictating peace terms in the burned out wreckage of Confederation Headquarters back on Earth. That's why Banbridge decided to make you expendable. That's what the *Tarawa* and other ships like her were built for."

"I understand that," Jason said quietly.

"If you were all volunteers maybe I could deal with it. But you're not. I suggested that route but Fleet security said asking for nearly fifteen hundred volunteers would be a dead giveaway that something was up, and besides there simply isn't time."

"So we got picked."

"You got picked."

Jason didn't know what more to say.

"Son, I'm not going to leave you out there. I'll do whatever I can to get you out and that is a promise."

Jason felt his eyes start to sting. He had never really known his father, but he found himself imagining that he was most likely cut from the same cloth as the man in front of him.

Jason nodded his thanks.

"Can I ask one favor?" Tolwyn said.

"Anything."

"Tell me about Kevin."

Jason sighed and looked back at the Admiral. He couldn't give anything less than the truth and he told the admiral about the arrogance, the spoiled haughty displays, the loss of the Sabre, and how he had grounded Kevin until further notice.

Tolwyn's features reddened.

"O'Brian grabbed me in the corridor and told me about it, but his version was rather different," Tolwyn said quietly. "Claims you were riding him too hard."

"I'm riding him hard because I think he's got the makings of a first-rate combat pilot. He'll get his wings back and he'll do well, once he gets that pampered defiant streak out of him."

Tolwyn smiled.

"My sister-in-law," he said, shaking his head. "All caught up with the family name and wealth. Wants the lad to be a nice clean career officer, an adjutant in some safe brownnosing job where he'll reach admiral through the political route. Gods, how we've fought over that boy."

Tolwyn looked away for a moment.

"Tell me about O'Brian."

"Sir?"

"I want the straight line, no butt covering for a superior."

"I don't think he can cut it, sir. He's going to crack before we're done. That briefing scared the hell out of him."

"Exactly what I thought. But he's the fair-haired boy of someone back at headquarters who made sure his efficiency reports look like they were written out in fourteen-karat gold. He's also got more than one enemy and I think that's why they put him on the *Tarawa*. Figured you're all dead anyhow once the show starts, so why waste a good officer."

"Can you get him transferred out?"

"Too late. I told Banbridge what I thought, but all he saw were those reports and he wants him to stay. Though I hate like hell to think about what I got you into, at the same time I'm glad you're on that ship to balance things out a bit. I hate to put you in this spot son, but if O'Brian should crack you know what you'll have to do and I'll back you all the way."

Jason nodded.

"Anything I can do for you, son?"

Jason shook his head. He had no real life outside the fleet. The only woman he was really interested in was going out there with him. His mother? At least the insurance would go to her. Damn, she had given everything, a husband, one son, and now another. A lot of money from a grateful nation, three blue stars hanging in her window, and loneliness. He could imagine the letter that Tolwyn would send, to be folded away with the other two. No, there was nothing the admiral could do now.

He realized Tolwyn was the same in a way. Wife and sons killed early on in the war. Nothing except the fleet, and one spoiled nephew. He hesitated and then decided to go ahead anyhow and make the offer.

"Sir. I've grounded Kevin as you know. If you want I could transfer him off the *Tarawa* for an evaluation and discipline review. He'll get cleared—hell most pilots have pulled similar stunts at one time or another. We'll be gone and you can transfer him over to *Wolfhound*. Put him in with Hobbes' unit, that Kilrathi is a damned fine leader."

Tolwyn's features grew dark and Jason instantly knew that he had made a mistake,

"I'll be damned if I'm going to show favorites," the admiral growled. "The boy's assigned to the *Tarawa* and by God that's where he'll stay. A Tolwyn doesn't run from a fight. I'd rather lose him than have to live with the shame both for myself, and for him."

Jason felt a warm glow of pride for his commander and he drew up stiffly.

"It's always been an honor to serve under you, sir," he said softly.

Tolwyn nodded, and then extended his hand.

"Good luck son, and good hunting."

• CHAPTER VI

Jason paused for a moment and waited. He felt the shudder and didn't even bother to look at the shifting starfields on the other side of the launch bay airlock. Seconds later the ship's nav computer announced successful jump and started the countdown for the next jump which would hit in just over eleven hours.

So they were on their way in.

He turned back around.

"No way, no damned way, I need a cleared launch area and taxiway for my ships. Now either that landing craft gets moved or I'll order it pushed over the side right now!"

"Listen here, young sir," Merritt growled, stepping up closer to Jason. "These ships are my responsibility, and if I don't have them I don't land. And I'll tell you this, if you lay a hand on that landing craft I'll kick your butt from here to Earth and back."

"You damned grunt," Jason growled. "If you don't have fighter cover, this carrier will get cooked before you're even out of the airlock."

He could sense that the entire deck was going quiet. Hundreds of marines were bunked out under the wings of the Sabres and in any spare corner that could be found. Tension was already high and they would most likely enjoy a good demonstration of hand-to-hand combat just about now to break the boredom.

The deck was crowded beyond anything he had ever imagined possible. Each of the landing craft was damned near the size of a Broadsword, capable of carrying up to a hundred men, two M-77 light ground assault vehicles, an array of medium caliber weapons, with a full battery of ground bombardment missiles slung to the undercarriage. That alone gave him the creeps. Ten landing craft, each loaded down with enough missiles to rip the *Tarawa* apart a dozen times over, were sitting fully exposed on deck. Except for the hot-loaded planes, all armament aboard *Tarawa* was stored in blast-proof lockers beneath the flight deck, only to be hoisted out and loaded on just before launch. But no one in the design of the carrier had envisioned the addition of ten marine landing craft. There simply was no place to store the armament other than on the racks of the ships, a fact which Jason felt was the equivalent of handing a lit bomb to Maniac and then telling him to go blow something up—sooner or later something would indeed blow.

If the Sabre lost in the training flight crashed on the deck now, it would ram straight into several of the landing craft—and the *Tarawa* would simply disappear.

"Ah, sirs?"

Sparks, moving fast, pushed her way in between the two.

"Just what the hell is it, Sparks?"

"I've been thinking, sir. Take a look straight up."

"Damn it, Sparks, not now."

"Look up, sir. See them hooks on the ceiling? They never pulled them out when this ship was converted over from a transport. We could hang eight of the landing craft up there, and there'd be just enough room underneath for the taxiway. If we jiggle the other planes around, we'll be able to squeeze in the other two landing craft and still have room to spare."

"What the hell are you talking about?" Merritt snapped. "Each of those craft weigh nearly a hundred tons unloaded."

"I know that, sir. I was thinking, though, we could rig up a null gravity unit inside each landing craft. Move it up there and it'd hang weightlessly. How the hell do you think they do it on cargo ships?"

"Well I'll be damned," Jason sighed.

He looked over at Merritt who broke into a grin of approval.

"Make it so, Sparks," Jason said, and he started to walk away, glad that his body was still intact.

"Commander."

Jason looked back and Merritt came up alongside and put a hand on his shoulder.

"Care for a drink?"

"Maybe later, Colonel," Jason said coldly.

"Look, Commander, I'm sorry. I'm used to getting my way. It's part of being a marine I guess. I know you were trying to do things right, I just wanted to see how you'd do it."

"Checking me out, is that it, sir?" Jason retorted.

Merritt smiled.

"Don't blame me. I know the odds on this mission. I guess you have to have a death wish to be a commando to start with. But the other missions I've been out on, I always figured there was a fair chance of coming back. I just want to know if I can count on you in the pinch."

"And I pass the grade so far, right?"

Merritt smiled.

"Svetlana's told me a lot about you already. You're all right in my book," and he made a display of shaking Jason's hand so that everyone on the flight deck would see it.

Jason realized he had been manipulated in a little morale-boosting game, but he couldn't help but like the blunt forthrightness of this squat plug of a man who didn't just cut his hair short but rather shaved it bald—an affectation that many of his troops followed. Jason was glad that at least Svetlana hadn't picked that marine habit up. Merritt broke into a grin that showed several chipped teeth and Jason found that the smile was simply far too winning, like an ugly dog that suddenly had broken into a fit of tail wagging.

"I'll take that drink with you later, sir," Jason said, playing the game as well so that his own people would hear him.

"By the way," Merritt asked, lowering his voice to a near whisper, "I heard that your captain used to run a transport."

"That's right, sir."

"Then why the hell wasn't he down here to supervise this loading? He's got the experience; he could have figured this problem out in a second."

"He's most likely busy right now," Jason said, keeping his voice even, not willing to admit that the captain had stayed locked in his cabin since returning from the briefing.

"Well, my reading is he's so damned scared it'll be a week before he can unplug."

"I can't comment on that, sir," Jason replied.

"See you for that drink later, Commander," and with a heavy pat on the shoulder Merritt stalked off, pausing for a moment to cut loose with an excellently chosen string of expletives aimed at a group of commandos sleeping under the wing of a Sabre.

Jason looked around the flight deck and couldn't decide whether he should stick around or simply just give it over to the deck officer. He decided for the latter and walked off, checking out the marines as he passed. He knew they were putting on a show for the "blue suits," as they called fleet personnel and they were certainly going all out. Most had their personal and combat gear stacked up around them, and were lounging on their equipment, sharpening knives and cleaning weapons. Few of them carried the standard issue M-47 semiauto laser gun. A couple had neutron mini guns, which pumped out a thousand bursts a minute, with shoulder slings to help carry the thirty kilos of weight. Others were armed with mass driver scatter guns, which fired five hundred naillike flechettes in a single burst. Others carried a bizarre assortment of non-military sporting equipment including a couple of sniper scoped Stenson Drakon rifles, capable of dropping a twenty ton Vegan saber tooth from a mile away, and near all of them had at least one or two Kilrathi items, especially the famed claw knives which could disembowel an opponent with the mere flick of a wrist. Those not working on their weapons had pried open the lids of self-cooking meals and the deck was filled with the scent of standard ration packs.

"Care for a souvenir, sir?"

Jason looked over at four marines who were sitting in a small circle playing cards. They were all wearing the standard adjustable camo which, chameleonlike, would sense its surroundings and then shift the color of the uniform to match, so that all of them, for the moment at least, looked as if they were dressed in deck plate steel gray.

"Not really," Jason said politely and started to move on.

"Just a moment, sir," and a marine reached into his duffel bag and pulled out a small gem-encrusted gold statue. Jason looked at it. It was a beautiful work of art, with a free flowing style representing a Kilrathi female, but it was done in an abstract so it was hard to tell for sure. It conveyed a sense of felinelike grace and beauty that he found appealing. It was a side of the Kilrathi he tried never to think about, the fact that beyond the war, they also had private lives, had their own literature, music, and art traditions that were even older than that of humans. He had once heard a cycle of Kilrathi poetry, about the loss of a lover, being read by Hobbes, and found it strangely moving.

He looked at the statue and could not help but admire it. Though he wanted it, he also felt that its presence in his room would be disturbing. In his war, the killing of Kilrathi was impersonal, except for an occasional taunt on the comm link. There were no bodies, no wounded, only the quick and the living, and those who were dead. The statue threatened to somehow put a face and feelings on the enemy, something he could never afford to let happen.

"Got it out of that furball palace. A real nice bargain for three hundred."

He was tempted anyhow but shook his head.

"I'll pass."

"Well maybe this will interest you," a female marine said, grinning sardonically, and her friends started to chuckle as she reached into her duffel.

She pulled out a small loop of braided rope, half a dozen dark leathery circles hanging from the coil.

He knew better than to ask but had to find out.

"What is it?"

"Cat ears," the marine said, "cut 'em off myself. Now one set still smells a bit, got it on Vukar, but the other two sets are nice and cured, fifty for the lot. It's a great gift to send home."

He wanted to explode but knew he was being set up.

"I'll skip it, Marine," and he kept on going, ignoring their low burst of laughter.

Damn. It made him sick. What was this war doing to us, are we becoming like them?

He left the deck area and headed for the ready room. Doomsday was sitting in the room alone, nursing his usual cup of overbrewed coffee.

"How you doing?"

Doomsday looked up.

"One of the problems with being a manic-depressive is that you know that someday you'll be right and the crap really will hit the fan."

"Oh, that's great to hear," Jason replied, pouring a cup of coffee for himself and settling in beside his friend.

"We've got a coward for a captain for starters."

Jason nodded. He seemed to have real luck that way. He'd already been in one mutiny against a total jerk, now he was stuck again, but this time in the hands of a coward rather than a ruthless tyrant.

"And we're on a one-way trip."

"You can say that around me buddy, but not around our pups."

Doomsday nodded glumly.

"They already got it figured out in spite of the security lid. Oh, they'll do the old stiff upper lip routine around you, try and look like a bunch of John Waynes."

"Who the hell is that?"

"Didn't they teach you any history in school?"

Jason shook his head.

"From the rather self-contradictory film records it's believed he was a great war hero. But anyhow, it's almost reassuring to have some depressed people around me for a change; it could actually cheer me up."

"Just great," Jason replied.

He suddenly didn't feel like hanging around. Doomsday was one of his closest friends and also had that rare ability to accept a friend, especially one far younger, in a command role. It's just that he wasn't the most cheerful of company at times and Jason felt as if he needed a real cheering up.

"After the next jump there's nearly a twenty-hour transit time to the following point. Things should be squared away on the flight deck by then and I want our people out and practicing convoy defense and strike runs against capital ships. You and the other Sabres will be the aggressors; Janice and I will run the defense, so come up with a good simulation of a Kilrathi attack pattern."

"I've seen enough; it'll be old hat stuff."

Jason nodded and left the room. He was tempted to go back and join Merritt for that drink; there wouldn't be any flying for twelve hours. He thought for a moment of Svetlana, after all she was now on his ship, but pushed the thought aside; it was better to just let that pass. At the moment sleep seemed awfully tempting and he turned instead to go to his cabin. Before relaxing he settled into his chair and pulled up a flight line status report on his computer to check on the progress of repairs.

There was a knock at the door.

He groaned inwardly. The last thing he needed was someone else barging in wanting to talk.

"Enter."

"I could come back later."

He looked over his shoulder and felt the old heart skip again.

"Come on in, Svetlana."

"I figured since we'd be taking this little cruise together, there was no sense in avoiding each other."

She reached into a duffel bag and pulled out a bottle, two camouflaged field cups, and a corkscrew.

"Delighted," Jason sighed, closing up his computer

and pulling the one other chair in his office around for her to sit in.

She uncorked the bottle and poured out two drinks. A warm cinnamon smell filled the room.

"Got it in that Kilrathi palace. Can't read the label, even our translator was stumped; for all I know it might be furniture polish, but here goes anyhow."

She tilted the glass back.

Jason took a cautious sniff and then followed her lead. It hit like a sledgehammer and he felt his eyes water.

"Damn, those furballs sure can make a potent brew."

"Another?"

Jason smiled and shook his head. "I think I'll just nurse the rest of this one," he gasped and she laughed softly.

They sat in awkward silence for nearly a minute. He found that he wasn't really sure of what he should start talking about. Business? There'd be plenty of time later to go over the strike plans. The past? Far too dangerous. Damn, you couldn't even lead off with the weather.

"I'm sorry about blowing on you the other day," she finally ventured, "It's just, well, Jason it took a long time to get over you, and then suddenly there you are, that damned boyish grin of yours. It tore me up."

"It's OK."

There was another long silence.

"Do you like the marines?" he finally asked.

"Sure. They're good. I wanted to be with the best. Since I couldn't fly, I figured I'd pound the ground. I'm proud of them."

"They're a hell of a tough bunch."

"What do you mean?"

He hesitated.

"Go on," and she smiled.

"I just had one of your grunts, a woman no less, offer to sell me some Kilrathi ears."

"So it turned you off. A little too brutal?"

"I thought we were fighting for some basic standards in life, and it struck me as something straight out of the middle ages. Though the Kilrathi might do it, we still play by certain rules, treat prisoners fairly and with respect, and non-combatants are off-limits. Hell, I put my career on the line once over that issue when I refused a direct order to dump a Kilrathi freighter loaded with women and children who wanted to surrender. I believe we can fight this war without becoming barbaric."

"And what the hell else is war, a tea party?"

"You're not following me."

"For you it's nice and clean—end of the mission you come back to white sheets, a hot meal, and a nice young, clean, and well-scrubbed ensign or lieutenant with stars in her eyes to warm your bed."

She spit the words out angrily.

"You know it's not like that at all."

"I've been in sixteen landings," Svetlana said, her voice suddenly sounding hollow. "Every friend I had in my first company died on what was to be my third assault. I was down wounded and missed that little jump on what was supposed to be a cold target. They said the landing craft covered a couple of square kilometers when the dust finally settled from the impact."

"Wounded?"

She pointed at the thin scar across her temple and back to her ear. He realized it was a surgical cut and didn't want to know what they had to go in for and dig out of her brain.

"In a typical landing we lose too much. And I've done it sixteen times. The last one you saw was a piece of cake. We lost ten percent and thought it was a joke. I've retaken four human worlds that the Kilrathi occupied. If you'd seen what I saw, you'd take ears too. You know what they did to the civilian population on Khosan? Jason, I was on the team that retook that place. You want a couple of details about what Kilrathi do to women and children?"

He shook his head, unable to reply for a moment. The holo images of the torture and massacre, filmed by a Kilrathi propaganda team, had been captured after the fight. It was sickening. And there was the other part about Khosan that hurt as well.

She looked at him and a pained look came over her features.

"I'm sorry, I forgot your brother was part of the defense team that got caught."

"It's all right," Jason said quietly, "the letter said it was quick and clean."

"Of course," and her words were a bit too hurried, though sincere.

There were certain things in life that you clung to, even when you suspected they were lies. The letter to his mother from Joshua's sergeant, which described a heroic death, cut down painlessly by a neutron blast, was one of them. He didn't want to think of the alternative, the fact that his brother might have been taken alive.

"What has this war done to us?" Jason said sadly.

"It's made us killers. As good as the Kilrathi. Maybe someday, those who come after us, maybe they'll live a soft life of peace, grow up, stay in school, love music and art, fall in love, and never know fear. Maybe they can live by the standards you talk about. And the funny thing is, someday they'll even forget about us, never knowing just how thin the line was between freedom and slavery."

Her voice was filled with an infinite sadness.

"But for us?" she smiled. "You and I know what it's done."

"I wish it'd been different," Jason said. "I mean, that we could have stayed together."

She shook her head.

"I wanted to see action as much as you; the marines were a guarantee."

She laughed softly.

"A real guarantee."

Svetlana looked down into her drink for a moment and then back at Jason.

"Tell me honestly. If it was a choice now. If Tolwyn came along and said, 'All right, Jason, you can take the girl and go home, but you'll miss all the action,' what would you do?"

"I'm not sure."

"Liar." She smiled again. "Once you've been in it, you can't let go. I'm so scared about this next mission I can't sleep. Hell, that's why I'm drinking. But I wouldn't miss a crack at their home world for anything."

He nodded his head. He knew that he was as good as dead already, but just for once, it would be good to be able to give it to the Kilrathi, to hit them right in their own backyard, rather than this endless war on the frontiers. It was worth everything, and he knew he'd go nuts if he ever passed it up.

"So we're in agreement then," Svetlana said with a sigh, and she poured another drink, and then downed it.

"Maybe when the war is over," Jason said quietly. "Maybe then we can make another try at it."

"Old lover, when this war's over, you and I will be dust."

Her voice was hard and cold.

"You sound like a damned marine."

"I am a damned marine and don't forget it," and

there was a slight slurring to her voice. "You lousy blue suits look down on us like we're animals or something, but you don't know what it's really like. Honey, if you ever saw war the way I have, you'd puke your guts out."

"All right, all right. You choose to be a macho grunt; you don't have to prove it to me."

"Prove something to you? Flyboy, I don't need to prove anything to you. Go ahead and fly your lousy fighters, but it'll be the marines that take the planets and win this war."

"Without top cover, you're nothing but target practice. I'm not the instructor who washed you out of flight school, so don't keep trying to prove something to me now."

Her eyes went cold and hard and she stood up.

"Go to hell," and she stormed out of the room.

"Hey, you forgot your bottle . . ."

The door slid shut and he sat back in his chair.

"Nice going, Jason," he sighed and was tempted to pick the bottle up and pour another drink.

The door slid back open and she stormed back into the room, came up to where he was sitting and pointed a finger in his face.

"And another thing, you egotistical bastard—"

Suddenly the whole thing seemed totally absurd and he started to laugh.

She looked down at him, her eyes filled with rage. And then it all started to melt away.

"You were about to say," Jason whispered, looking up and smiling.

She hesitated and then her words came out as a whisper.

"Can I spend the night with you?"

"All right Blue Squadron, pair off with your wingmen; let's get a couple of thousand kilometers between each pair and practice some head-to-head dogfighting."

"That's more like it, sir!"

"Cut the chatter, Mongol," Jason said, a grin crossing his features, unable to blame Mongol for his enthusiasm.

He was amazed at how they were doing. The simulation of the convoy defense had gone flawlessly, with four of Doomsday's Sabres marked off as "kills" before they had even closed within five thousand clicks of target, and not a single simulator torpedo getting through. Jason could tell that Doomsday was still seething about getting waxed by Lone Wolf, who had nailed him as he closed and was waiting for computer lock on the *Tarawa*. The accountants back at fleet headquarters would most likely go nuts if they ever found out that the new planes assigned to *Tarawa* had clocked over two hundred hours of flying time in the last thirty days. Planes aboard frontline carriers were expected to last a minimum of fourteen months before their thousand-hour strip-down and rebuilding check, a process which grounded the craft for a month and cost a cool million just in parts. But the thought of it made him want to laugh, as if any of these planes would even last that long.

"Lone Wolf, you're with me."

There was a moment's pause.

"Aye, sir."

"Stick to me like glue," Jason said and he winged over, kicking on afterburners. He looked back over his right shoulder and saw Kevin closing in to follow. Jason banked right, watching, and Kevin nudged in a touch of extra throttle, following Jason through the turn. Jason opened his throttle full out and Kevin stayed close, reacting as Jason nudged his throttle up and down, Kevin following suit almost simultaneously.

"All right Lone Wolf, break left now!"

The Rapier turned over on its side and banked away.

"Switch on your combat simulation system, as you complete your circle; the game's on!"

Jason broke hard right, toggling up his own combat simulator which would fire his lasers and neutron guns at a one percent setting, with shields now programmed to simulate all hits as if they were full impacts.

As he turned he watched his screen, Kevin's ship now highlighted by a red blip. Kevin pulled out of his turn, snap rolling to throw off Jason as to his intended direction of banking. Jason pulled a high yo-yo, coming up over in a climbing bank, attempting to line up on a deflection shot. Kevin broke out of his climb, coming in straight at Jason, firing off a salvo. Jason, caught momentarily off guard by the gutsy move, pushed his stick forward, thus missing the incoming, and then pulled straight back up again, firing a volley which caught the underside of Kevin's ship.

"Damn!" and Jason grinned at Kevin's discomfort as he pulled up hard, snap rolling again and then breaking hard left. Kevin followed, punching in afterburners. But Kevin was on afterburners as well and yanked his ship into a skidding turn. As he rotated through, he lined up on Jason and fired several rounds, two of the three hitting squarely, shields forward snapping off, the computer reading that a quarter of the ship's armor was gone.

"Nice shot, Lone Wolf!" and he zoomed through his turn, catching Kevin with another deflection shot.

"Ouch!" and Jason smiled, sensing that Kevin was actually enjoying the encounter and a chance to nail the old man.

The swirling fight continued for nearly a quarter hour and Jason found himself grinning with delight at the challenge. But there was a predictable pattern to

Kevin's actions, a problem with new pilots who found a couple of maneuvers that worked and then stuck to them. If a fight was over quickly, it didn't matter, but in a long drawn out duel, predictability could be deadly.

Twice he was able to nail Kevin as he snap rolled and then broke out to port and the third time he went into the maneuver Jason positioned himself to nail the young pilot with a full deflection, but this time Kevin broke to starboard, skidding through his turn with afterburners blazing. Jason started to turn as well and then looking up in his rear projection mirror he saw Kevin roll out not a hundred meters behind him. Jason pulled up hard and Tolwyn stayed glued to his tail, a volley just skimming overhead. The second volley impacted full on the rear shields, and the computer simulated a full shield shutdown.

Jason took a deep breath, then slammed his throttle off, cutting all power. Kevin raced up on him, skimming just a couple of meters over Jason's canopy, the shields of both ships snapping.

He lifted his nose slightly and slammed a volley straight up Kevin's tailpipes and Lone Wolf's engines shut off.

"I'm dead, sir," Kevin said quietly.

"Good fighting, Kevin; let's head back to the hanger."

Clearing the airlock of *Tarawa* behind Kevin, Jason nudged his ship in through the tight quarters and touched down. As he climbed out of his Rapier he saw Tolwyn standing to one side by himself, while the other pilots gathered in a circle, talking excitedly, waving their hands back and forth to show their maneuvers.

Kevin walked up to Jason.

"A good fight, sir," he said.

"You don't like getting your tail waxed, do you?" Jason said quietly.

"I'm not used to it, if that's what you mean."

"Top scorer in flight school, even beat out one of your instructors if I remember your efficiency report correctly."

"Yes, sir."

"Look, Kevin, this wasn't some little demonstration to prove to you that I'm a hot pilot and you're not. I got past that kind of crap years ago. I want you to come out of your next fight alive. You might be facing Imperial Guard and you don't get to be an Imperial Guard pilot unless you've killed at least eight Confederation ships. I don't want some bastard over there painting your kill on the side of his plane."

"It'd be hard to tell that one to my uncle, wouldn't it?"

Jason put his hand on Kevin's shoulder and led him off to a quiet corner of the crowded deck.

"I want you to cut that crap out, Kevin," Jason said, forcing himself to not blow up at the insult. "I've got a hell of a lot of respect for your uncle, but the fact that you're his blood doesn't cut it with me. Aboard this ship, and in my command, you're Kevin Tolwyn, a damned good pilot, who is also one arrogant pain in the butt, and nothing more. Get that clear, mister, once and for all. I don't care who else aboard this ship has been kissing your butt or kicking it because you've got an admiral for an uncle, but you're not going to find that with me.

"I know you've got a tough road, people hear your name and their eyes go wide. I'll confess it confused the hell out of me the first time I saw you."

"I know that, sir."

"And you didn't make it any easier on me if you remember it. If I was rough on you, it was to kick the props out from under you, so that the other pilots in this wing knew you'd be treated just like them."

Kevin was silent.

"I know all of you are wondering where the hell we're going and why the tight security; the only thing I can tell you so far is what you already know, that the mission is damned important and you'll be facing the best the Kilrathi can throw at us. I can't tell you where, or why yet, but I can tell you it'll be one of the most important missions you're ever going to fly, and if you get out of it in one piece, it'll be something to tell your grandkids about. I want to make sure you fly at your best and get that chance to live. I owe you that not as Kevin Tolwyn, a nephew of a god almighty admiral, I owe you that as Kevin Tolwyn, a pilot in my wing. Do you read me clear on that, mister?"

Kevin looked at him quizzically.

"OK, sir," he said, his voice quiet.

"I'm putting you back on the combat flight roster as of now," Jason said quietly. "You made a mistake that cost Jim Conklin his life, but I think it was an honest mistake."

Kevin breathed a sigh of relief.

"Thank you, sir, I didn't want to miss the next show."

"Just remember one thing though."

"What's that, sir?"

"Remember every time you go out there, that it's not just you riding in that cockpit that you have to worry about. The life of your wingman, the crew of this ship, perhaps even an entire fleet might be in your hands. Think with your brains and with your heart, not with your guts. Do that and you'll be a hell of a pilot some day if we survive this next fight."

Kevin nodded, unable to reply.

"Now let's go get a cup of coffee."

Jason patted him on the shoulder and they started for the hangar door.

"One question, sir."

"Go on?"

"That maneuver of yours, slamming back the throttle when I was straight on your tail. In training school we were forbidden to do that because of the risk of collision."

"Well this is the real universe now, Kevin; it's a favorite trick with some of the Kilrathi aces. You see, in their training school they don't care if a hell of a lot of people get killed. They've learned that maneuver by heart. If they die getting rammed, at least it takes an enemy down with them. If not, chances are they'll have you dead in their sights and you're history."

"Yeah, I'll remember that now. But I could have rammed you."

"I trusted you, Lone Wolf. I know you've got the makings of a damned good pilot and I trusted you wouldn't."

Kevin broke into the first smile Jason had ever seen.

"Thank you, sir, I appreciate the trust."

Trying to suppress a yawn, Jason studied the holo map intently.

"If you're bored, Boneski, we can find someone else to fly this mission," O'Brian snapped.

Jason shook his head, making sure to avoid eye contact with Svetlana. It'd been five wonderful days since she had come back to his room. It was wonderful and yet filled with a sad poignancy, as both of them tried to forget all that had been lost, and also just how short a time they had left together.

"It's nothing, sir," and he looked over at the *Tarawa*'s intelligence officer who was giving the briefing.

"Are you sure the base is on that planet?"

"I can't promise, sir," the young lieutenant replied, "I'm just working off the computer data feed into our banks. The information came from Kilrathi who've defected. We haven't even got a remote surveillance drone in this far."

Jason studied the map intently. They had been running flat out for nearly five days, the supply ship, loaded down with extra fuel having just unloaded and turned around. Jason punched a control key and slowly rotated the map, studying the red line that was tracing their route through the next system. So far, intelligence had been right. They were coming up a back alley that the Kilrathi didn't even suspect the Confederation knew about. The only traffic they had encountered was a lone transport, which Doomsday took out, hopefully before it could get a distress signal out. With the next jump, however, the mask was supposed to be pulled off and it would be his job to go up, knock on the door, and announce their presence.

"All right then," Jason said quietly. "I'll take a Ferret out alone. I'll act as if I'm on standard sweep, and cross the flank of that station. The furballs will scramble and then I run and lead them straight back here."

"I still don't like that," O'Brian said. "Suppose they launch a torpedo strike."

"As I said before," Jason said quietly, "they'll be out in pursuit of a light recon fighter. They won't be loaded for a heavy ship hunt. Their standard procedure is to first find out what they're dealing with before coming in with the heavy armament. We want them to see us, and report it in. By the time they rearm and relaunch we'll be out of the sector."

O'Brian pursed his lips, and looked around the room. Merritt, Grierson, and the other ship commander looked back with disinterest. O'Brian cleared his throat.

"All right, but if they come at us with torpedoes I'll note in the log that you had promised otherwise."

Jason found himself still laughing about O'Brian's threat as he punched through his nav point and turned in towards the Kilrathi base.

He had maneuvered through an asteroid field on his approach in, using it as a shield to block their scanning. As he cleared the field he punched it up and continued his approach, pulsing out a radar scan ever minute, as if doing a general pattern search, knowing that the Kilrathi base would pick up the pulses, analyze them, and realize that a Confederation ship was in the area. It was the equivalent of hanging out a huge sign that said "kick me." And it didn't take long to get the response.

He rolled his ship over and started to race back, half a dozen Kilrathi light fighters on his tail at ten thousand kilometers.

"*Tarawa* combat control, I've got six Sartha behind me, coming in for a snoop."

"We are launching now," came the reply.

"That's not the plan; we want them to get a visual on *Tarawa*, hold on that launch."

"I have been ordered to launch a defense team," combat control replied, her voice strained.

"Is the captain there?"

She hesitated.

"Yes, sir."

"Then put him on the line."

There was a moment of silence.

"Doomsday is leading out a strike," she finally said, "and the captain states that you are to follow his orders."

"Damn it!" and he snapped the comm link off.

O'Brian was blowing it; it was essential that the Sartha see the convoy and then escape to report. If they were engaged forward the information might never get back.

"Doomsday, do you copy?"

"Right here."

"Switch to commlink 2331."

"Copy."

"All right old friend, you with me?"

"Got ya."

"You know the plan. The old man wants you to engage and destroy at fifty thousand clicks out. I want you to run, and keep pulling back. We need those Sartha to see the ship."

Doomsday laughed.

"Oh, will we be in for it, but I'll take care of it."

The Sartha were starting to fall behind, and Jason snapped his engine on and off, mimicking that he was starting to overheat. He scanned through Kilrathi frequencies and finally locked on to them. They were calling to each other excitedly, and it sounded as if some sort of argument was on.

He clicked on his mike.

"Your mother eats used cat litter," he shouted in what he hoped was good Kilrathi.

There was an explosion of roars from the other side.

"Bugs Bunny screws his mother," a Kilrathi taunted back in broken English and Jason roared with laughter. Apparently the Kilrathi had picked up some old Earth television transmissions that had been slowly traveling outward at light speed for hundreds of years. One fragment they had picked up had been analyzed by their psychological warfare department and they believed that this ancient animated character was a great folk hero of Earth. A number of taunts had been built around it and he remembered how crestfallen his friend Hobbes was when he was informed that such a taunt produced hysterical laughter from human pilots, since it had been one of Hobbes' favorites when he was still serving the Empire.

Jason exchanged a few more taunts, the responses leaving him in stitches and he found himself hoping that the pilot he was facing would survive their upcoming encounter. He almost hoped that someday they could share a drink and he could tell him just how comical he really was.

The *Tarawa* was less than fifty thousand clicks out, and he hoped that the Kilrathi were finally picking it up. There was a moment of hesitation from his pursuers when they detected eight ships coming up, another round of shouted arguments and then they pressed on in.

"All right, Doomsday, break back in."

Doomsday turned his ship around, several thousand clicks ahead of Jason, and started back for the *Tarawa*. The commlink channel from *Tarawa* flared to life and Jason switched the link off and smiled. He could imagine that O'Brian was going berserk when he saw that the fighters were running straight back home with only six Kilrathi Sarthas on their tail.

Jason watched his screen, knowing that he had to put on some sort of convincing show, both for O'Brian and for the Kilrathi who might grow suspicious.

"Ten thousand clicks we break back," Jason announced.

As they crossed the line he switched back up to full power and yanked back hard on his stick while punching in the afterburners to produce a skidding turn.

As he turned, the Sarthas broke into an open formation and the fight was on. He bore straight in on the lead ship, rolled ninety degrees, punched some more afterburner in, and turned again, coming up on the portside rear quarter. He squeezed off a sharp double burst, and fragments rained off the enemy.

Another burst would kill him but he held off. The enemy turned to try to circle in and Jason kicked on his afterburners as if he had panicked and was now trying to escape. The Sartha turned in behind him. Doomsday streaked past, with his fighters behind him slashing into the other ships.

Jason continued to run straight back towards *Tarawa*, the Sartha behind him, trying to close the range. He pivoted and rolled to avoid the incoming, struggling with his own instincts and training to fake a pull-up, then roll over and dive under, coming up beneath his opponent. No. He had to lead him in.

Three small dots appeared straight ahead and within seconds started to take form. The Kilrathi, intent on what he thought would be a kill, continued to bore in, still firing. Good, his gun cameras would definitely be on, recording what was straight ahead. Jason dived straight for the fleet until a blind man could not help but see what was ahead. The Sartha slowed and Jason grinned, imagining a rather panicked cry of "oh damn!' from his opponent.

To his amazement the *Tarawa's* long range laser cannon opened fire and Jason ducked his ship out of the way.

"Damn it, turn those guns off, this turkey has to report home!" Jason roared.

The Sartha pulled up and away. Jason turned after him, pursued briefly and then jerked his throttle up and down to simulate engine trouble.

"Doomsday, one heading straight back, let him get through. He's scared to death but he's got the information."

"We've scratched four of them, feels strange to not finish 'em."

"That's not the mission, form up and return to base."

Jason turned back in to the *Tarawa*, lined up for

approach and came in to a smooth landing. As he shut down his engine and Sparks helped him out of the cockpit, the deck loudspeaker clicked on.

"Commander Bondarevsky, report to the bridge at once."

"I guess you're in for it now, sir," Sparks said with a grin.

"Tell me something, Sparks, just how the hell is it that you always seem to know what's going on all the time?"

"I keep my eyes and ears open, that's all," she said quietly.

"I see."

She hesitated for a moment.

"For what it's worth, sir, I think that marine captain's a mighty fine lady."

Jason looked over at his crew chief and could only shake his head. They had tried to keep their relationship secret. Fleet policy, though it didn't officially ban such "fraternization," certainly didn't approve of it either. Couples were expected to be discreet and, outside the privacy of their rooms, to show military decorum at all times.

Embarrassed, Jason forced a weak smile.

"And she's awfully lucky as well."

He looked at Sparks and sensed that there was a twinge of jealousy in her comment. She stood before him, a streak of grease on her cheek, her hands dirty, her uniform a baggy pair of maintenance coveralls. But for the first time he also realized that she was an extremely attractive young lady.

"Ah, yeah, ah thanks, Sparks," and he quickly left the deck.

As he walked down the corridor, still in flight gear, the ship's crew that he passed looked at him and then lowered their eyes. As he opened the airlock door onto the bridge he could hear O'Brian's high voice:

"I'll have his stripes for this."

"Reporting as ordered, sir," Jason said quietly.

The entire bridge was as silent as the grave as O'Brian turned, his features flushed.

"You disobeyed a direct order to engage those Kilrathi beyond the range of this ship."

"Sir, can we discuss this in your wardroom?" Jason asked quietly.

"No! We'll discuss it right here!"

Jason walked past the captain and pulled open the wardroom door.

"Sir, this might involve issues of security and you know what Admiral Banbridge said about that."

Jason knew that it had nothing to do with security at all. Before entering the system the crew had been briefed at last on their mission. That alone had nearly driven Jason to distraction, since O'Brian's briefing was short on inspiration and long on the perils involved. But the last thing he wanted were witnesses to what he was about to say.

Fuming, O'Brian stalked across the bridge, his shoulder brushing against Jason, forcing him to step back. Jason followed him into the wardroom and slammed the door shut.

"I ordered you to engage those Sartha beyond range of the *Tarawa*."

"Sir, under the mission guidelines established by Admiral Banbridge we were to engage the Kilrathi in this sector, in such a manner as to lead them back to the *Tarawa* so that our position would be revealed."

"Banbridge is not out here now, mister, and I made a decision based upon the current threat."

"Six lousy Sartha a threat to an escort carrier, a destroyer, and corvette?"

"Don't you question my judgment, mister."

"I am questioning it," Jason snapped angrily.

O'Brian, his features flushed, waved a finger at Jason.

"Oh, I know all about you and that *Gettysburg* affair. You're a mutineer. You got away with it last time, but by God you won't this time."

Furious, Jason struggled for control to not say anything else.

"I've decided to cross this sector without detection. If we spring into Kilrah unannounced we'll smash them, by God. Now they know we're coming and I have a good mind to call this mission off thanks to you."

Jason turned away for a second. He felt his hands shaking with rage and then he turned back.

"If you do that, sir, our main task force will be jumped by ten carriers. They'll be destroyed and we will lose this war!"

He slammed the table with his fist, afraid for a second that he had actually broken his hand.

O'Brian blanched and stepped backwards.

"I'm grounding you; you are confined to quarters and we are pulling back now that the Kilrathi know of our whereabouts."

Jason felt a rising temptation to simply kill O'Brian and be done with it.

"At least the captain of the *Gettysburg* was not a coward, I'll give him credit for that."

"You are under arrest," O'Brian snarled.

"Listen, O'Brian. You were at the briefing. You know what's at stake."

"Our lives are at stake."

"Your miserable hide is all you're thinking of. If we don't do this next jump in towards the heart of the Empire, they won't divert part of their fleet. Over fifty thousand men and women are in our task force. They're all that stands between the Kilrathi and our homes. All of them will die if the Kilrathi don't turn back part of their fleet! You'll go back home to nothing."

"We're pulling out."

Furious, Jason turned away. God, was he going to have to initiate another mutiny? He had barely gotten through the last one. No one in the fleet would accept or believe that he was forced to do it twice in spite of Admiral Tolwyn's promise of support and O'Brian could change his story later, something he would most certainly do if they ever got back.

There was a knock at the door.

"Go away!" O'Brian roared.

The door opened and Grierson stepped in.

"Thought I'd come over here and congratulate young Jason on a job well done," Grierson said quietly.

O'Brian looked at Grierson in confusion.

"You lured those furballs straight in. It was masterful. I bet at this very minute the damned Kilrathi are going nuts. I had to come over and let you know how I felt."

Grierson spoke quietly, not even looking at Jason, his attention focused on O'Brian.

"Sir, I'd suggest we push this little fleet up to flank speed and head straight into the next jump inward as quickly as possible. Captain Teng just called me from *Kagimasha* as I was coming over and suggested we do that as well. It's how we'd react if this raid was supposed to be trying to sneak in and suddenly got discovered."

He paused for a moment.

"Don't you agree, sir?"

O'Brian's features dropped, his face going as pale as rotten bone.

He nodded his head, unable to speak.

Grierson turned to look back out at the bridge, the door into the wardroom still open.

"Hey, you there, communications, pass the word to the other two ships, bring her up to flank speed, head straight for the jump point. Helm, get a move on there and throttle her up!"

The entire bridge crew was standing in a tight cluster, looking at Grierson in the doorway as if he were a ghost.

"Well shake a leg and get moving! We're about to scare the living daylights out of the entire Kilrathi Empire. Hell, I'd sell my soul just to see their damned Emperor's face when he hears that we're coming for a visit!"

"Aye, sir," and grinning, the crew returned to their seats.

"Well I best be getting back to my ship, that little shuttle craft of mine can barely keep up."

He reached over to Jason, shook his hand, and then patted him on the back.

"Good work, son."

Jason looked back at O'Brian.

"May I return to my duties, sir?" he asked quietly.

"Return to your duties, Mr. Barnosky. Dismissed."

Jason followed Grierson off the bridge and back down the corridor to the flight deck.

"Your quarters nearby, son?"

Jason, still shaken, nodded towards the door and the two entered his room.

Without unzipping his flight survival suit Jason collapsed down on his bunk with a sigh.

"Rather fortunate you came along, sir," Jason whispered, almost afraid to speak too loudly.

"I was tuned into your commlink and heard the exchange. O'Brian exploded when you turned your radio off."

"Then you know what he wanted to do?"

Grierson nodded.

"I know your reputation, son; I also know the truth

about the *Gettysburg* incident and I fully supported what you and your friends did. O'Brian was setting you up while at the same time trying to find a way to squeeze out of this little crack we got caught in."

"Hell, if he pulled out, you and everyone else would live to see your next paycheck."

"Don't insult me," Grierson said coldly. "I know what the hell the stakes are, same as you, and I'll be damned if some coward kills a hell of a lot of my friends back at Vukar and brings down the Confederation just to save his lousy hide. So I figured I'd better get over here, cover your butt, and lean on him a bit. As long as he knows that he has two other captains watching him, he'll be forced to play according to the plan.

"Now I've got to get back to my ship. If you've got a problem again, here's a secured commlink channel which routes straight in to me," and as he spoke he jotted down the number on a slip of paper and handed it to Jason.

"Thank you, sir."

"Stay sharp, son, and for God's sake stay alive. You're the one counter we've got against him aboard this ship."

"Just great," Jason sighed.

Grierson smiled.

"Find that young lady of yours and take the next watch off and try to relax a bit."

"Just how the hell do you know about that?"

"Hey, juicy gossip is the fastest traveling news of all," Grierson said with a laugh and with another friendly handshake he left the room.

Jason switched off the lights, lay back on his bunk and closed his eyes, not even bothering to get out of his flight suit.

He wouldn't have even noticed someone else in the room if it hadn't have first been for the faint scent of honeysuckle, a smell which took him back so many years to when he was in flight school.

"Svetlana."

"Captain Grierson dropped by my landing craft on his way out and said you wanted to see me."

Jason smiled. Grierson was all right; if only he was the one running this mission, there'd be no worries, other than what he knew they were finally going to face when part of the home fleet closed in.

"The perfume?"

"Our good friend Janice loaned it to me."

"Perfume on a marine? Come on."

"Just shut up and follow my orders," she said as she started to unzip his flight suit.

• CHAPTER VII

"It is too neat, far too neat."

Prince Thrakhath clicked the holo film back to the beginning.

It was shaky, the Sartha pilot incompetent, and overcontrolling his ship as he attempted to line up on the Ferret. But there, clearly visible, were three ships. He froze the image and looked back at his intelligence officer.

"Are you sure?"

"Quite sure, sire. Magnification of the image confirms that it is *Tarawa*, one of their new class of light carriers," and the intelligence officer ran off the specs of the ship.

Thrakhath settled back into his chair and looked around the room.

"And the course?"

"Confirmed. A remote sensing drone picked up traces of a jump in the Jurbara Sector. The timing would fit precisely into the passage of these three ships."

Thrakhath looked at the strategic map display hovering in the middle of the room, and ordered the intelligence officer to trace the route in.

"From the Gmarktu Sector where the film was

taken, then into Jurbara. They're heading straight into the heart of the Empire," Thrakhath whispered.

The intelligence officer nodded.

"Get out."

Saluting the staff officer left the room.

Thrakhath looked at the map one more time, and then replayed the film again.

It didn't smell right. If they were indeed going for a raid, why bother to send out patrols that just so happen to stumble on a base, thus triggering a sortie which leads straight back to their fleet? They could have slipped through, their passage perhaps never detected. Secondly, they knew they'd been found out, yet still they were pressing in. Suicide. Such an act was ofttimes expected and honorable for a Kilrathi, but for humans it was rare.

He looked back at the map again.

Vukar Tag.

Was there a connection?

He walked around the strategic map which hovered in the middle of the room, telling the computer to plot arrival times for the fleet to Vukar and back to the center of the Empire. Six days back at flank speed, five days and a half out to Vukar.

Next he checked the *Tarawa*'s course. Just under six days as well if they were indeed going for Kilrah.

It was all too pat.

He called up his order of battle on the opposite wall and studied it once again. Ten carriers, over twelve hundred fighter and bomber craft, one hundred and twenty major ships in escort.

There was a knock at the door.

"Enter."

He looked up as Baron Jukaga entered the room, followed by Kalralahr of Fleets Rusmak and Kalralahr of the Imperial Legions Gar.

"You've heard?" Thrakhath asked.

"The audacity," Gar snarled. "First the home of the Dowager, and now they strike straight at our heart."

"And why? How does it fit together?"

"A defilement born out of desperation," Rusmak growled. "All our projections indicated that this war would be finished within another year, their precious Earth turned into an extinct and lifeless husk. They are doing this as revenge raids, to hurt our pride."

The Baron looked over at Rusmak and chuckled softly.

"Spoken as a true warrior, my good Kalralahr."

"Do you see it differently?" Rusmak snapped.

"It is not desperation; it is cunning," the Baron replied softly.

Rusmak snorted with disdain.

"I am eager to hear the wisdom of an intellectual such as yourself," Rusmak said sarcastically.

"Strike first at the Dowager to force the home fleet into a sortie. When the backdoor is thus left unguarded, sneak in and ravage the Kilrah system and thus place us in this little quandary."

"Are they even aware that the Imperial Fleet has sortied?" Gar retorted. "Have you proof that they are anticipating a counterstrike? We do know from our secret outpost on Vukar Tag that their own imperial guard is digging in, building plasta-concrete bunkers, fortifying. A ship landed yesterday loaded down with heavy armor and ground defense equipment. That indicates to me that they are following their standard procedure of fortifying what they have taken and then converting it into a base."

"The second carrier that struck Vukar, it is this other one we have now sighted," Baron Jukaga said quietly.

"How do you know that?" Thrakhath asked, taken by surprise and embarrassed as well that he had not considered that possibility and checked on it.

"I studied the magnification of the images from the Sartha and also from the ground station on Vukar that recorded the beginning of the assault. They are one and the same."

"Then that means they know of a jump line that we thought was secret," Thrakhath said. "By standard run it would take thirty or more days to circle down beneath the Empire and then slash up."

"Precisely."

The Prince let the thought digest for a moment. He turned to look at the back screen in the room, ordering the computer to bring up whatever intelligence data it had on the new carrier.

"Its design is weak," Rusmak sneered. "Only one launch deck apparently built on the frame of a medium transport. It shows they are losing the war of production and are reduced to refitting transports. It is nothing but a sign of desperation."

"For a desperate act perhaps," Thrakhath whispered.

"We have two choices," the Baron said quietly.

"And they are?"

"We split off part of the fleet to head back into the heart of the Empire to hunt this raider down and destroy it."

"Or?"

"We totally abandon the liberation of Vukar for now, and deploy the entire home fleet in a defensive posture."

"Impossible and ridiculous," Gar roared. "You are talking about the Imperial honor. Vukar must be avenged as quickly as possible. And secondly you heard the intelligence report. They are fortifying the planet. They know we will not use high-level weapons to bombard it, that we will land and take it back in a straight-out fight. Give them thirty days and they could very well have reinforcements brought in, and it will cost ten legions to dig them out. Those are my legions; I will not shed one drop of blood more than is necessary. If we wait, it will cost us our finest troops. That, I think, is their real plan, to make us bleed white in the retaking. Each day of delay will mean thousands more casualties for the Imperial Guard units."

"Nevertheless I stand by my analysis," the Baron replied, "and quite frankly, General, I don't even see why we should bother to retake Vukar in the first place; it is a boring and dusty world," and as he spoke, he languidly examined his talons as if looking for some minor imperfection in their lacquered polish.

"You are a fool," Gar replied. "There is no need to send the entire fleet back. We sortied together as a show of vengeance; a force of seven carriers will be as good as ten. All ground assault forces can continue on. With the remaining three carriers you can send one carrier straight back and two to flank and seal off any escape."

"Split the fleet?" the Baron asked quietly.

"Seven carriers are still an overwhelming force."

"And suppose it is a trap?" the Prince asked quietly.

The Baron smiled but said nothing.

"Nonsense, sire," Rusmak interjected. "A trap with what?"

"Vukar is bait," the Baron said. "I've suspected from the beginning that the humans have a plan within their plan. We know we are drawing the sack in around the humans for the kill. Their losses have been horrendous. If it was not for this little adventure of theirs, already we would be moving into our next operation, which is to seal off the entire Enigma Section from the rear and then to drive straight into the heart of their Confederation. They must know that as well. When you see defeat staring you in the face you take chances and I see this maneuver of theirs as that, a gamble to lure us into a killing match on their terms."

Rusmak laughed.

"You attribute too much to these humans."

"Yes," the Baron said coldly, "I do attribute much to these humans. I have learned to respect their intellect, their cunning, their bravery and skill. Our history of conquest has been far too easy; the other races we have subjugated have been technologically inferior and morally weak. These humans, however, are neither. Never approach them with contempt, Rusmak."

"You sound as if you love them," Rusmak laughed. "While you're at it, why not give your daughter in mating to one of them?"

The others in the room went silent at the insult.

"So she could beget a fool like you? I doubt that she would lower herself to have such a child."

Rusmak snarled angrily and came to his feet, hand on dagger hilt.

"Enough of this," the Prince said, extending his hand. "Both of you be silent. We are talking of a battle, not your philosophy Baron, nor your childish insults, Rusmak."

Rusmak glared angrily at the Baron, who smiled and ignored him as if he were so insignificant as to not even be worthy of consideration.

"Baron, I do agree with Rusmak that you attribute far too much cunning to those animals," Gar stated.

The Baron laughed softly.

"They know we will fight for Vukar, though it is worthless in a strategic sense. I daresay they attacked it because they have learned the high value we place on honor and vengeance; though in this war I consider such things to be superfluous."

"You say honor is meaningless?" the Prince asked, unable to hide the surprise in his voice. "You saw the holo of the obscenity their commander performed."

"A good bit of theater that. Come, come, Prince Thrakhath, don't you think he knew there was a surveillance camera filming that for your consumption? Their detection gear is as good as ours, in some ways even better. They most likely know the station sending out the burst signals is there but have decided to let it live."

"So what do you think will happen?" the Prince asked, growing increasingly annoyed with the Baron's attitude.

"We send our fleet in, expecting to launch a ground assault and their carriers appear, striking us while we're tied to a ground operation. If we turn to engage and abandon the ground attack all they need to do is get a handful of fighters in amongst the transports and landing craft and we lose our legions. If we attempt to defend the transports and ground assault, our counteroffensive capability against their carriers is crippled."

"We have a track on all their fleet carriers," Rusmak replied. "Two raid at Oargth, one in Bukrag, one is down for repairs, and their four remaining heavy carriers are gathering in Enigma anticipating our thrust in that region by our third fleet."

"And eight of them are destroyed," Gar announced proudly.

"So they are desperate," the Baron said.

"And this raid of theirs is a desperate action and nothing more," Gar retorted.

Prince Thrakhath leaned back in his chair and closed his eyes. He plotted out the lines of movement as if searching for a mathematical answer. There had to be a connection between the two attacks. It was obvious he could not ignore this *Tarawa*, but how to respond? The thought of splitting his fleet left him uneasy. If part of it should ever be lost, the political consequences could be devastating. He opened his eyes for a moment and looked over at the Baron.

You'd just love to see the home fleet disappear, wouldn't you? he thought. Your side of the family has always hated us, our bloodline not as royal as yours, and you'd just love the chance to grab the throne.

Yet to turn around with everything and abandon the counterstrike? It would make him look foolish, ten fleet carriers to swat down this fly, even though the fly was threatening Kilrah, the first time such an audacity had ever been offered to the Empire in all its long millennia of conquest. Never had enemy eyes seen the home world, unless it was as dishonored prisoners brought home as slaves or for public executions.

But if there was a trap at Vukar? What could they have waiting? He calculated yet again.

He had to do both; there was no avoiding that fact, and it made him uncomfortable. The other fleets on the front were too far away to be diverted back to home defense so it would have to be the Imperial Units. Besides, it was never wise politically to have units which might be loyal to other clans located closer to the throne than the Imperial Fleet. As for the retaking of Vukar Tag it was out of the question for any units other than those of the Imperial Command to avenge that point of honor, for to do otherwise would be to show a weakness before the other families.

He also thought of the secret memo on his desk from the Emperor, ordering that the raider must be dispatched but the Imperial honor was to also be avenged if Thrakhath believed that both could be done at once. Somehow a copy of the holo showing the humans taking Vukar was leaked to certain members of the court, the insult to the Dowager Empress causing howls of derision. She was never accepted across all these years, viewed as an upstart from the perhipery of the Empire and this insult was whispered by some to be a fitting revenge for her audacity in mating her way into the Imperial line.

Even though it was not a direct order from the Emperor to press the counterattack, just a strong suggestion, it made this debate moot, but he was curious to see how his underlings would act.

"Three carriers detailed to return and hunt this interloper down," the Prince said, his voice sharp. "I'll decide within the hour which ships it will be."

He opened his eyes and looked at the Baron.

"You disagree?"

"How can I disagree with a decision of the Imperial blood?"

"But you do disagree?"

"To split a fleet is never a wise tactical maneuver, especially when confronting a potential unknown. I still maintain that the assault on Vukar was intended to be more than just a mere insult to the Dowager."

"An assassination attempt a mere insult?" Gar snarled.

"Yes, precisely that," the Baron replied, laughing softly. "These humans are smart enough to know that killing the Dowager would cause a burial of all rivalries for revenge in spite of how some of the royal line feel about her means of gaining power. They undoubtably knew she was not even there and that the destruction of the palace would, as a result, simply be a humiliation rather than a call for full blood vengeance. And besides, the palace was old, decrepit, dusty. A mere frontier outpost. If I owned it I would have destroyed it as an embarrassment long ago and if the humans destroyed it I'd view it as a favor to improve the view."

Thrakhath detected the political taunt in the Baron's words, the implication that the line of the Emperor was not royal enough, the Emperor's mother of petty nobility, her claim to the Emperor's father one of mere beauty and attractiveness, and nothing more. He wanted to spring across the table and drive a claw dagger into the Baron's royal blue-blooded throat for that insult.

Not now, we can't afford this rivalry now. Let the war with the humans be finished, and then in the glorious aftermath the rivals can be purged. Damn this war, he thought. It had forced a burial of old rivalries in the face of a common foe and as a result the tension was festering, unable to be lanced and cleansed until the humans were destroyed.

"Sire, I do not wish to miss the strike on Vukar," Gar announced.

The Prince looked over at the commander of the Imperial Legions.

"You will not, nor will you, Rusmak."

He closed his eyes again. The retaking of the planet and the gaining of vengeance was just that, a mere retaking and exacting of vengeance. Little glory there. But to bag the interloper, to save the honor of the home system, that would be the game at the moment.

"I will personally lead the three carriers covering the home world. Baron, you will be in charge of the assault on Vukar."

Thrakhath smiled at the sudden discomfort of his rival who realized that he was trapped, forced now to redeem the honor of a woman and family he despised.

"I am not a fleet officer," the Baron said quietly.

"Rusmak will be in charge of all tactical decisions; you will represent the royal bloodline, nothing more."

He looked over at the Baron and smiled. If there's glory it will be to the loyal Rusmak; if dishonor it will be yours, he thought, and he knew that the Baron was already aware of what he was thinking . . . that was why he hated and feared him.

"Come on in, Tolwyn."

Banbridge, smiling, came out from behind his desk and extended his hand.

"What brings you over to *Wolfhound*?"

"Just a short chat before the fight, that's all."

Banbridge nodded his head.

"How are things on *Concordia*?"

"They're eager, ready. All available craft are loaded for a heavy strike; the pilots anxious for the show to start."

"I just got a courier in from Big Duke One. They're dug in up to the eyeballs. They're finishing up some bunkers that can take direct hits from matter/antimatter, even old atomics, and they'll still be sitting there waiting. Those fur butts are going to get one hell of a reception when they start heading down to land."

"Duke always did love a fight like this, the old leading of good men in a desperate battle against impossible odds. He was like that even back in the Academy, wanted combat up close and personal. Well, tomorrow they're going to get it."

"You saw the latest drone reports."

"Still no confirmed count of carriers," Tolwyn sighed, "to be expected that they'd find that scout drone while clearing the mine field. It's a trick we used once too often, hiding a surveillance drone in a mine field, and then expecting them to simply avoid the field."

"Whoever is commanding them is smart, damned good."

"Think it's Thrakhath?"

"I'd love it," Banbridge said, slapping his open palm with a closed fist. "To really clean that bastard's clockworks . . ."

"Suppose it's him that comes to clean our clocks?"

Banbridge looked over at Tolwyn.

"Not getting pessimistic are we?"

"I just like to consider all alternatives."

"No room for defeatism in my command, Admiral."

Tolwyn, sensing he had been reprimanded, let it drop. Banbridge leaned against the front of his desk.

"Sorry, Geof. Stress of waiting. I always hated the waiting before a battle. Once I get into it, it's just fine; God forgive me, I even love it, but the before part grates on the nerves."

Tolwyn smiled.

"It's always been that way. Ever read Henry V, the night before the battle of Agincourt? The fear, the waiting, the not being sure if all would go as you planned. It has always been that way on the eve of battle."

"You Brits and your history," Banbridge said with a smile.

"We British also have some other traditions."

"Don't start on that again," Banbridge said, his voice suddenly going cold.

"I'm just asking this, sir. If, excuse me, I mean *when* we kick their butts in front of Vukar, let me take my task force, jump down through the line the *Tarawa* took. The Empire will be off balance after losing most of their home fleet. Just let me go in and try and cut a hole for them to escape through.

"No."

"But, sir—"

"You heard me, Tolwyn. No, damn it! We're risking any hope for victory on tomorrow's fight. Chances are that even if everything goes according to plan we're still going to lose at least one carrier. If it doesn't go to plan, then the point is moot anyhow. I'm not going to throw *Concordia* away after a victory, in the forlorn hope of pulling out a ship that's most likely already dead."

"You're talking about fifteen hundred men and women as if they're pieces on a chessboard."

"I'm talking about the survival of the Confederation, Geoffrey. I didn't like sending those kids out any more than you did. But, by God, Geof, we're on the ropes and fighting for survival. Our carriers are the thin line between tens of billions of people and the vengeance of the Kilrathi. We have a grand total of seven fleet carriers left to cover the entire front, Geof; we've lost nine in the last year and it'll be another year before they finish repairing *Austerlitz* and our new heavy carriers come on line. They have at least twenty and God knows how many more coming into the fleet.

"You remember the budget fights long before this war ever started, when we were begging like paupers for the money to build the shipyards which would turn out capital ships? Now we're paying for it. It takes ten years just to build a yard and train the construction personnel, and five years after that to build a carrier in that yard. It kills me; those same political bastards who denied us the funds now blame us for the defeats.

"The Kilrathi were ready for this war, we weren't, and we're still playing catch-up after thirty years of fighting. I don't like it, but given the alternatives, we have to sacrifice *Tarawa* if we're to have any chance of winning, to even up the odds and buy time for our next generation of ships to come on-line. Geof, you more than most know what will happen if we lose any more carriers and the Kilrathi get in amongst some of our civilian centers."

Tolwyn nodded, and lowered his head for a moment, his features hard.

"Sorry to bring it up, Geof; your wife was like a daughter to me. I'll never forgive those bastards for what they did to you, to her, to all of us."

"You don't see it though, Wayne," Tolwyn finally said. "If that's what it takes to win, sending our kids out on suicide missions, then I think the Kilrathi have won anyhow. They've made us like them."

"Damn it, no; that's a final order and if I go down tomorrow I expect it to be obeyed. I've already told Fleetcom the same thing if something happens to me. You'll take over my command, Geof, but Fleetcom will issue you a direct order not to go in after them. No rescue attempt."

Tolwyn stood defiant.

"That stinks to holy hell and you know it, Wayne. Just what the hell has happened to you?"

"Would you feel the same about them if your only living heir to the family name was back here instead of out there?"

"Damn you to hell, Wayne," Tolwyn roared. "How dare you even suggest that?"

"More than one has," Banbridge snapped in reply. "And if I hear another word I'll find some other admiral to run *Concordia* in tomorrow's battle."

Tolwyn, enraged beyond the ability to speak, stood defiant, unwilling to back down.

Banbridge's paging line started to beep and he picked up the headset next to his desk. He listened intently.

"Very well, signal by laser link, all ships to maintain full radio silence but condition moved up to yellow."

He put the headset back down.

"Eight Kilrathi destroyers have just jumped into Vukar. Six have opened a bombardment of the planet, one is moving towards the jump point which we'll enter through to set up a picket, the other is holding station at the Kilrathi entry jump point.

"It's started, their classic opening move," Tolwyn said. "Within six hours their main fleet will jump through."

"You better get back to your ship, Geoffrey." He hesitated. "I'll forget what was said here."

"I can't forget," Tolwyn said coldly.

The two old comrades looked at each other for a moment.

"Damn it, just get back to your ship. You know I didn't mean what I just said. I just wanted to let you know what some people who aren't all that friendly to you are saying about your desire to rescue *Tarawa*."

Tolwyn nodded and started to turn away.

"Geof?"

Tolwyn looked back.

"Damn it, Geof," Banbridge said softly. "We've been friends a long time. It's been twenty-five years since you showed up in my class at the Academy and first came to my quarters for that party where you met Elizabeth. I want our friendship to keep, no matter what."

Tolwyn nodded and finally extended his hand.

"Good luck Wayne, God knows we're going to need it."

"Scared?"

"No," and she sighed, snuggling in closer to his side. He realized yet again that the military didn't have to signal its rather puritanical values any more directly than in the way they made bunks. Two people in one was uncomfortable if not outright impossible. There was a standard joke about how once you made admiral you got an oversized bed in your suite to make room for all the people you slept with on the way up.

"I'm just so sorry it's over."

"We knew there wasn't much time to start with," Jason whispered.

"There never was, lover. Not back in school, not out here."

He felt his stomach knotting up again. Never had he faced the beginning of a mission with such a grim certainty that he would not be around at the end of the day. It was a strange feeling. To know that the universe would go on without him. That friends would still be here, would hear the words spoken, shake their heads and mumble a few lines about "poor Jason." There'd be a couple of sad but laugh-filled stories of remembrance, maybe one or two tears shed in private, and then they would go on with their living, their fighting, and their own dying.

And he so desperately wanted Svetlana to live. That was the hardest part. She would go down as well this day. There wouldn't even be that to leave behind. At most, a short note in the home news bulletin, and another blue star for his mother, and hers, to hang in their windows.

He felt cheated. So many others had their moment, to fall in love, marry, raise a family, leave something behind. Not him, and not Svetlana.

He felt something damp on his chest, and knew that she was crying. She did it so quietly; there was no shaking, not even a muffled sob. Just silent tears.

He held her closer, not saying anything, feeling the beat of her heart. The ship was all so quiet, the occasional voices in the corridor muffled, as if everyone aboard was holding a silent service for himself.

"Svetlana?"

The voice was soft, metallic.

She sighed, reaching over the side of the bed to pick up her fatigue blouse which was on the floor. She held the collar up and pressed her insignia button.

"Here, sir."

"It's time, kid."

"OK, sir."

She dropped the blouse and snuggled back in against Jason's chest for a moment.

"Merritt?"

"Hum-uh. He told me to spend what time we had

left with you; he'd call me when it was time to start suiting up."

Jason put his arms around her and held her tightly. She returned the embrace and then ever so slowly pulled away. In the shadows he watched her dress and neither spoke. She sat back down on the bunk to lace her boots and then leaned over to kiss him one last time.

"I'll see you at the end of the day," she whispered.

"Yeah, the end of the day. Take care, love. Tell Merritt he's all right, and we'll be there to cover you."

"Don't take any chances."

Jason tried to laugh, but couldn't.

"I love you," he whispered.

"I've always loved you, I always will," and then she was gone, leaving Jason alone, to sit in silence, waiting for the signal that the final jump through into the heart of the Kilrathi Empire was about to begin.

• CHAPTER VIII

"All pilots, man your planes."

Jason looked over at the communications screen in the ready room. The young flight control officer was obviously agitated and on edge. The feeling in the ship was like a hot electric current. There was an almost hysterical aura of excitement over the fact that they were attacking the home world system of the Kilrathi Empire, mixed in with a sense of dread of what was coming.

"All right people, good luck, good hunting, now move it!"

The pilots came out of their seats, and started for the door.

"Battle stations, all hands to battle stations!"

The alarm klaxon echoed through the ship, the red emergency battle lights coming on in the dimmed corridors as *Tarawa*'s combat control system started to suck every available bit of energy for the shielding and guns.

Jason looked back at the screen.

"Scout report?" he shouted.

"Starlight's reporting twenty plus Kilrathi fighters and three corvette-class ships on intercept approach."

"All right, going to my fighter now, I'll hook back in with you there."

He joined the rush down the corridor. They'd been on full alert when the jump into the Kilrathi system was pulled, but to his incredulous surprise only half a dozen fighters and one light corvette were covering the approach. The battle was over before he had even launched. He had then ordered his people to stand down, to conserve their ships, and their own stamina, until they were within attack range.

Now it looked like the Kilrathi were coming out to block the way in.

He reached the flight deck. The marine assault troops were loaded into their landing craft and the deck suddenly seemed almost spacious. Merritt, dressed in full battle gear, with a standard issue laser gun slung over his shoulder, stood next to his landing craft, which was squeezed into the slot where one of the lost Sabres had been parked. Seeing Jason, he snapped off a formal salute and then a thumbs-up. Svetlana was by his side. He almost wished that in a melodramatic scene she would rush up to stand by his fighter as he took off, but discipline held.

She raised her hand in a wave that seemed almost childlike and sad. He waved back and then forced himself to turn away.

He hit the ladder and scrambled into his cockpit.

"Kick some fur butt, sir!" Sparks shouted as she pulled the ladder away and signaled for the tractor to pull him up to the flight line.

"*Tarawa* combat control, what's the situation?"

"One of our recon craft already lost. Starlight reports many, repeat many bogeys on sortie from the second moon, three corvettes approaching as well. Captain O'Brian has ordered our escorts to move forward and engage.

That was standard procedure at least, but it bothered him that Grierson was not behind the *Tarawa* to sort of nudge O'Brian along.

"Deck flight officer!"

"Here, sir," and her image appeared on his comm-link display.

"Push Doomsday up ahead of me on launch; I want at least one ship with torpedoes out there as quickly as possible."

"Aye, sir," and she turned away to shout the orders.

Jason switched back to the combat information center on the bridge to keep an eye on developments. His tractor pulled him up towards the flight line and then came to a stop as Doomsday's Sabre cut in ahead of him, the squeeze so tight that for a moment he thought that their wings would hit.

The crew was improving. He'd never have pulled a change in launch sequencing only a week or two before. But now that the heat was on they seemed to be moving like clockwork. The hot launch fighters went out the airlock, Mongol, followed by Round Top and Lone Wolf, and then Doomsday was moved up to the catapult. The Sabre snapped out and then Jason was moved into position.

He leaned back as the launch officer pointed forward and he was out, kicking on full afterburner, leaping straight ahead to catch up to Doomsday. Switching over to Janice, he called in for a report.

"This is Starlight. Pulling back fast, we've got at least twenty-five of them coming in hard, Dralthi, Sartha, a couple of Grikath, and three Kamekh corvettes!"

"Any carriers?"

"That's the mystery. Several of these fighters have ground camo paint schemes and no bloody carrier in sight."

"Hot damn!"

"I know. Damn it, Bear, we got within a hundred thousand clicks of the second moon before they finally scrambled. Kilrah was straight ahead a million and a half clicks away. God what an awesome sight."

"Defenses?"

"Full planet defense screening was up on Kilrah. A dozen orbital bases, their commlink channels going wild. But no carriers. I got a good scan of everything before they came off the moon."

"Beam the info back to *Tarawa* now. Send it straight into Combat Information, set up a side band to Svetlana, and get it to those marines as well."

"Got it going now."

"Good work. Head back in, rearm for combat support of landing operations."

Less than a minute later Janice shot past at full throttle, with only one wingman. Two down, Jason realized. Straight ahead he was already getting preliminary lock on the incoming wave and it seemed as if the entire screen had turned red.

"Intrepid?"

"Grierson here."

"Why don't you break back, wait for more fighter support?"

Grierson laughed.

"Going in harm's way, son. We've got to keep them away from *Tarawa*."

"We'll support. We've got one torpedo load, will take on their lead corvette," Jason replied.

"Hot work there; why not hold back for more fighter support?" Grierson replied.

"No time, *Intrepid*."

Seconds later he shot past the two escort ships, moving in line abreast formation.

"Doomsday, I'm on your port side. Pick your target and I'll support."

"See you in hell," Doomsday shouted, and even as he spoke the first Kilrathi Sartha, moving as a forward screen, opened up. The shots were close, even when fired from maximum range and Jason realized at once that these were not second line pilots.

Doomsday rolled his ship, kicking on afterburners; Jason followed suit. He heard Round Top, Mongol, and Lone Wolf calling out their targets as they waded into the head of the attack, trying to suppress Kilrathi defenses while the lone Sabre went in.

The space around Jason was crisscrossed with laser and neutron blasts, mass driver shots, and dozens of missiles. Pulling in directly behind Doomsday, so that he could almost see the color of his tail gunner's eyes, he watched his screen as three missiles tracked in and started to close.

"Missiles coming in!" Jason shouted.

"Setting up torpedo lock on their corvette, can't break!"

Jason watched the shots close in. When the warheads were within seconds of impact he popped off a spread of chaff and flares, two of the missiles detonating. But one came straight through. He pulled on afterburner and shot straight up as the missile, sensing the greater heat display of Jason's engines, followed, ignoring Doomsday. Jason pulled into a skidding turn and then shut down his engines to present the cold silhoutte of the forward half of his ship. The missile streaked past and he breathed a sigh of relief. And then it started to turn back as well.

He watched in horror as the missile weaved for a second and then picked up on the heat discharge still dissipating off from his engine nozzle. The furballs must have noticed that trick of turning and shutting down and reprogrammed their missiles to pick up on it. He started to fire up but knew that he was a dead man as the missile streaked straight in at him.

The missile detonated so close that he felt the jarring blow and it was several seconds before he realized that

Lone Wolf, in a brilliant deflection shot, had destroyed the missile that was closing in for the kill.

"Good shooting, Kevin."

"What I'm paid for, sir."

Jason smiled and waved as Lone Wolf shot past, breaking astern to hold off the next wave of fighters. His knees felt like jelly and he took a deep breath, struggling to get calm and kill the gut-wrenching fear.

"We've got tone! It's away!" Doomsday shouted.

Jason rolled his ship and looked over his shoulder as a spread of torpedoes streaked away from the Sabre and leaped in towards the lead Kilrathi corvette. The corvette sent out a spread of shot and then turned straight in to present as narrow a target as possible. The torpedoes detonated across the bow, splitting the ship open and it disappeared in a silently spreading ball of incandescent fire.

"Scratch one, Doomsday. Good shooting; now get the hell out."

Doomsday continued straight in and Jason followed, shouting a curse. He felt an almost surreal sense take hold, as if instinct were guiding him. No longer even thinking on a conscious level, he weaved his way through the swirling engagement. A Grikath weaved in front, attempting to gain a lock on Doomsday and Jason fingered off a dumb shot missile round straight into the Grikath's tail, blowing the ship apart, and he slammed through the spray of wreckage, his shields shorting out from the high-speed impact. He felt a whoosh of air as his canopy cracked from the blow. A spread of torpedoes, outbound from one of the Kilrathi corvettes, streaked past, inbound on *Intrepid*.

"You've got torpedoes inbound!" Jason shouted.

The point defense system of the *Intrepid* kicked into action, sending out a spray of mass driver bolts, blowing two of the torpedoes apart, one of them striking a glancing blow as Grierson turned straight into the attack.

Jason looked over his shoulder to watch and then turning back, yanking his stick into his gut as one of the Kilrathi corvettes loomed up directly in front, diving down in an evasive roll. The ship suddenly disappeared, hit by a spread of torpedoes launched from *Kagimasha*, debris ricochetting out in every direction.

Breathing hard, Jason arced downward, kicking on full afterburner to avoid the wreckage, catching a brief glimpse of a Kilrathi, still alive, tumbling through space, arms flailing, mouth open in a silent scream.

He looked around and realized that nothing was around him. He had lost Doomsday in the confusion and was now heading straight in towards the second moon.

Nothing else was coming up.

Was this everything they had?

He switched through the commlinks. The third Kilrathi corvette was under heavy bombardment, most of the enemy fighters engaging the *Intrepid* and *Kagimasha*, with only six breaking on through to *Tarawa* where four of his fighters were holding their own while the rest of the squadron continued to launch.

He aimed straight in at the moon and accelerated for a quick look.

He pushed on in past the ten-thousand-click mark and down to five thousand, turning on his gun cameras, switching the image to his battle information screen.

Damn, it was a massive shipyard, and he started to count off the construction slips and docks spread out across several hundred square kilometers. And then he saw them, six carrier dockyards, each one occupied by a ship in various stages of construction, well protected inside durasteel bunkers with overhead phase shielding. A spread of missiles appeared on his screen, fired by ground defense, a light patter of long range laser guns joining in. He started to pull back up. As he turned across the surface of the moon the home planet of the Kilrathi Empire came into view. It looked similar to Earth, a beautiful blue green sphere, hanging in the blackness. He was tempted to push on in but knew it was useless, and besides, there was a far more important target right here.

He turned and headed back out, the missiles continuing in pursuit but far to the rear.

"*Tarawa* Combat Information,"

"*Tarawa* here."

"How goes it?"

"Incoming fighter attack destroyed, lost one fighter, one seriously damaged."

He didn't want to ask who was going to be scratched off the list.

"Uploading additional information on the second moon. Found one hell of a fat and juicy target. Here comes the information; be sure to pass it on to the marines."

He hit the upload and within a second a burst signal forwarded the data.

As he continued to climb back out he passed through where the swirling battle had been, only moments before. Several Kilrathi fighters were still making sweeps on *Kagimasha*, which had taken a hit to its main engine. As Jason closed in, a wing of four fighters from *Tarawa* closed and within seconds the fight was over.

"Grierson, you get the transmit of camera footage?"

"Saw you going down, so I thought I'd listen in."

Jason smiled. Grierson was definitely on top of things, the type of commander who knew when and where to listen and when to move.

"We could set the furballs back months, maybe two or three years, balance the odds up a bit. Not just the carriers but the work yards as well. It's the best damned target I've ever seen!"

"I'll start to soften 'em up."

Pushing the afterburners up, Jason headed back to the *Tarawa*.

"Let's go for it," Merritt said, grinning with delight, slamming his fist on the hard copy photos spread out on the table.

"How long will it take?" O'Brian asked quietly.

"Those are hardened sites; capital ship bombardment won't do it. Oh, it'll loosen things up, but we want the machinery, the docks, the stuff that makes the ships, and yes, the trained construction personnel as well. Each one of them is far more important in this war than any Imperial Guard soldier and has to be treated that way."

He looked over at Jason.

"They're in this war as well, even if they aren't carrying guns."

"I know that," Jason said quietly, hating to agree but realizing that Merritt was right.

"That means going in, placing matter/antimatter mines, blowing it apart piece by piece from the inside. We're just looking at the surface stuff in these photos. I'm willing to bet there's a hell of a lot more buried underneath.

"That moon's got a thin atmosphere, but not enough to support life for long. Smash the barracks and living facilities while we're at it and really mess them up."

He scanned the computer-generated map which was covered with tactical symbols that to Jason were something of a mystery, but to ground assault troops defined every detail of what they were going in to hit.

"Thirty hours standard should do it all. I've got ten

landing ships, five hundred people. There's at least a hundred or more juicy targets down there."

"I thought just six, the carriers," O'Brian replied.

"Those ships go through a series of assembly and fitting-out points. We're going for the lot, including the cruiser construction and fighter assembly. Thirty hours."

"Damn it. We made it here," O'Brian snapped. "I say we sweep past, bombard, and get the hell out. Swing by Kilrah and launch a missile spread, then we can claim to be the first to have ever hit their home planet. We'll be heroes. We could do that within an hour and be on our way. Their carriers could be popping through at any time and when they do I plan to have us out of here."

"I'm in charge of ground operations," Merritt replied softly, "and I'm launching to nail the fleet base. Gods, there isn't a marine alive who wouldn't beg for this chance to kick those furballs right between the legs, and here it is. I was itching to get at their capital and smash it up a bit too, but this is more important, this is the stuff that will affect what happens out in the real war rather than some stupid headline-grabbing for propaganda. Think of it, man, a couple of marines with a mine killing a carrier, something it'd take an entire fleet to do in a standup fight if those ships ever get operational. We could even the war up and do a job that would—if we got lucky—cost tens of thousands of lives if those carriers ever get a chance to fly."

"I'm ordering you not to."

"Go to hell," Merritt said with a grin. "Either you bring this ship into launch and support range or by God I'll shoot you right here and do it myself."

Jason swallowed hard, looking over to O'Brian to see how he'd react. O'Brian started to sputter, his mouth opening and closing like a fish out of water.

"When we get back I'll see you shot for this," O'Brian finally hissed. "I will stay alive if only to bring you back in order to see that."

"Getting back," Merritt laughed. "You've got to be kidding. Now pass that order and I'm not threatening you, Captain. I'm dead serious about this."

Jason noticed that Merritt had casually unsnapped the flap of his pistol holster, the weapon fully exposed.

O'Brian finally turned in his chair and punched the commlink channel to the bridge.

"Move us up to a one-hundred-thousand-kilometer strike range against the moon," he barked, and then slammed the channel off.

"Now clear the launch area or my people will do it for you."

Jason looked over at Merritt and grinned.

"See you down there, sir."

"Jump transit in ten minutes, sire."

Prince Thrakhath, trying to suppress a growing rage, nodded at his new astronavigator. The navigator was obviously nervous.

"Just do it right," the Prince said coldly.

He turned and stalked away.

It happened, there was nothing he could do to change that. Every once in a while a transit jump point shifted unexpectedly or simply closed down. Now, of all times, why now? The last jump, which should have taken them into the home world, putting them there hours ahead of the *Tarawa*, had gone awry, and they had instead jumped to the next system beyond Kilrah, forcing them to turn around and try it again. The last navigator was dead in atonement for what might have been simple bad luck. But in war some individuals were lucky, others not, and he had no room on his staff for the latter.

* * *

Jason circled back out around the *Tarawa*, watching as the last of the marine landing craft lumbered out of the docking bay.

The landing craft turned, kicking up its afterburners. "Going in now!"

"We're with you, Cat Killers," Jason said in reply, trying to keep the lump out of his throat as he watched Svetlana's ship turn in towards the moon.

Intrepid and *Kagimasha* had pounded the moon for the last hour, suppressing ground-to-space defenses enough to allow *Tarawa* to close within a hundred thousand clicks. A steady stream of Kilrathi fighters were coming up from the main planet, and down from a base orbiting a gas giant which was over a hundred million clicks away. But they were coming in disjointedly, in small waves of not more than eight or ten. He had lost four fighters and four recon so far in defense, but they were still holding their own. From the way the Kilrathi were flying, he suspected that they were now sending in trainee pilots scrambling up from flight school bases. It was a murderous waste of future talent, and he was glad to dispatch them now, rather than have to face them when they were fully honed for combat.

He started to realize as well that his own pups were no longer pups; they were flying and fighting like veterans.

"Now crossing into limit of ground defenses," Merritt announced.

Jason, flying point cover for the ten landing craft, focused his attention forward. The moon was twenty thousand clicks away and closing. As they crossed fifteen thousand a scattering of heavy neutron bolts came up and *Intrepid* moved to bombard the defenses.

"Green Leader, let's take 'em out."

"With you," Doomsday replied.

Eight Sabres and four Rapiers led by Jason kicked up their afterburners and started down, diving straight at the moon's surface. The moon seemed to race up, filling all of space until surface details were clearly visible, the huge spread of the base a series of lines cut into the dark gray surface.

Jason dove past the position of *Intrepid* and continued straight in. He started to randomly jink his fighter to throw off enemy aim and to his horror he saw a Sabre move straight into a heavy neutron bolt. The ship disappeared and for a second he thought it was Doomsday.

"Try and stay alive till you drop your munitions; each of these new missiles cost more than an entire ship, so let's not waste Confederation property," Doomsday's voice crackled on the comm.

They pressed in through a thousand clicks and then down to a hundred, boring in through the thin atmosphere.

"Break now!"

The remaining Sabres turned, following their nav screens in towards the preprogrammed targets which the computerized mapping analysis had indicated were potential ground-to-air defense systems.

Kilrathi jamming swept through the frequencies, attempting to mask their ground defense radars. Each of the seven Sabres dropped four air-to-ground anti-radar missiles, each one then breaking into fifty submunition rounds that locked onto individual radars, radio links, laser trackers, point defense guidance systems, and subspace transmitters. The missiles in turn fed back their target selections to Doomsday's ship, which was mounted with a command system for this major launch. This system automatically prevented overlapping of targets and reassigned missiles to priority hits if the first missile tracking in should be knocked out.

Fourteen hundred matter/antimatter warheads streaked downward. A spread of Kilrathi point defense guns kicked on, sending up thousands of marble-sized mass-driven rounds. Hundreds of missiles were hit, detonated anywhere from ten clicks up, all the way back down to the surface. But hundreds more got through, some of the missiles weaving and breaking to higher priority targets to replace those that were lost. The surface of the planet erupted.

The Sabres pulled up and away, streaking back towards *Tarawa* to reload.

Jason pulled out, circling around, waiting. There was a moment of silence on his tracking system and then more Kilrathi systems, which had stayed off the air, but were now switching on after the strike, came on. He squeezed off his one anti-radar missile, watching as it leaped ahead, then broke apart, the fifty small missiles turning and diving off in every direction. There were more detonations, the surface five kilometers below blanketed with flashes of fire.

"Bring 'em in!" Jason shouted.

"Going in now and thanks, Blue Leader."

"Godspeed, Svetlana, I love you and take care."

He couldn't help himself and he knew that everyone was listening in but at that moment he didn't care.

The ten landing craft streaked past, spreading out to hit their first targets. From under each ship the air-to-ground suppression missiles were streaking out, the barrages blasting into the surface, shattering point defense systems. Yet still there was some fight in the Kilrathi and Jason watched as a landing craft suddenly split open, nailed by a rain of mass-driven shot. He kicked on afterburner, diving down, trying not to look at the shattered, flaming craft as he streaked down past, lining up on the mass driver battery, dodging the hoselike river of rounds coming up. Another battery opened on his flank, but he ignored it, putting the first battery into his crosshairs and squeezing off a dumb fire missile which streaked straight in. A jarring blow rocked his ship, his starboard shielding clicking off, and he heard the howling shriek of shot tearing into his durasteel armor. He turned inward, the gunner following him. Jinking down, he pulled out just above the surface of the moon and streaked in ten meters off the ground, pouring in fire on the battery, blowing it apart. Behind the battery he saw a geysering mushroom of fire as the landing craft dived into the ground and exploded.

Jason passed over the ship, throttling back. It was obvious there were no survivors.

He clicked back onto the marine channel and drew a sigh of relief when he heard Merritt's voice on the air, directing the assault. Merritt's landing craft hit the surface next to the hardened silo for a carrier. Jason circled above them, watching as the front and rear doors of the ship sprung open, the top turret of the craft pouring out suppressive fire as marines, clad in light atmosphere pressurized suits, scrambled out the rear, armored assault vehicles pushing out the front. A firefight instantly flared up at the entryway to the hangar and Jason, coming to a near hover, pointed his nose down and fired off an extended volley until his charger went down to zero. He caught a glimpse of the ship inside and he felt a mad, insane glee. It was a Kilrathi carrier, near completion, and totally defenseless. Unable to contain his joy he raised his nose slightly and pumped a shot straight into the ship's bow, laughing with delight as durasteel armor peeled back in a vaporized flash.

"Save your juice, Blue Leader." It was Svetlana.

"First time I ever got this close without feeling like I was going to die of fright."

He pulled back up as marines stormed into the

hanger, fighting every step of the way with ground defense units. Circling back up, he held station ten clicks above the battle. Another flight of Dralthi sortied from the home planet, moving towards *Tarawa* and Jason listened in as Starlight, who was positioned as forward defense, handled the battle, losing one more of her Ferrets and a Rapier in the engagement, but stopping the assault a good fifty thousand clicks short of *Tarawa*.

Jason kept a mental note of his losses. Five Ferrets, a Sabre, and five Rapiers down so far, twenty five percent losses. Even though they had dropped fifty Kilrathi fighters and bombers, along with four corvettes, he knew the battle was shifting against them.

He circled above the battle for another hour, vectoring in on several ground targets and watching with a sense of envy as Doomsday, returning with a fresh load of munitions, led his Sabres in on a suppression of secondary targets, unmasked as the marines started to shut down some of the phase shield generating systems. The attack ripped apart barracks and construction areas, the heavy single-missile matter/antimatter warheads tossing up debris twenty kilometers above the moon's surface.

"Blue Leader this is *Tarawa* Combat Information."

"Blue Leader here."

"We are under attack from Kilrathi Stealth Fighters. Repeat we are under direct attack."

"On my way."

The screen scrambled and distorted for several seconds and then the combat information officer came back on, her voice high and strained.

"Blue Leader. We have detected one heavy carrier, repeat one heavy carrier and eight escort ships inbound at flank speed," and the screen distorted again.

Jason spared a quick look back down at the moon's surface.

"How long before carrier arrival *Tarawa*?"

There was no answer for several seconds.

The image finally came back on, and he could see that the combat information room was on fire.

"We've taken a hit, Blue Leader. Repeat question."

Jason kicked on afterburners and started straight back up.

"How long on that inbound report?"

The screen went dark again.

"Jason?" It was Grierson on the *Intrepid.*

"Grierson, you copy on that?"

"I've got them on long range scan. I bet they came through a jump point screened by an asteroid belt and launched their stealth fighters. I'm reading their carrier as being here in three and one-half hours."

"Copy on that."

He switched back to Svetlana.

"You copy that last report?"

"What the hell's going on up there?"

"Tell Merritt he's got three hours tops and then we're getting the hell out of here. One carrier confirmed, they're hitting us with Stealths now."

"Damn, we won't get all the targets."

"Tell Merritt get the damned carriers on the ground, and whatever else he can, but this bus is definitely gonna leave in three."

"Copy that, Blue Leader."

"Blue Leader?"

It was the Combat Information officer again and he breathed a sigh of relief.

"Blue Leader here. How we holding out?"

"Under heavy attack." The woman looked away from the screen for a moment, nodded reluctantly and then stepped away to be replaced by O'Brian.

"Blue Leader, where the hell are you?"

"Coming back in. Will arrive in five minutes."

"I am initiating emergency withdraw for our exit jump point immediately."

Jason looked at the screen, stunned by what he had just heard.

"The marines, sir. They'll never catch up."

"They are expendable," O'Brian snapped, "Tell your people to come back in and catch up. When we hit jump point we will not stop for stragglers."

"You bastard!" Jason roared. "You're leaving the marines behind. We've got time to recover them, just hang on!"

"We are leaving, mister. You are relieved of command and are under arrest for insubordination."

"You filthy coward, I'll kill you if I ever get aboard that ship," Jason snarled and he snapped the channel off.

He slammed the afterburner throttle forward so hard that for a second he thought he had broken it clear off. A Kilrathi stealth started to materialize off to one flank and he ignored it, heading straight in.

The *Tarawa* finally was visible, tail already turned to the moon, engines up to full throttle.

"Bear, what the hell is he doing?"

"Grierson, he's running out!" Jason shouted.

"Damn him, I'm moving up to stop him."

"Cover the marines; try to land and pick them up if I can't stop that damned coward."

Grierson hesitated.

"Copy that."

Jason continued the chase, gradually catching up to Doomsday's squadron which were returning back from their second attack and were now spread out in a sweep to engage the Stealths.

Jason weaved his way through the battle swirling astern of *Tarawa*, barely noticing the explosions, streaking missiles and laser burst. Moving up parallel to *Tarawa*, he clicked his radio back on.

"Blue Leader coming in to land."

"Acknowledge, Blue Leader."

He swept up over the ship, seeing where several dozen heavy mass driver hits had scorched the ship's hull. He banked hard around, diving for the landing bay, Round Top coming in to drive a Stealth fighter off his tail. Jason slammed through the airlock, ramming into the safety net.

He popped his canopy, stood up, and without even waiting for Sparks jumped down, hitting the deck hard and stood back up.

The deck launch officer came running up to him. "Are we bugging out?"

Jason nodded savagely and pushed past her.

He hit the main corridor and started down it at the run.

The ship's intercom was alive with shouts and commands and then, as if from far away, he heard a high-pitched voice on the channel.

"He's closing in, he's closing. Top guns get him, get the bastard! Get . . ."

The deck beneath Jason's feet seemed to drop away and then slam back up, knocking the wind out of him, driving him to his hands and knees. A high-pitched squawking echoed through the corridor, the hull breach/depressurization alarm. He felt a whoosh of air mixed with fire race down the corridor and he covered his head. The blast of heat raced overhead and then, as if playing out in reverse, slashed back up the corridor in a hurricane gale, dragging Jason along with it. He slammed his helmet visor back down and his pressure suit kicked on.

He continued to slide down the corridor, drawn along by the reverse blast of decompression. Hitting the shattered airlock door, which led into the bridge, he grabbed hold of the side and looked in.

The bridge was gone.

He looked straight up and saw the blackness of empty space, a Sabre streaking past, pursuing and nailing a Stealth just as it started to wink out. He looked straight in at the wreckage and fought down the desire to vomit. The entire bridge crew was dead, what was left of them splattered against the durasteel bulkheads. The floor of the bridge was blown out, the next deck down, torn open as well and blasted with wreckage. Electrical cables sparked in the pure vacuum. Fragments of a shattered Kilrathi fighter were embedded in the deck below. A kamikaze hit, Jason realized. He stepped into the wreckage and looked around and then he saw him, or what little was left of O'Brian, the lower half of his body gone. If he had not had a helmet on, he realized that he would most likely have spit on the corpse.

He turned, climbed back out of the wreckage, and started back up the corridor. A damage control team came racing down the corridor and he pressed up against the wall to let them pass. At the end of the corridor, back out into the hangar deck, an energy airlock field had been established and he stepped through and then unsnapped his helmet. A crowd of deck personnel was gathered around, looking back down the corridor.

"Damn it, get back to your stations!"

The group looked at Jason.

"The captain and all the bridge officers are dead," Jason announced and they looked at him in shock.

He hesitated.

"Flight deck officer."

"Here, sir."

"We're going to establish a new bridge and combat

information center in your command center. Hook into the ship's computer log and . . ."

He found it almost impossible to say the words. He took a deep breath.

"State that as of this moment I, Jason Bondarevsky, as senior officer of *Tarawa* hereby take command of this ship."

The officer looked at him.

"And my first order is that we are turning this ship around and getting the hell back into the fight!"

"This is Admiral Tolwyn. Pilots, man your planes, pilots, man your planes."

Admiral Tolwyn switched his main screen back to the forward relay broadcasting now from Big Duke One's headquarters down on Vukar Tag.

The entire plateau was a mad confusion of explosions, swirling dust, and wreckage. The camera operator aimed straight back up again and jumped the image through one thousand magnifications with full computerized enhancement. As the image expanded out, Geoffrey Tolwyn held his breath.

The entire Kilrathi home fleet hovered in space above the planet. Hundreds of tiny dots were detaching from the transports, winging down to the assault, escorted by hundreds of heavy Kilrathi fighter bombers.

"I tell you all hell's breaking loose down here," Big Duke shouted, trying to be heard above the staccato roar of explosions and the slashing thunder of ground-to-air missiles lifting off.

"Hang on, we've got more incoming!"

The camera mounted on the surface above the bunker swung about, dropping its magnification back down and pointed close to the surface.

A wall of ground suppression missiles came in, kicking on their ground penetration booster engines which could plow the warhead through twenty feet of plasta concrete before detonation. For an instant Tolwyn saw the swarm of landing craft behind the missile barrage and then the image winked out.

"Jesus, that hit hard," and Big Duke was back on the air, this time only with audio signal.

"Count six, a possible seven carriers now supporting the ground assault. Wait a minute, another volley coming straight in; they've got lock on our transmission signal. At least three hundred landing craft behind this one. Damn, this looks like . . ."

The signal winked off.

Tolwyn waited for several seconds.

"Get me Banbridge."

The comm officer snapped a laser communications line on to *Wolfhound*'s antenna.

"Big Duke's getting hit hard," Tolwyn said.

"A couple of more minutes, just a couple of more to let them land their first wave and get their heads in the noose and then we jump through. Your pilots ready for launch?"

"In their cockpits."

Banbridge turned and looked back at his own comm screen and then turned back to Tolwyn.

"We've just got a report Big Duke's headquarters took a direct hit. Not confirmed though."

Tolwyn nodded and said nothing. He had been friends with Duke ever since their Academy days. The name Big Duke was hung on the marine because of his diminutive five-foot height, which was offset by a pugnacious attitude, always looking for a fight.

"Geof, initiate your jump; we'll be right behind you."

Tolwyn smiled grimly.

"See you on the other side."

He turned and looked over at his helm officer.

"Start us into the jump point, sound battle stations, we're going in!"

• CHAPTER IX

"Damn it all, get that screen back up," Jason shouted, bracing himself against a bulkhead wall as *Tarawa* banked into a sharp turn. The hit to the bridge had damaged the inertial dampening system, which insured that the artificial gravity field inside the ship reacted simultaneously with the hull of the vessel as it maneuvered and turned. Though the delay was marginal, less than one thousandth of a second, it made all maneuvers noticeable, slamming the crew back and forth as the ship went through evasive action. It was inevitable for fighters, given their size, but a carrier wasn't built to take it

The screen before him snapped back to life, showing a wavery image of Grierson.

"What kind of track are you getting?" Jason asked.

"The enemy carrier is closing in at flank speed, with a spread of two cruisers and four destroyers forward and two corvettes to the flanks. Will arrive in twenty-seven minutes. We have a second wave of inbound fighters as well, fifty plus."

Jason groaned and looked over at his ready board.

He had seven Rapiers, six Sabres, and eight Ferrets left that were still flyable, not counting his own Rapier. Two thirds of them were dry on missiles and would have to be recalled and turned back around in time to meet the next attack.

"How's damage control?" Grierson asked.

"Still without any long-range scan so you'll be our eyes, *Intrepid*. We've established a ring of airlocks around the hull rupture. Shield generation is still down, engine room is still cut off, but we've managed to patch a radio link in to them, our inertial dampening is out of phase and we're not sure on the jump engine. The jump control officer is dead, the non com chief says it'll be hours before he can be sure we're up and running in that department. The entire bridge is out, along with the infirmary, and forward crew bays." He hesitated for a moment. "We've lost a fifth of our crew, over a hundred dead, forty wounded."

"You're still lucky to be afloat, Captain. We picked up two marine crews on the surface before lifting back off. We lost one trying to lift off, and another is damaged on the ground, its crew shifting to another landing craft. Two marine landing craft will externally dock with us within the next ten minutes and we're dumping the landing craft; Merritt's ordering the surviving three landing craft up now."

"Kagimasha?"

"Here Commander," and the ship's captain was in the viewscreen, a bandage covering one eye.

"How are you?"

"We got a bit scorched, shielding's down to thirty-two percent, but engines are fully back on line."

"We'll swing in for a rendezvous; you two cover us."

Grierson grinned.

"That's my job," and the screen blanked.

Jason looked over at his new combat information officer, who was sitting in front of a portable holo screen, which was now tapped into the ship's main computer. The launch control office overlooking the flight deck was now standing double duty, with helm, combat information, communications, weapons control, and damage control wedged into the room, their portable gear plugged into the main system through a maze of fiberoptic wiring. All combat ships were outfitted with a reserve bridge in case of a hit like the one *Tarawa* had just taken, but as a converted transport, that fallback system had never been built in. Without the supply of portable holo screens, which usually were on board a ship for briefings, and entertainment, they would be totally blind now.

Jason looked around the room, promising himself that if they ever got back he would certainly raise one hell of a stink concerning this oversight, and even as he though about it, he had to laugh at the irony of even worrying about such things at a time like this.

"Signal Doomsday and Starlight to bring the birds in for rearming. They've got ten minutes, so make it smart."

"Aye, sir."

Jason walked over to the plastishield which provided a view of the launch deck.

The first Sabre, Doomsday's, came in fast, touching down at the end of the launch ramp. The ground crew raced over to the ship, running alongside of it as the tractor pulled it off the ramp. Crews, pushing missiles on small null gravity trailers ran up to the ship, locking them into the external pylons, while hoses were snaked into the ship's fuel tank and cables latched in to top off the energy supply. Doomsday climbed out of the cockpit, waving for his co to stay, and ran up to the control center.

He came through the door and looked at Jason appraisingly.

"So you've got the helm now?"

Jason nodded.

"How's she holding up?"

"Patching it together, though one more blow like that and she'll split apart."

"We'll keep 'em off your back but for heaven's sake, man, we've got to turn and get the hell out now or they'll block the jump point."

"Merritt wants five more minutes. They've got mines strapped into five carriers in their construction bays rigged to go, along with a cruiser assembly building. He's rigging the last carrier and construction bays right now."

"Damn it Jason, we're going to go up with them if we hang around."

"Five minutes."

"We've replaced a coward with a gung-ho maniac, just great." Then he slowly started to grin.

More ships came in, and Jason watched the landings, nodding an agreement when the deck officer marked two of the fighters off as unfit to fly and had them pulled to the far corner of the hangar where repair crews swarmed over them. A Ferret, with a wing completely sheered off came in, trailing a tangle of wires which hooked into the side of the airlock, spinning the craft around. Jason groaned as the ship broke apart, parts spraying down the deck.

The deck officer leaped from the command room, racing across the deck, screaming for crew members to manhandle the wreckage out of the way and within a minute the next fighter came in, slipping within inches of the Ferret's shattered cockpit where an emergency rescue crew was hosing the ruins down with fire retardant, and pulling the unconscious pilot out.

The last ship landed and Doomsday returned to his craft, ready for launch.

Jason punched up the ship's intercom.

"All hands," and he hesitated for a moment, "this is the captain speaking."

"*Intrepid* reports inbound fighters, fifty plus, less than fifteen minutes away and closing. Nine capital ships are five minutes behind them, two Fralthra cruisers, four Ralatha destroyers, two corvettes, and one heavy carrier. We should run for it right now, but there are still four platoons of marines down on the moon, getting set to blow half a dozen damned carriers and lord knows what other equipment from here to hell where it belongs. We're giving those people five more minutes because this ship does not leave its people behind. Engine room, get ready to pour on the fire when I give the word. Keep up the good work, people, and the Empire will learn to cover its butt and crawl away when they hear the name *Tarawa*."

He clicked off the intercom and suddenly felt foolish for having delivered what he felt was a hackneyed speech. From the corner of his eye he saw that his make due bridge staff were grinning and nodding their heads with approval. Embarrassed, he turned away to watch the forward monitor screen which was filled with the image of the moon.

"Merritt, you with me?"

"Copy that *Tarawa*. We are lifting off now."

"Starlight, you on them for air support?"

"Four ferrets and one fighter lined up above them."

"A and B craft will be up first, C landing craft under Major Svetlana Ivanova will follow us out. We've had some unexpected resistance down here trying to get out."

"Major?" Jason asked.

"Hell, we're all getting battlefield promotions out here today," Merritt said. "I figured I'd toss a couple around as well. Company C's top hand is down, knocked out, and she's got the job now."

Even as he spoke Jason could hear that Merritt was

caught up in the middle of a firefight as he loaded the last of his grunts on board.

Jason looked over at the short range radar scan and saw the first blue blip come off the surface, followed a half minute later by the second.

"Come on, damn it, move it, move it!" Grierson snarled. "Those fighters are kicking in afterburners; they'll be here in less than five."

"Get three Sabres out there and then clear the deck for landing craft recovery," Jason ordered, trying to keep his voice calm and businesslike.

Doomsday slammed down the launch ramp, and the crews pushed the second craft into line, sending it out less than thirty seconds later.

The rear sweeping short range scan, which had survived the kamikaze hit, started to turn red on the outer limit of search; the enemy wave was closing in.

"Merritt, move it, damn it," Jason said softly, still trying to force an outward appearance of calm.

"We're shoveling coal into the engines as fast as we can, *Tarawa*."

"C Company lifting off now!" Svetlana called and Jason breathed a sigh of relief.

The first landing craft, coming off the surface at full throttle, came within visual range, afterburner flame rippling behind it.

An alarm started to ping on the combat information board and for a second Jason thought that the incoming fighters were already trying to achieve missile lock, even though they were still thousands of kilometers out. And then he saw the threat display, a red box snapping to life on the moon's surface below.

"Svetlana, take evasive!"

"Outbound heat seekers," Starlight shouted, launching suppressive fire.

"Svetlana, shut engines down. Blow chaff!"

Four missiles streaked up, converging in on the

landing craft which was just within visual range. Jason shouted for the petty officer running the display to jack up magnification. He felt helpless; as captain of a carrier he was reduced to simply watching a life-and-death struggle being played out on the holo screen.

The landing craft turned, a shower of chaff and heat flares blowing out the stern. The first missile closed and detonated half a click astern, the second and third disappearing into the fireball and detonating as well. Jason breathed a sigh of relief and then the fourth missile emerged from out of the explosion. The missile closed.

"No!" Jason screamed, grabbing hold of the side of the console as if by sheer force of will he could somehow turn the missile aside. It detonated just astern of the landing craft.

"*Tarawa*, *Tarawa*, we're hit and going in!" Her voice was strangely detached and calm as her image appeared on the screen.

Sickened, Jason watched as the landing craft, trailing fire, started to spiral back down to the planet's surface.

"First landing craft clearing airlock door," and he looked up to see Merritt's craft coming in, touching down hard, the sides of the ship fire-scorched from the intense battle down on the planet's surface.

Before the craft had even skidded to a stop a side hatch was opened and Merritt jumped out, running up to the control room, pushing his way in, dropping his helmet on the floor.

"Svetlana, try and gain orbit!" Jason shouted.

"No joy on that, *Tarawa*, we're going down, only one engine still good." Behind her, he could see the pilot struggling with the controls, the copilot of the landing craft slumped over in his seat, the back of his head a bloody mass. The ground rushed up and then the image snapped off.

"They've impacted next to one of the carrier hangers," the combat information officer shouted.

"Landing craft C, landing craft C, do you copy?" Jason shouted.

A crackling hiss filled the air and then a voice drifted through on the static, the visual image barely discernable.

"*Tarawa*, we're still with you; we've touched down, many casualties on board."

"Thank God," Jason sighed and he looked over at Merritt.

"*Tarawa*, it's time to leave this neighborhood," Grierson announced, coming on-line. "Do you copy on that? The rear screen is red with incoming!"

Jason felt as if his heart had suddenly gone to ice. He looked at the situation board, the holo displays and monitors. *Tarawa* was seriously wounded, but she still had four hundred and fifty aboard and, as the second landing craft came in, more than a hundred marines. On a side monitor the computer had zeroed in on the crashed landing craft, reading out injuries as reported by the individual marine's life-support systems. Thirty-five of them were still alive, including Svetlana.

"The Confederation doesn't leave its people behind, not while *I'm* in command," a voice whispered in his memory. "I'll do what it takes to get you back," and he felt as if Tolwyn were standing beside him.

Never leave someone behind, the pledge goes both ways.

He looked over at Merritt who stood with a pained expression.

"Jason, if you try and pick those people up, we all die." Jason tried to run a quick calculation to think it through. *Intrepid* could attempt to land, a tricky maneuver on the crater-pocked surface. She had pulled it off once to pick up two companies of marines, and had been scorched by ground fire in the process. It would mean bringing her speed down to zero, and then having to climb back out against gravity. She'd be caught coming off the planet, not only by the fighters but by the capital ships.

Send the Sabres in; they could cram several people into the rear storage hatch. That'd save twenty maybe. Relaunch a landing craft and try to hold the fighters off.

"Damn it to hell!" Jason snapped.

"They knew the risk," Merritt said quietly, "they knew it when they signed on."

"And the deal goes both ways," Jason shouted. "We're going in after them."

"*Tarawa*, do you copy?"

"We're here, Svetlana, just hang on. We're scrambling the Sabres in to pick up half your people, a landing craft is being turned around now for the rest."

There was a pause on the other side.

"Nice try, *Tarawa*, but I don't think so."

"Just hang on, Svetlana."

"Jason," and there was a pause for a moment. "Listen Jason, you're running the show now. A thousand people are counting on you to get them out. We're finished. Don't sacrifice yourselves to save us. I know what the score is and so do you. If you hang around now, you're all going to be lost. Get the hell out now!"

"Shut up, Svetlana. We're coming in."

"Colonel Merritt?"

"Here, Svetlana."

"What's the firing code?"

Merritt closed his eyes and lowered his head.

"Double Alpha, Fox, Tango, Three," he said, his voice low, barely audible.

"Double Alpha, Fox, Tango, Three, copy that," Svetlana said quietly.

Jason looked back at Merritt.

"The matter/antimatter mines were rigged to fire on a one-hour delay so we were well clear," Merritt whispered. "They can also be fired manually."

He looked straight into Jason's eyes.

"I'm sorry son, but she's right. God help us all, but she's right."

Jason turned back to the commlink which was again showing a wavery image.

"Svetlana, don't. Wait, just wait."

"Double Alpha, Fox, Tango, Three," she repeated. "Firing trigger is armed."

"Svetlana!"

She turned and looked back at the screen.

"Jason, honey. Save your fleet. Maybe some other time, some other life, we'll see each other again. I've always loved you, Jason. I'll always be with you."

"Svetlana! No!"

The screen went blank.

He looked up at the forward monitor as dozens of white snaps of light mushroomed across the screen.

He stood in mute horror, watching as the explosions ripped the naval station apart, white hot walls of fire racing outward, mushrooming up into the sky.

The control room was as quiet as a tomb, except for the steady chatter coming in from the other ships, and Doomsday's squadron, which was positioning to cover the *Tarawa* from the rear.

Jason suddenly realized that all eyes were upon him.

"Son."

Jason looked over at Merritt who stood with tears in his eyes.

"Son, you're the captain now."

Jason nodded and walked over to the control display, trying to blink back the tears.

"Holo tactical display," and the image came up and floated before him. The Kilrathi fighters were spreading out and the heavy capital ships were closing as well, two of them maneuvering to block the path to their intended retreat point.

Though long-range scan was not yet back on-line he could surmise that an additional capital ship would be stationed directly at the jump point. With the condition *Tarawa* was already in, there was no hope of fighting through and at this point, even if they did make it to the jump point, there was no guarantee that the jump engine would work correctly. They were cut off. He had to do something else, and damned quickly.

"Pull up a map of this system," Jason said quietly, and the image appeared alongside that of the tactical. He studied it intently for several seconds. He traced out a line with a laser pointer and then looked over at the computer nav system which automatically took his course plot and changed it into a heading while compensating for the gravitational effect of the moon, and all the other planets in the system.

"Helm officer, bring us around to a heading of 331.3 by negative one degree to solar axis standard. Engine room, let's see what you've got. Signal our intended path to our escorts and the Sabres. Close down the ram scoops ninety-five percent for full acceleration. Let's get the hell out of here," and he felt his voice start to quaver.

He looked over at his staff who looked at him in confusion over his command, which was heading them nowhere near a jump point and then they leaped to work.

Jason looked around the room, feeling the ship start to shudder as she turned and powered up full afterburners.

"*Tarawa*, what the hell is this heading?" Grierson shouted, coming back on the commlink. "You're taking us straight into the willywacks and no jump point is in sight!"

"All points are undoubtedly covered by now," Jason said quietly. "We're going straight for the gas giant, where they have an orbital base. Most likely all their fighters have been expended."

"So big deal, we smash a lousy base, then what?"

"We need time for repairs," Jason announced, "our shield generator's still out, jump engine is doubtful and all our wiring is shot to hell. We need some time."

Grierson suddenly smiled.

"OK, *Tarawa*, we're with you."

The rearmed fighters aboard *Tarawa* sortied back out, forming a protective screen to the rear of the ship as it climbed up and away from the Kilrah system.

"We've got a long run," Jason said quietly and he went over to the deck officer's chair and settled down.

By the end of the first hour a steady battle was being waged a thousand kilometers astern of the *Tarawa* as Starlight and Doomsday struggled to keep successive waves of faster enemy fighters and strike craft from closing in to engage their crippled carrier. Another Sabre went down, along with two more fighters and three Ferrets which were going head-to-head with Grikath and Jalkehi fighters, in exchange for a dozen enemy fighters and a single torpedo hit to a Kilrathi destroyer which forced it to drop out of the chase.

By the third hour of the long stern chase *Intrepid* and *Kagimasha* were trading long range volleys and launching torpedo spreads against the enemy Ralatha destroyers, one of which seemed to carry an improved engine system that enabled it to afterburner up to a dozen clicks a second faster than *Tarawa*. With ram scoops almost fully retracted, speeds went up past six thousand clicks a second.

Throughout the chase Jason sat in silence,

occasionally issuing a terse command, but saying nothing more. Fighters, short of ammunition and fuel, would break off and sweep back in for refitting and sortie back out. Jason watched the pilots who did not even bother to climb out of their cockpits, and saw their pale, sweat-streaked faces, lined with fatigue.

"Enemy base orbiting the gas giant is now within five hundred thousand kilometers and closing," his combat information officer announced and he finally stirred.

"Any fighter activity?"

"You guessed right, sir, they shot their whole wad trying to get us. She's defenseless except for her guns."

"Signal *Intrepid* and *Kagimasha* to take her out and then form back on *Tarawa*. Order all ships to extend ram scoops for additional braking manuver and hang on!"

Though the damage control crew had been working on the inertial dampening system, main priority was still on the jump engine and shields. The delay was down to a hundred thousandth of a second but when the energy field of the ram scoops was suddenly extended back out, the ship felt as if it were being torn apart as it went into a thirty gee deceleration.

The *Intrepid* shot past, diving in towards the station which sent up a spray of neutron rounds. A volley of torpedoes dropped out of the destroyer and the enemy station disappeared.

"Helm, take us straight through the blast and then snag us in tight to orbit around the planet."

"Captain, just what the hell are we doing now?" Merritt, who had stood by his side throughout, finally asked.

"You'll see."

The expanding cloud of debris seemed to race up and Jason winced as fragments of the shattered base slammed against the durasteel hull, the *Tarawa* groaning from the impact. The nose of *Tarawa* rose up, skimming just above the outer atmosphere of the giant.

"All fighters recover now!" Jason shouted.

"Say, Jason, did I hear you right?" Doomsday replied.

"You heard me, get in now damn it!"

"Copy that, *Tarawa* but those furballs will be on us."

Jason leaned over and switched back to *Intrepid* and *Kagimasha*.

"You know the game, rendezvous at . . ." and he looked up at the clock on the wall, ". . . exactly thirty hours from now at 17:24 hours and be ready to haul ass."

"Copy that *Tarawa* and good luck." Grierson said, grinning with delight.

"*Tarawa* out."

The first Ferret came in, followed at twenty-second intervals by the surviving recon and light fighter craft, and then the remaining Rapiers and Sabres followed suit while Janice circled outside, providing tight-in cover for the landing ships.

"We've got a hell of a lot of incoming," the combat officer shouted.

"Keep the fleas off our back," Jason said, toggling back over to his escort ships.

Intrepid moved in directly behind, and Jason found that he was starting to drum the arm of his chair nervously.

Half a dozen Grakhi bore straight in and slowed.

"Torpedo attack imminent."

A spread of torpedoes dropped out from each of the Kilrathi fighters.

Jason turned and looked over at Merritt.

"Still got any mines on board?"

Merritt nodded. "A couple in each of the landing craft."

"Set a landing craft on autopilot, and once we've recovered our last ship I want the mine activated and the landing ship out the airlock door on automatic pilot."

"Got you," and Merritt dashed out of the room.

On the downward looking screen Jason watched as the boiling upper atmosphere of the gas giant raced by, not ten kilometers below. The magnetic distortion created by the atmosphere made communication almost impossible with his escorts and he watched as they attempted to cover his stern.

The six Kilrathi heavy fighters pulled up and away, their spread of torpedoes closing in. Jason heard the high-pitched ping of a solid guidance lock.

The stern anti torpedo guns kicked on, attempting to gain a lock in turn, sending out a hail of mass driven shots and in turn the Kilrathi torpedoes popped out small bundles of chaff and signal distorters to throw the guns off. The anti torpedo missile mount on the bottom of the carrier launched a round, the missile streaking forward and then turning to race astern.

Two of the torpedoes were detonated but four continued to bore in.

"They've got definite lock," the combat information officer shouted. "Computer analysis estimates one will break through and hit in twenty seconds . . . fifteen."

The collision alarm kicked on.

The rear guns and firepower of the escorts crisscrossed space, knocking one, and then two more torpedoes down.

"Impact in five, four . . ."

"Oh Christ!" the officer screamed, and, stunned, he looked up at Jason.

The torpedo disappeared in a flash, exploded by

a Ferret which had dived straight into the weapon, detonating it just astern of *Tarawa*.

Jason, unable to speak, looked up at the situation board and saw the status report for Janice's ship wink off.

"She knew how to pick her death."

Jason looked up at Doomsday who had just landed and had quietly watched the drama played out while standing in the corner of the room. "I'd have done the same, so would you."

Jason felt as if he could not take it anymore. He closed his eyes.

"Last fighter in."

"Launch that landing craft and have it turn astern of us."

"Landing craft on full autopilot and away."

Merritt came back into the room and leaned over a comm channel and started to punch in a code. He stopped and looked over at Jason.

"Escorts, you still copy."

The two ships responded, voices and images distorted almost behind recognition due to the heavy magnetic field around the planet.

"Initiate dive into the atmosphere on my count. Five, four, three, two, one."

He looked over at Merritt and nodded and the marine colonel slammed down on the key. A heavy matter/antimatter mine detonated half a dozen clicks behind the fleet, directly between them and the Kilrathi's, blasting out an electro-magnetic pulse that overloaded all surveillance equipment.

"Dive! Helm, point us straight in!"

As the electro-magnetic pulse of the explosion mushroomed out behind them, the three ships pushed over and dived straight in on the gas giant, hitting the upper atmosphere. The *Tarawa* started to buffet and rock, and he could feel the ship twisting and straining beneath his feet.

"Ten clicks into the atmosphere, twenty, fifty."

He watched over the helmsman's shoulder as they continued to go deeper in, ordering a leveling out when they were a full five hundred clicks down into the storm of frozen ammonia and sulphur. The surviving external sensing systems were off-line, picking up nothing but clutter from the intense radiation, and magnetic storms sweeping the upper atmosphere of the planet.

"Level us out, signal engine room, just enough power to maintain orbit."

"Leveling out, sir; engine room reports throttling back to eighteen percent power."

"Rig ship for silent running. No transmissions of any kind. Passive listening devices only."

"Ship rigged for silent running."

He looked over at the main screen of the combat information officer. It was awash with static. A ping line drifted across the screen and then another. The combat information officer looked back at him, her eyes wide.

"They're sending out high energy microwave bursts, looking for us."

"Well let 'em look," and Jason held his breath.

The pinging moved on; they hadn't picked him up, and he slowly exhaled.

"Ship's intercom."

He picked up the microphone.

"All hands. We've managed to elude the Kilrathi attack by diving into the upper atmosphere of a gas giant where their sensing devices can not find us due to atmospheric interference. As you can guess, any type of visual search is like looking for a feather in a blizzard. We will rendezvous with our escorts in a little less than thirty hours. In those thirty hours we are going to repair our ship and our damaged fighters and we are going to come back out kicking. Congratulations on a job well done."

He lowered his head for a moment.

"Merritt's marines smashed half a dozen carriers under construction and a hell of a lot of equipment. Our task force has downed over seventy enemy fighters, four corvettes, one orbital base, along with a number of probabilities and damaged. I'm proud of you, and the Confederation is proud of you. All damage control officers, weapons officers, and engineering officers report to the temporary bridge in one half hour. Thank you and keep it up, *Tarawa*. I'm damned proud to be part of this team."

He clicked the intercom off, not even noticing the looks of pride in his staff.

"I'm taking a half hour off," he said quietly. "Call me if anything comes up."

He left the bridge and went into the tiny cubical that now served as his wardroom and closed the door. Jason lowered his head, covering his face with his hands, and wept.

Prince Thrakhath turned away from the holo screen.

"It won't be a pleasure reporting this to the Emperor," he said quietly, looking over at the Khantahr in direct command of his flagship.

"Sire, might I remind you that you expected the enemy carrier to use the planet as a slingshot, that they would loop around and come straight back towards Kilrah, not to dive into its atmosphere."

Prince Thrakhath looked at the Khantahr.

"I admire courage, and I admire truth," he said. "You are right."

The Khantahr visibly relaxed.

"Is there a probability that they have gone around

the far side of the planet, masked by the EMP of the antimatter explosion?"

The Khantahr looked over to his executive officer in charge of navigation.

"If so, they will emerge from under the south pole of the planet within the next ten minutes. If they should then choose to close ram scoops and go to full acceleration, they could leap ahead, perhaps even close on Kilrah before we can stand back to defend her."

Prince Thrakhath looked over at the holo display as the navigator plotted out a possible course.

"Masterful maneuver. I expected them to dive straight back to Kilrah, to seek death while doing maximum damage, now that we have covered their probable exit jump point. Now I am not sure if they are hiding beneath us or at this very moment are circling around."

He studied the screen intently.

"Pull the carrier back to a high polar orbit around Kilrah. Detail the destroyers to orbit this planet and to try to pick up a trace if they are indeed down there. The cruisers and corvettes are to form a picket line between here and Kilrah. If they are going straight back now, I want to be ahead of them. If they are hiding below us, we'll wait them out. They'll have to come up sooner or later and when they do we'll finish them."

The Khantahr nodded his agreement and left the room followed by his staff.

The commlink on Prince Thrakhath's desk blinked. He looked over at it, noticing the bright yellow flash that meant it was a scrambled message from the Imperial Palace. He took a deep breath and punched down on the button.

The image of the Emperor appeared in the middle of the room.

"Yes, Grandfather."

"The enemy carrier?"

"We've lost it for the moment, sire. It has either dived into the atmosphere of Igrathi to hide, or even at this moment is circling around for a return attack. I am pulling back to cover Kilrah. If he is hiding, he'll have to come back up at some point, and then we will close for the kill."

"I have seen the damage reports. I am not pleased."

Prince Thrakhath was silent.

"Six carriers, six construction yards, a cruiser construction center, and four thousand of our best trained technicians are casualties. Do you know what this means?"

His voice reached a cold pitch of anger.

"Yes, Grandfather, I am fully aware of what it means."

"A third of all our carrier construction facilities smashed by this noisome fly of a ship, and you let it elude you!"

"Sire, if you had followed my recommendation and pulled the entire home fleet back this never would have happened. And tell me, Grandfather, what is the latest from Vukar?"

Prince Thrakhath waited.

"The landing is still going according to plan, but there has been a problem detected."

"And that is?"

The Emperor hesitated.

"What is it, Grandfather?"

"An enemy fleet has been detected, closing in on the landing operations, the first report just came through."

Prince Thrakhath felt a sudden chill of dread.

"Order them to retreat at once!"

The Emperor shook his head.

"By the time the signal arrives the issue will already be decided."

"I will find this carrier, Grandfather. It will not replace what we have lost, but at least it will pay for its crimes."

• CHAPTER X

"All right, let's have the status reports," Jason said wearily, struggling to keep awake after nearly two days without sleep. He gratefully accepted the cup of coffee from Doomsday, trying to hide the fact that his hands were shaking slightly, either from too much caffeine or just from simple exhaustion.

He looked over at the damage control officer, who, by good fortune for the *Tarawa*, was an old petty officer with twenty-five years fleet experience; another transfer from the *Concordia*. His senior, a young cadet straight out of the academy, had died on the bridge, and as a result the most qualified person had risen to the job.

"We've welded durasteel plating over the breach in the hull, your suggestion of cannibalizing it from that wrecked Ferret was a damned good one. It's definitely not air tight, so I'm keeping the airlock force fields up, and I've ordered everyone still working in that area to keep their pressure suits on, even though we've pumped air back in.

"Shield generation is ready to go back on line, though the phase generator is still not synching quite right, so I don't suggest pushing her up to the max power setting."

"How high then, Jim?"

"Seventy-five percent and that's pushing it."

"Keep working on it."

"I've got people on it now.

"We've reestablished a pressurized and secured corridor back to the engine room, and the last of the electrical fires was tracked down and contained in the aft crew quarters. Still some toxins in the air though, both from the fire and from the ammonia and sulphur atmosphere leaking in, so I think crew quarters should be off limits for at least another couple of days till our air filtration cleans it all out. Also, anyone in the aft deck areas should wear filter masks as well."

Jason sighed and looked around the room.

"I take it that's the good news, chief."

Jim nodded and blew out noisily.

"We've got structural cracks running down three of the six main keel beams—this ship is leaking air like a sieve from hundreds of microscopic structural cracks. We could very well start running short on air pressure by the time we get home. I've talked with our environmental chief and he's dropping internal pressure down to 4.5 pounds per square inch and jacking up the oxygen content but increased oxygen means increased chance of fire if anything flares up again. If we take any neutron hits and they get through the shielding, the resulting electrostatic discharge could cause a flare out."

"Then we jack the pressure back up and lower the oxygen when we know we're going into combat."

"And lose air. It'll be tricky as well because if we fluctuate air pressure and particularly nitrogen content we could cause the entire crew to get the bends. The environmental officer is trying to work something out."

"I think they called it robbing Peter to pay Paul, chief."

"That's how I see it, sir."

"Bridge control status?"

"We've run some more wiring into the launch control room but our long-range scanning array is wiped out. We'll have to rely on *Intrepid* and *Kagimasha* for that data. Helm control, combat information, navigation, and damage control stations are now fully operational."

"A damned fine job," Jason said. "Chief, we couldn't have pulled it off without your skill."

"Hell, Captain, I just want to get out of this scrap alive; three months and I'm up for retirement."

"I'm just glad you didn't retire before this cruise."

"I wish the hell I had," the chief replied, and Jason laughed in commiseration.

"I think we all kind of wish that at the moment, chief."

He turned and looked over at his old comrade.

"Doomsday, how are our planes?"

"Twenty-three pilots left, not counting you, sir. One of the marine shuttle pilots and his co were both checked out on Ferrets so we do have two backups though it'd be murder to send them out against Kilrathi fleet pilots. Five Sabres, eight Rapiers, and seven Ferrets left."

Jason had been mulling that one over and now had to make a decision.

"All right, Doomsday, you're promoted to wing commander."

"Just what I always wanted, sir," he said dryly. "They live about as long as new pups."

"You'll also continue to run the Sabre squadron. Round Top takes over the Ferrets," he paused for a moment, "and Tolwyn runs the Rapiers."

"I don't like that, Jason."

"I didn't expect you to, but the kid proved himself out there, he dumped four of them and saved *Intrepid*'s butt from a torpedo strike."

"I wish we had Mongol."

"Well, we don't," and he thought of all the fresh young faces now gone: Mongol, Flame, Ice Wind, Nova, Eagle, Talon, Thor, and Odin, all the heroic young names, now dead.

He looked up at the chronometer which was ticking off the time.

"It's an hour to scramble and rendezvous. The galley's promised a hot meal for everyone, and the crew's to eat at their posts. People, we're going to get out of here, we're going to get home, just remember that, and tell your people that as well. It's time for the service, so let's get out on the deck and look sharp."

He rose up from his chair and walked out of the makeshift bridge, his staff following. Out by the airlock the crew was waiting, both the living and the dead. The bodies were wrapped in nothing more than the standard fleet navy blue bodybags and covered with bed sheets. Some of the forms were at least recognizable as having once been human; those lost on the bridge were far smaller bundles. For those who had been vaporized or blown into space, the old fleet tradition of "burying" their uniform served as a substitute. How the damage control and infirmary team had ever dealt with the task of cleaning up from the blast was beyond Jason.

Their bodies were now lined up by the airlock.

Jason walked up to the line of corpses and turned to face those crew members who could be spared from damage repairs to attend.

He was at a loss for what to say, though he had attended far too many of these services in the past.

"We don't have time to say much," he said quietly, "and I don't think our comrades would want us to take that time right now. When all of this is over, perhaps then we can gather together again and do this properly."

He turned away from the crew and faced the line of bodies. He reached into his pocket and pulled out a copy of the Bible and read the 23rd Psalm. Finishing the prayer he lowered his head.

"You were our shipmates, and our friends. Though it might sound strange to say it, I want to thank you for us who still live, both here, and across the Confederation, for it is through you that humankind will live, will endure to final victory, and will finally achieve peace.

"Sleep well, my friends, until that day when space shall give up her dead."

He came to attention, saluted, and the haunting refrain of "Taps" echoed through the ship. Details of marines stepped forward and as gently as possible picked up the bodies and stepped up to the airlock field, pushing them through one after the other. With the ship running stern first, as the bodies hit the atmosphere outside they tumbled away into the green blue ammonia soup sky and disappeared. Colonel Merritt came forward after the last body disappeared, and stepped up to a helmet and jump boots which Jason knew were symbols of all the marines who had died in the assault. He saluted and then two sergeants picked up the tokens and pushed them through the airlock as well.

Jason turned back to face the crew, standing ramrod straight.

"We pull out of here in thirty-seven minutes. Now let's get the hell out of this system and kick some fur butt on the way!"

Stunned, the Emperor lowered his head, motioning with a wave of his hand that the messenger was dismissed.

How could this be, how could this ever be? Just what had gone wrong?

Five carriers of the home fleet gone, sixteen support ships gone, nineteen troup transports and four legions of the guard annihilated down to the last warrior. Rusmak and Gar, two of his finest commanders and both of the royal line dead as well.

How could this ever be?

Who was to blame?

And the family, the vast extended family of the imperial blood, what would they now say and do with the bulwark of their home fleet gone? He could well imagine the casualty lists. So many sons of the royal blood would have been lost and the family would look for blame.

He thought for a moment of the various factions, each jockeying, pushing, positioning to destroy its rivals.

A klaxon sounded in the distance and he stirred from his contemplation.

A screen sparked to life, an action which would be permitted only in an emergency.

"My lord, forgive the intrusion."

The Emperor looked at the commander of the palace guard who stood at rigid attention, head lowered.

"Go on, then."

"Sire, the enemy carrier. It has lifted out of the atmosphere."

The Emperor, furious, said nothing.

"Sire, it is accelerating rapidly with ram scoops fully retracted and making a course which will intersect with Kilrah within the hour. Prince Thrakhath advises that this might be a suicide attempt to crash into Kilrah."

The Emperor nodded. Outside of a close circle of the high command and the warriors directly involved in the fight, not a single individual living on Kilrah knew that a human strike force had penetrated into the heart of the Empire.

"Thrakhath's fleet?"

"Moving to intercept."

"No alert is to be sounded," the Emperor said quietly.

"Sire?" The commander hesitated.

"Go on."

"Not even for those residing within the Palace?"

He paused. If a strike should indeed get through, the likely target would indeed be the palace compound. Tens of thousands who might survive in the shelters would die. But to even admit that danger was this close? And the home fleet smashed? He could face a coup before the day was out.

"No one is to know. I want to speak to Thrakhath on a secured scramble line."

"As you desire, my lord."

He turned away from the screen which went blank for a moment. First a high-pitched hum and then a scramble code followed.

"Sire."

The Emperor turned slowly to face the Prince.

"You have heard of Vukar?"

Thrakhath did not reply.

What is he thinking? the Emperor wondered. After all it was I who insisted that the assault continue and the fleet be split. His own position is threatened now. Could he in turn then be plotting against me?

"We must do three things," the Emperor said finally.

"And they are, sire?"

"One, no strike must ever reach Kilrah. Not a single missile, nothing. You are to block this human scum no matter what."

"Sire. A close in direct attack will finish them now."

"You lost a third of your fighters yesterday. If you close assault, can you assure me that no ship will penetrate?"

Thrakhath hesitated.

"No, you cannot, that is obvious. Assume a defensive position ahead of them and block their attack. You have two other carriers maneuvering in through different jump points to seal off escape. We will kill this human fleet in revenge, but it must not succeed in reaching this planet. Do I make myself clear?"

"Yes, sire. And the other two items?"

"We shall increase the size of this enemy fleet in our reports to match what we have suffered both in lost construction and in the home fleet."

Thrakhath smiled and then shook his head.

"But those of the family will know the real truth."

"That does not matter. Finally, we must find one at fault for Vukar, let him take the blame, and divert attention."

"The Baron."

The Emperor nodded.

"Fine."

"Grandson, you must succeed. If not," he hesitated, "far too many will then start to look to you as the cause of their problems."

He switched the screen off without waiting for a reply.

"Captain, their carrier is maneuvering in from the flank."

"Their course bearing?"

"Positioning above their first moon, between us and Kilrah."

Jason smiled.

He looked over at the helm officer.

"Our speed?"

"Crossing through eight thousand clicks a second and climbing, sir."

"Prepare to launch remaining landing craft and pilotless Ferret. Communications, signal our escorts to stand close. Alert tractor beam crew to get ready as well."

Jason looked over at the strategic display map. They were surrounded by a circle of Kilrathi ships. Six in pursuit all the way back from the gas giant, two closing in to either flank. And the carrier positioned ahead and several million clicks out from Kilrah.

He settled back into his bridge chair and watched the display. With the ram scoop energy fields completely closed down, the *Tarawa* continued to accelerate. He was going to burn damned near every ounce of fuel reserve aboard ship in the next twenty minutes; if the furballs didn't fall for the maneuver they'd get nailed at the jump point when they were forced to slow back down to insure a correct alignment for jump entry. But it was the only plan he could come up with and Grierson had chuckled with delight when first told.

"What are they doing?" Prince Thrakhath whispered, not really addressing his question to anyone in particular.

He watched the data screen. The three ships were accelerating with ram scoops closed down . . . and they were aiming straight in on Kilrah.

"Project terminal velocity if they should ram the planet," Thrakhath said and he looked over at his combat control officer.

The data appeared on Thrakhath's screen.

Ten thousand and eighty kilometers per second. He sat back and allowed the information to sink in. The mass of the ship, striking at that velocity into the atmosphere would cleave straight down to the planet's surface, impacting with a force equal to several dozen matter/antimatter warheads. Three such strikes would kill tens of millions.

Was that his plan?

"Contact planetary defense, get shielding up to maximum and the hell with security. Prepare to position this ship on a collision intercept with their carrier. Scramble all fighters for point defense with same orders.

He left his chair, the battle station alarm screeching through the ship.

"Prepare to launch landing craft and Ferret," Jason announced and he looked down at the flight deck.

"Launch!"

The landing craft went out the airlock door, aimed on a ballistic trajectory straight in on Kilrah, followed by the lone Ferret, both ships on automatic pilot, both ships armed with old-style atomics which would be detected by the Kilrathi defense.

Kilrah, which only minutes before was nothing but a blue-green dot, was now a sphere hanging in the darkness.

"Coming up on maneuver change," Helm announced.

Jason settled back into his chair and strapped himself in.

"Hang on *Tarawa*, just hang on."

"Rotating ship for maneuver firing now!"

Jason felt the nudge of the thruster rockets which turned *Tarawa* to a line perpendicular to its flight path. Without the scoops, any form of aerodynamic maneuvering was impossible. It would all have to be done by the age-old method of space flight which was to burn fuel in order to turn.

"All engines firing!"

"They've launched atomic warheads!"

Prince Thrakhath leaped out of his chair and came up to stand behind his combat control officer. The telltale yellow blip was superimposed over the purple which marked two ships that were launching from *Tarawa*.

"Block them, shoot them, we must bring them down."

"*Tarawa* is shifting course!"

"Block the warheads!"

Creaks and groans echoed through the ship as the main engines, sucking up the hydrogen fuel at a prodigious rate, feeding it into the fusion reactor cores, started to change the trajectory that would have taken them straight into Kilrah.

The planet, displayed on the main monitor came racing up. Dozens of blips, marking the forward defenses of the Kilrathi, swarmed across the screen, positioning themselves to intercept what they thought would be the suicidal gesture of a planet ramming. But now, with every passing second, *Tarawa* was maneuvering dozens of clicks away from the anticipated path. Some of the fighters started to turn, while others continued to converge on the two drones, whose heavy mines clicking towards detonation were sending the Kilrathi into a frenzy.

"Planet loop in ten seconds."

"Navigation, you damn well better be right," Jason said, looking over at the nav officer who gulped nervously. "Are tractor beams ready?"

"Tractor beam standing by for computer firing."

"Velocity now at nine thousand, eight hundred and twenty eight kilometers per second."

Navigation looked over at her console and punched in the latest data which was instantly fed into the main nav computer. Tens of thousandths of a second later, adjustments were sent into the ship's helm control which minutely altered the engine firing.

"Landing craft rammed by a Sartha," combat announced.

Jason ignored the information, watching as several Sartha, moving now without their own ram scoop fields, attempted to close with full afterburners, coming in on ballistic trajectories.

"Projected impact on *Kagimasha*!"

Jason turned to look at the tactical screen.

It was over even before he could pick out the intersecting lines, a Sartha swinging straight into the path of the corvette, the two intersecting at nearly ten thousand kilometers per second. A white burst of light, far brighter than the sun, appeared on the starboard beam monitoring screen and then disappeared from view as *Tarawa* raced past.

"They never knew what hit them," Jason whispered.

The green-blue ball of Kilrah raced up and for a second Jason was convinced that navigation had screwed it, and they would impact.

"Tractor beam on now!" the navigation officer shouted.

Jason felt the shudder run through the ship. The tractor system was never designed for this, the idea being cooked up by Jim Bane, an old navigation petty officer. If the carrier used the beam on a fighter for recovery the mass differential between the fighter and carrier would be such that for ever meter the carrier might be moved towards the fighter, the fighter would be pulled in several kilometers. Now the beam was aimed straight at Kilrah, pulling the *Tarawa* straight in towards the planet; however, due to the ship's forward velocity it actually wouldn't go straight in, but rather loop in a slingshot around Kilrah, and, if all the calculations were correct, aiming them straight at their intended jump point. If it worked this would alter maneuvering tactics and close-in tactics forever!

They skimmed over the northern pole of the planet, fifty kilometers above the outer atmosphere, the planet's gravitational field bending their trajectory even further into a slingshot.

In less than ten seconds Kilrah was a hundred thousand kilometers astern.

"Damn," Jason sighed, "what a ride."

The bridge went silent as everyone turned to look at the navigation officer.

She continued to lean over her plot board, watching as the computer fed in the data, tracing out the line as *Tarawa* and its lone escort curved down and away out of the equatorial line of the Kilrah solar system.

She finally gave a sigh of relief and looked up with a grin.

"It worked, sir," she said, her voice shaking. "We are on-line up to jump point F-One. Will arrive in seven hours and thirty-two minutes. Will have a fuel reserve of two point three percent after deceleration to achieve jump."

Jason turned and looked over at combat information.

"Not a single ship has even emerged from the other side of Kilrah. Estimate a five million plus kilometer lead on them."

"People, we just might live till tomorrow," Jason said with a smile. "Stand down from battle stations, let's get some rest."

A round of self-congratulations went through the bridge and as he looked out on the flight deck he saw crew members and marines slapping each other on the back.

There was one problem though: jump point F-One took them out on a side track run and not closer to home, but it was the only one they could run to using Kilrah as a slingshot. The enemy carrier at Kilrah could elect to pursue or could take a jump into a parallel system, blocking their escape. And beyond that, there was still no word as to what else might be out there. He was in the dark and the entire Kilrathi

Empire would be mobilizing to hunt them down. They had managed to run, but they were no closer to home, and there was no place to hide.

"He's good, damned good," Prince Thrakhath thought, unable to prevent at least a brief moment of admiration for whomever it was that commanded the human fleet. The diversion, and he now realized that that had been the intent, of the two ships loaded with atomic mines, had momentarily scattered his defense, allowing them to run straight through while losing but one escort ship. They had never intended suicide at all and he realized that he had made the fatal mistake of not viewing the tactical situation from a human perspective. An opportunity to shatter part of Earth, even at the expense of one's own life, would win undying glory for those who sacrificed themselves. He found it almost inconceivable that they had not taken such a course and curiously found himself feeling almost insulted that the humans would not be willing to trade their lives for a chance to strike a blow at the home of the Kilrathi race.

As he studied the plot boards he realized that though the maneuver to run was brilliantly executed it was also an exercise in futility. The jump point they were taking was a single track line, going into a system with only a single jump point beyond it; the next system had but a single jump point exit as well. It was not until the system after that, that there were several jump points, one of which would lead back towards Confederation space. They had simply run into a cul de sac. The carrier *Karu* could be positioned to cover one of the exits. By following the more direct path he could arrive to cover the same exiting system in only three jumps to the four that the humans would need. Either their navigators were not aware of this, or they were simply trying to run the game out and cling to an extra day of life. It would have been more honorable to die here and destroy part of Kilrah. For a moment he actually felt a twinge of regret that the humans had not taken such a course. For after all was not the Emperor responsible for the fiasco, and it would not have been just the Emperor who died but thousands of the court sycophants as well. It could have produced an interesting result. The death of court hangers-on and bureaucrats would have been a pleasure to witness.

"Astronavigator, signal to the *Karu* that the humans have taken the Vuwarg jump. They are to block the jump line from Baragh to Rushta. Carrier *Torg* to move to block the jump point from Baragh to Xsar. We will close the line from Baragh to Lushkag. Signal the same to the Emperor. Have at least thirty reserve fighter craft from the palace guard on Kilrah to sortie and rendezvous with us to replenish our losses. We leave to jump from this system within two hours."

He turned to look at his staff.

"Let's finish this affair. The court historians can then practice their usual craft of lying and embellish it into a great victory rather than a miserable hunt."

• CHAPTER XI

Jason Bondarevsky realized that physically he was at the end of his rope. He looked into the mirror, trying to still the shaking of his hand as he finished shaving. The image that looked back at him was disturbing. His features were pale, eyes dark rimmed and bloodshot. Not since the beginning of the raid had he found a moment to hit the exercise room, a strict requirement for all pilots in order to stay in top physical shape. If he were in charge of anyone who looked like himself, he'd have sent him to sick bay, and ordered a stretch of R&R along with a couple of sessions with the psychological officer.

The nightmares just would not go away—the image of the fireball rushing in to smash the marine landing craft, Svetlana, ghostlike, turning to look at him as the flames swept in. Beside her, Janice and all the others whom he had lost.

He closed his eyes, nicking himself with the old-style razor.

The cold flash of pain from the cut startled him, and cursing, he took his towel and dabbed the wound. He took the small cup of water, which was all that was allowed for shaving due to water rationing, and tried to clean the rest of the soap off.

There was a knock at the door.

"Sir, Captain Grierson has landed. Colonel Merritt's already in the briefing room."

"Right there."

He wiped the last bit of soap off his face, and put on the now thoroughly wrinkled and stained uniform. The laundry room was an empty burned-out shell and all the crew had long since given up trying to look clean.

Jason looked back in the mirror one more time, forcing himself to achieve a certain look of confidence and he stepped out into the corridor. A work crew came to attention and he motioned for them to stand at ease as he squeezed past the welders.

"How's it going, Chief?"

"We're welding a durasteel brace in on that cracked keel spar, sir. It's a tough job getting at her though."

Jason looked down into the hole torn into the deck flooring. Flood lamps illuminated the work crew who were squatting on either side of the cracked beam, maneuvering sections of durasteel into place using hand held null gravity units. The chief was hunched over a portable holo display, which was loaded with the ship's blueprints, and pointed out the damaged section highlighted in red.

"Hell, sir, by the time we get home we'll be able to skip the dry dock and just keep right on going."

"Keep it up, Chief," and Jason patted him on the shoulder and continued on.

It felt strange to order men like the chief around, old-line fleet lifers who were in the service before he was even born. The man was pulling off nothing short of a minor miracle. *Tarawa*, after the hit, in any normal situation, should have been sent back into a rear area dry dock to either be scrapped or taken apart and rebuilt. Such work usually went from the outside in. The chief was doing it backwards, taking apart sections of the ship to get at the damage. Areas of the ship not essential for survival, such as crew quarters, were being stripped for parts, especially the precious durasteel, and then were sealed off and pumped down to conserve on air. The chief was also adding in some modifications of his own, and now with O'Brian dead, he didn't hesitate to point out criticisms in the ship's design, spiced with a choice selection of expletives aimed at fleet headquarters. Yet if anyone dared to agree and denounce the *Tarawa*, the chief and most of his crew would have to be restrained from pummelling the person who dared to so insult "the old girl."

Two days ago, on their sweep through the second system after Kilrah, they had encountered a minor Kilrathi orbital base and taken it out in a sharp attack led by Grierson, several Sabres, and a company of marines. Like carrion flies the damage control team had scrambled aboard the base, climbed over the still warm bodies of the Kilrathi and in under an hour stripped it of anything useful, pulling up sections of durasteel, emergency air canisters, a light shuttle craft, and then going so far as to cut out half a dozen of the base's mass driver mini guns, which were now being welded to the ship just forward of the landing airlock for point defense. The volunteer gun crews would have to go EVA to get to the open turrets but their additional firepower might make the difference.

Jason stepped out of the corridor and went across the hangar bay. Sparks was directing a double team of ground crews that were taking apart three Rapiers which had been condemned as unfit for further service, stripping out the good parts from each, and attempting to get one flyable craft out of what was left.

Any armor left over was immediately sent to the repair crews which were now using it to reinforce the forward bulkheads just aft of the armored gun bow, a section which the chief had declared to be a weak point.

Jason gained the bridge and went over to the combat information officer on watch.

"Still the same, sir. *Intrepid* reports two cruisers and four destroyers six hours behind us. They're scanning and have a lock on us," she said quietly, without taking a second to look up from the screen.

"Our next jump point?"

"Still looks clean."

He looked over at the nav officer on watch.

"Two hours and twenty eight minutes to jump point."

Jason nodded and went into the wardroom.

The men in the room came to attention and Jason smiled.

He realized that technically Grierson should now be in charge of this fleet; he was after all the senior officer. After the heat of action at Kilrah he had offered to turn it all over to him, but Grierson refused, claiming that Jason was doing well enough, that he was after all in charge of the largest ship in the fleet, and that as a destroyer officer he had no experience whatsoever with carriers. Jason had laughed at that, since until Kilrah the biggest craft he had ever run was a Broadsword. Grierson was a rarity; there were far too many officers who, qualified or not, would have shouldered him aside and taken control. Though technically in control of the two-ship fleet, Jason knew that in a pinch he would defer to whatever this older officer had to say.

"Those buggers still behind us?" Merritt asked.

Jason nodded.

"Just shepherding us along," Grierson replied.

"Making sure we go straight in to the next jump," Jason replied.

He looked around the room.

"Any suggestions?"

"I still think we should come about, go back in, and have a show down with those scum," Merritt stated.

Jason shook his head emphatically.

"Those are heavy cruisers. Each of them carries a squadron of fighters on board. That'll be at least thirty to thirty-five against our twenty. Our torpedo supply is just about used up; we've got enough for one more action and then we're out. Both of our ships are hurt. They'll eat us alive."

"At least we could take one cruiser down," Merritt said. "We're being run into the snare like rats trapped in an alleyway. I think it's kind of obvious that they must be racing ahead through a parallel jump line to position themselves in the next system."

Jason nodded and looked around the room.

"Look, our own nav information for this sector is sketchy at best," Grierson said. "Maybe this is the shortest route out. We do know that there's a jump point in the next system that will take us to the Jugara System. Once at Jugara we hook into that long jump which takes us damned near to Confederation lines. So let's not get to pessimistic here."

"Oh come on, Grierson," Merritt said wearily. "Don't you think they know that? Hell, it's their damned system. It'll be blocked by at least one carrier, maybe more. Here we're worried about facing thirty-five fighters, and I tell you that if we push ahead we'll be facing a major capital ship with a hundred and fifty fighters and bombers on board."

"The key question is," Jason interjected, "do the Kilrathi have a shorter route to the next jump point than the one we've taken?"

"I think we can assume so," Grierson replied. "Otherwise that carrier we faced at Kilrah would be dogging our heels right now.

"It's also possible that those two ships we launched

at Kilrah caught the carrier in the blast," Grierson continued. "That's something we don't know since the planet masked our view."

"That's a long-shot assumption," Jason replied. "Damn, it'd be nice to believe that, but in my old line of work we never were allowed to count a kill unless gun cameras got it, or we had a witness, and that's the way I'm going to play it now."

"So what's the game plan, Jason?" Grierson asked, and Jason suppressed a smile of thanks.

"We head for the jump point, go through, and make a run to the Jugara jump point. We can't go back towards Kilrah. Those cruisers would chew us apart. Even if we did defeat them, at best we'd come out crippled, with our ammunition supply depleted."

"And if we find a carrier on the other side of this jump, we're all dead meat," Merritt said.

Jason nodded.

"But we're not a hundred percent sure that the carriers will be there."

"And your gut feeling?" Grierson asked.

There was no sense in lying.

"They'll be waiting for us."

Merritt threw up his hands in exasperation.

"Just great."

Jason nodded slowly.

"Look, the moment we all heard about this mission we knew that we were dead meat, thrown away as a diversion. Damn it all, I'd give a couple of really important parts of my anatomy right now to know what really happened at Vukar. I guess we won't. We've done a hell of a lot of butt kicking though in our own right, with six carriers smashed on the ground thanks to the marines."

Merritt nodded a thanks and Jason forced the nightmare thought away.

"If we turn back we're a hundred percent sure

we're cooked. If we run ahead, there's a chance, just a small one, but there is a chance the way might not yet be blocked. Every second is precious. I'm going to run for that chance."

"And if you're wrong?"

"We'll die game," Jason said quietly. "If we find a carrier there, we go to flank speed, launch our fighters. We'll try to evade and fight a way through to the next jump. If we can't and it becomes obvious that we're finished, I intend to bore straight in. They won't be expecting that. They might take us down, but by God if Doomsday and his Sabres or *Intrepid* can get a torpedo lock on that carrier we'll rip it apart. When we launch our last torpedoes I want a carrier in our sights and not just some second rate cruiser. If need be I'll send the crew to the escape pods and ram him. We're going to take at least one more down with us."

"So that's it?" Merritt asked.

"Hell, what more do you want?" Grierson said with a grin.

"Jump transition in ten seconds . . ."

Jason settled back and silently prayed. He looked around at his bridge staff, and beyond the plastiglass windows to the launch deck. His fighters were all manned, standard procedure for jumping into any unsecured sector, ground crews waiting expectantly.

"They've fought so hard, so damned hard Lord, let 'em make it," Jason whispered.

There was a snap of light and he closed his eyes, waiting.

There were several seconds of silence and then the reports started to fly.

"Nav computer confirms correct alignment and jump."

"We have contact," combat information shouted. "Bogeys, repeat many bogeys bearing 021, positive three degrees, range one hundred and ten thousand clicks, closing at two eight zero clicks a second."

"Get me Grierson on the laser link."

The screen clicked on.

"You see them?"

"A hell of a lot of traffic out there."

"How's your long-range scan?"

"One carrier confirmed, parked on the edge of an asteroid belt. She's deployed out a belt of mines forward. One other carrier on the far side of the system, wait, we've got another just coming through on jump transit, on the far side of the system, but she's hours out from here."

"I'm also picking up indications of another jump in progress on the jump point leading back to Jugara, but it's blocked by the asteroids and heavy jamming."

Jason nodded.

"So what are you going to do?" Grierson asked quietly.

Jason swallowed hard.

"Engage the carrier. If we can get past, we'll run for Jugara."

Grierson smiled.

"I'll see you on the other side, son," and the screen flickered off.

"Launch all fighters," Jason said quietly.

"Confederation ship has just come through and is accelerating, moving straight at us."

Prince Thrakhath nodded.

"He has warrior spirit. It will be the death of him. Launch all reserve fighters."

Kevin Tolwyn, breathing hard, leaned back in his seat. The catapult slammed his Rapier down the length of the deck and he kicked on afterburners as soon as the airlock was cleared, aiming straight ahead.

Pulling out at a hundred kilometers he circled back around, letting the first Sabre go straight past; the second Sabre followed and finally the third and fourth. He banked up high, checking his nav screen, watching as two other Rapiers sortied out to form the rest of the escort. The strike group formed up and then started forward.

"Strike Group Alpha, follow my lead."

"With you, Doomsday," Kevin replied.

"Stay close to me, Lone Wolf, and don't break away."

Kevin sensed the dislike and rebuke in Doomsday's voice but let it pass, though he was tempted to cut loose with a couple of choice words.

Funny, it all seemed so strange now. This was never how he figured it would all end up—there had never been any challenge before. He felt his thoughts racing, aware that it was triggered in part by the adrenaline coursing through him. A swarm of memories floated through, the pampered world he had once known, the all-so-correct schools, the luxury vacations, the summer home in Scotland, Eton, and then Cambridge, all of it so correctly arranged by his mother and his dead father's family. The hardships of the war were outside his understanding, the shortages, even the rationing which his mother's family could so easily work around, what with so many of them properly placed in top positions in the government and in the military procurement industry.

His uncle? A strange duck in the family waters. The severe, reticent uncle who would come home on rare trips back to Earth, looking around with disdain, a disdain intensified by the fawning of hangers-on who wanted to meet the famous admiral.

As for the military, there was no real way to avoid it; after all the Tolwyns had all done their bit going back for fifty generations. It was part of the family tradition. It had killed his father in a training accident when he was an instructor at the Academy. His mother wanted to make sure there wouldn't be any such risks to himself.

He thought of his mother and her horrified reaction when he had insisted upon flight school, turning on her sternness and then the tears, pointing out how the Vice Minister of Armaments wanted a military attaché in his office, and with such a posting, there would be no reason to miss the theater season, or a chance to choose the right young lady from the proper family in London.

How the path weaves and changes, Kevin thought. Because I wanted to fly, to be like my father, I'm now getting set to die in this godforsaken corner of the universe, in a battle no one will ever hear of. He checked his instrument array, watching the growing spread of red blips, the thoughts still racing.

Mother and the family had made the most of his going to flight school, even arranging a holo station interview and magazine articles to show how even the best of families were doing their bit for the war effort, while quietly arranging that he would never get anywhere near to where there might be some real danger. That was still the mystery though. This mission had been in the planning for months, so why was he assigned to *Tarawa*? Was it vengeance on the part of a political rival to the family, an accident, or even done innocently, mother pulling some strings, believing that the ship would never see action, and after his tour of duty he could report back to headquarters, do his bit, and reach admiral without ever having to hear a shot fired?

He'd never know—and he didn't give a damn. He banked slightly to look down at Doomsday's ship a hundred meters below and then straightened back out again.

There was something about these people he had never experienced before in his entire life. They didn't give a good damn who he was; out here on the edge the name was meaningless. There were only the quick and the dead, the comrades you could trust to risk everything to pull you out, and those who weren't worth a damn. He could now see that for nearly all of his twenty-two years, he had not been worth a damn. He thought of Jason, only three years older than himself, a wing commander, his ascent based upon nothing more than ability and moral strength—and now he was an acting captain. He knew that even if Jason had hated and despised him, he still would have put his life on the line to save him.

He had finally come to realize that the only thing that counted was whether you could be relied upon or not. He had suddenly found that he wanted the approval of the other pilots in the ready room, not the sucking-up approval when he had first arrived aboard *Tarawa* and treated all of them to free meals and endless free drinks at their last port of call. That was crap. He wanted instead the steady-eyed look of understanding, and especially from Jason.

Jason had given him the chance to change it all, even after his mistake. The mistake . . . again he looked down at Doomsday's Sabre and then straight ahead. Jim Conklin had been an amiable sort from some back hill farming town in America, not the type he would have ever invited to the club if they had met only half a year ago. And now Jim was dead. Jason was right; he should have stayed close, and forgotten about the kill. He had even heard Jason's orders to turn back, just before the radio winked out, never knowing until afterwards that Jim and the tail gunner were about to die.

Never again, never again, Kevin thought to himself.

"*Tarawa* control." It was Doomsday.

Kevin looked down at his commlink visual.

"*Tarawa* control here."

"We're going for the carrier," Doomsday said.

Kevin felt his gut tighten up. A cruiser, two destroyers, and a host of fighters were between them and that target. (Never again, indeed. Never anything.)

And yet if that were the case he would die with him and not regret it in the slightest.

This was where he wanted to be.

"Strike Force Alpha, good luck," and it was Jason on the line.

"Always figured I'd wind up in a fix like this, *Tarawa*, now get the hell out of here."

Doomsday chuckled softly.

"All right Alpha, suck it up and stick to me like glue."

Kevin nudged his throttle up a notch, edging forward of the strike force, arming his IFF missiles. Kilrathi fighters, spread out in a screen in front of their task force, started to turn on an intersect line with the attack, while more than fifty of them continued straight on in, passing twenty clicks to Kevin's port side, afterburners flashing, moving to attack *Tarawa* and *Intrepid*.

The radio started to crackle as Round Top passed out orders to the screen of six Ferrets, two Rapiers, and two Sabres which were marshalling to form a defensive screen.

"Strike Alpha switch to commlink 2282,"

Kevin turned the dial to the proper channel which eliminated the chatter from the defensive squadron.

The first Drakhri dived in, executing a brilliant roll and loop, followed by a section of three more fighters. Kevin banked around hard, turning up for a side approach and then pulling over, following the last Drakhri in. The enemy fighter broke off from its attack, banking out and away. He ignored him, closing in on the third fighter in line which broke as well when a salvo of neutron bolts slammed into its stern. The first two fighters continued on in against the Sabres.

"Sabres break left," Doomsday called, and the four ships banked hard, the Drakhri slashing down through empty space. Cleared of the Sabres, Kevin unleashed an IFF and pulled back up on his stick, breaking off the pursuit to cut back upwards for top cover on the fighter-bombers.

"Good work, Lone Wolf," Doomsday clicked, and then he was off the screen again.

"With you, Doomsday," Kevin replied.

The Drakhri fighters, more than a score of them, set up a regular attack pattern, sections of four breaking in on the group, one striking from above, another from either flank or astern, while others maneuvered for position.

"Line on the lead destroyer, activate torpedo lock then break it off at ten kilometers and roll in on a heading for the carrier!" Doomsday called.

The group turned, following their leader, except for one Rapier that disintegrated in a burst of light.

The enemy fighters continued to harry the flanks, pulling tight circles at the edge of the group, leaving the front open as the Destroyer's long-range lasers opened up, and with the range closing were joined by the ship's neutron and mass driver guns.

A direct hit nailed the second Sabre in the formation, a curtain of debris flaring out. In the momentary confusion a Drakhri dived into the group, and Kevin followed him in, unloading an IFF at point-blank range, the missile slamming into the enemy ship's engine. He thundered through the debris, watching his shields wink down.

He circled back out, meeting two more fighters head-on and within seconds scored his second kill of the day with a quickly toggled dumb fire bolt that impacted on the enemy fighter's cockpit.

"Break, break!" Doomsday shouted, and the attack swerved off from the enemy destroyer and banked hard around, dropping to a direct line up on the enemy carrier a thousand kilometers away.

"Forty seconds," Doomsday cried, "get early lock, and run 'em in, too many fighters to slow down for standard launch."

The turn away from the destroyer momentarily threw off the Kilrathi defense, but even though the outer wave was now astern, the enemy still had fifteen fighters positioned directly in front of their carrier, which now sortied up to meet the threat.

Seconds later another Sabre disintegrated, caught by a volley of missiles which intersected the formation from both sides, the doomed pilot banking away from one shot and thus turning straight in on the other.

Two Sabres were now left and Kevin was shocked to hear Doomsday singing what he could only surmise was a mournful death chant.

"Twenty seconds, initiate lock!"

Kevin heard the high-pitched whine of the torpedo guidance systems kicking on even as he broke to starboard to throw an enemy fighter off his tail. A Drakhri was directly in front of him, racing away from the Sabres. He fought down the temptation to gain an easy kill, flipped over, and dived back towards the Sabres, winging a Sartha which broke off from a line up on Doomsday's tail and fled.

"Ten seconds to torpedo launch; hold it steady."

The two Sabres flew a straight line in, not deviating in the slightest from their course, the enemy carrier now clearly visible. The first proximity mine was passed, the weapon gaining a lock and moving to strike the attacking Sabres, Kevin bursting the weapon with a well-aimed particle cannon shot.

A spread of missiles started to track in, launched by a light destroyer which was providing point coverage for the enemy ship.

"Hold it steady, hold it steady!" Doomsday shouted.

Doomsday's wingman disappeared in flames, an instant later his own ship was flipped over by a near burst, his torpedoes firing off on a wild trajectory.

"Doomsday!"

"Damn! Torpedoes auto fired, damn it!" Doomsday shouted, even as his ship continued to spiral down and away.

Kevin winged over, following him, turning to threaten a Drakhri which sensed an easy kill, but backed off in an evasive turn as Kevin fired off his last remaining IFF.

"Lost my copilot, we're in trouble here!"

"Head back for *Tarawa*, I'm with you!" Kevin shouted, "just fly the damn thing, don't worry about anything else."

"Damn it, go for the carrier!"

"With what, my fists? Not till I get you back home; now fly damn it!"

Kevin looked back over his shoulder, wanting to slide down lower in his seat as the incoming missile alarm blinked on his screen. He popped off his chaff while maneuvering at the same time to avoid a mine. The missile turned and streaked away. "Blue two, you with me?"

There was no response and Doomsday was the only friendly blip on his screen. He saw Doomsday start to turn as if attempting to regain an attack position on the carrier.

"Damn it, Doomsday. If you want to die, make it worth something. Your ship won't get within a hundred clicks of that carrier before they rip you apart. Now head back to *Tarawa* and trade your junker in on something that can still fly and fight!"

Doomsday's image flashed on the commscreen, his cabin filled with smoke.

"All right Wolf, help me get home."

"With you all the way, Doomsday, with you all the way. Let's just hope we've got a ship to go home to."

Jason stood transfixed, watching the screen, listening to the battle reports coming in. Damn, to be stuck here on the bridge when I should be out there.

"*Tarawa*, this is Grierson."

"Go ahead."

"Alpha Strike's wiped out, two survivors breaking off. Head over the top of the asteroid field; there's a bit of a hole there in the Kilrathi defenses, you might have an open run. Get your pups back in; there won't be any carrier on your table for lunch today."

Jason nodded dejectedly.

"All right *Intrepid*, follow me up."

"I'll be along shortly."

"Grierson, what the hell are you doing?"

"What the hell do you think? Covering my carrier; now get a move on, son."

"Helm, bring us over to clear the asteroid belt."

"We've got ten more Gratha fighter bombers coming up out of the asteroid field," combat information shouted.

Jason turned to look at the tactical display as the blips emerged out of the clutter of the asteroid debris field.

"Seven torpedoes are out and running, coming straight down our throats!"

"Where's our combat cover?"

"Still astern and engaged sir!"

Jason turned to look out from the bridge. Beyond the forward airlock he could see the enemy fighter bombers breaking to turn away.

Point defense keyed up, the forward laser guns

setting out a rapid fire staccato of bursts. A torpedo detonated ten thousand meters forward. The mass driver guns cannibalized from the Kilrathi base kicked in, the recoil shuddering through the ship and the second torpedo exploded. Four more exploded in rapid succession.

"Five seconds to impact. One torpedo's got a definite lock."

Jason wanted to cover his ears, to drown out the high-pitched shriek of the torpedo guidance system coming in through the combat information audio link.

"Three seconds."

"Brace yourselves."

The blow slammed him to the deck and then back up. The bridge went dark, and he felt himself floating as the artificial gravity generator shorted out. Jason waited, instinctively holding his breath, expecting the hull to split, spilling him into the vacuum of space.

Emergency battle lamps snapped on and then he slammed back down on the deck as the gravity generator kicked back in. A deep hollow booming echoed through the ship, sounding as if the *Tarawa* were being pounded by a giant's hammer.

"Damage control. This is forward turret," cried the voice edged with hysteria. "We've taken a direct hit to the forward bow. We're sheering off!"

Jason staggered back up to his feet and looked out the forward airlock.

"Merciful God," he gasped.

The forward twenty meters of the armored bow was peeling back. A fiberoptic communication line to the bow was still intact and the screams of the crew trapped forward echoed on the bridge. The bow continued to tear back and a howling shriek echoed through the ship as the durasteel frame buckled and finally snapped. The bow tumbled off. For a brief instant Jason saw a body tumbling end over end, floating out of the bow into the vacuum of space. The bow disappeared astern. What was left of the forward part of the ship was flame-scorched and blackened. The minigun crews outside of the airlock were gone, the position torn apart by the spray of shrapnel.

Jason scrambled back up to the bridge and looked over at damage control.

"Chief, are we holding?"

"We shouldn't be, but the third bulkhead back from the bow seems intact. One airlock is compromised; we're leaking a hell of a lot of air though. I've got crews heading there now to shore it up."

"For heaven's sake how?" Jason asked.

The chief looked back at him.

"The armor bow was an add on for the forward turret; remember this was designed as a transport, and additional positions were simply welded on," he hesitated for a moment. "Plus we added those reinforcements in late yesterday. Lucky for us."

"How many crew in that turret?"

"Thirty-five, sir. At least it was quick."

Another series of shudders ran through the ship as combat information called in the latest strike information, half a dozen fighters strafing, hoping to break down what was left of the phase shielding, which was down to eight percent. A bolt slammed against the forward airlock and for a fraction of a second the lock failed. A mass driver round slashed down the length of the deck, impacting on the far wall of the hangar, sending out an explosive shower of shrapnel, cycling down ground crews that were working feverishly to turn the last few fighters around. The fuel tank of a Ferret cooked off with an explosive roar, sweeping the deck in a fireball. Fire alarms wailed and the fire control system kicked on, spraying down the deck with a blizzard of white foam. The pilot, still inside the Ferret, was struggling to get out of the exploding ship when the ejector seat detonated, slamming him into the ceiling of the hangar.

Jason stood on the bridge, barely aware that the plastiglass shield that separated him from the flight deck was hit by the shrapnel. Cracks raced across the shield. It disintegrated, cascading back into the bridge in a shower of broken fragments. The bridge crew struggled to sweep the broken fragments off their instruments, several cutting their hands in the process.

Another mass driver bolt penetrated the forward airlock, the Kilrathi fighter appearing to hover directly in front of the *Tarawa*. The round impacted close to where the last had hit, and punched through the wall, slashing into the interior of the ship. The Kilrathi fighter opened up with a full salvo, a stream of rounds pouring in, the forward airlock shimmering, phasing in and out, air rushing out with a hurricane force as the airlock pulsed on and off, the rounds smashing through the aft wall of the hangar deck, shrapnel shrieking. The deck was a nightmare of explosions. A blast of flame blew through the bridge and Jason ducked down, covering his face with his hands, feeling the hair on his head and eyebrows curling and burning from the heat. The wave of fire pulsed down. Instrument panels exploded, electrical fires snapping out of control panels.

The bridge went dark for a moment and then the emergency lighting came back up, the room filled with dark acrid smoke.

Coughing, Jason turned to shout an order to the combat control officer to order a fighter in for protection. But the woman was gone, her headless corpse lying on the floor of the bridge. Everything was disintegrating into smoke, fire, and confusion.

There was a stunning flareup of light from forward of the airlock and the Kilrathi fighter disappeared.

Through the fireball Jason saw a Rapier arcing up and away, attempting to shake off two Drakhri on his tail.
"Something's not right here, sir."
Jason looked over to a marine sergeant who had stepped in to take the dead officer's place.
"We're getting readings of a fourth carrier, closing in from the other side of the asteroid field. IFF shows it to be Kilrathi, but it's not in our computer register."
Jason went over to look, the wavery image suddenly snapping off, the holo image disappearing. The marine sergeant looked up.
"We're blind, sir, all surveillance systems shot."
"What about that other carrier?"
"Last I saw she was coming out of her mine field in pursuit."
"Helm, how are we?"
"Losing speed, sir."
"Close in the scoops."
"Sir, we won't have enough fuel."
Jason looked over at the helmsman's screen. Fuel was at less than five percent. With scoops closed they'd run dry within minutes.
Another shudder ran through the ship.
"Engine room reports impact of two missiles on the stern, one exhaust nozzle blown off."
The damage control board was lighting up, showing red from one end of the ship to the other. Even as he watched, the neutron turret on the bottom winked out, its power cables shorting off.
"Sir, rear turret reports Grierson's turned around and is heading back in on the enemy fleet."
Jason picked up the communications officer's headset.
"Grierson, stay with us!"
"Grierson!"
"Damn it, somebody get me a laser beam comm lock on Grierson!" The image of Grierson winked in

and out. His friend's image was wavery, his mouth moving, but no audio was coming through. And then he disappeared as another shudder ran through *Tarawa*, throwing the laser lock off.

The enemy fighters which had been circling *Tarawa* like a host of angry hornets turned back towards *Intrepid*.

"Helmsman, can you bring us around?"

"Steering is marginal, sir."

Frustrated, Jason stood on the bridge, powerless to intervene.

"Grierson!"

"Outside radio links are dead, sir," the comm officer said, his voice slurred with shock.

The marine sergeant now in charge of combat information was under the control panel, swatting down an electrical fire. A grainy, two-dimensional image came back up on line. The *Intrepid* was moving in on the cruiser covering the enemy carrier. Jason watched the screen as the drama was played out. A spread of torpedoes leaped out from both ships nearly simultaneously and at point-blank range.

The two ships disappeared, and Jason lowered his head.

"Sir, they didn't get the carrier but they sure as hell smashed the cruiser," the marine whispered.

Jason nodded.

"Carrier still coming on."

Through the airlock a Sabre came in, sparks raining out from its port wing which was nearly torn loose from the fighter bomber's hull. The Sabre skidded through the fire retardant foam, slamming into the safety nets. Seconds later, without waiting for clearance in all the confusion, a lone Rapier came in as well, skidding down the deck through the foam, jockeying to one side of the Sabre, narrowly avoiding a collision.

Jason looked up and watched as Doomsday scrambled down from the cockpit and raced to the bridge, Tolwyn behind him.

Another explosion rocked *Tarawa*, knocking Jason to his knees as a second wave of fire swept through the hangar deck. He wasn't even sure where it had come from.

He stood back up and looked at the situation board. Combat information was blind again, the nav station a shambles, the officer curled up by the console holding a badly fractured arm; tactical display was gone, all outside links down. The room had a surreal look, smoke filled, illuminated by fire and the red battle lamps, acrid smoke swirling about him. He felt a trickle of blood running down his face, but no pain, not even sure if the blood was his or somebody elses.

The damage control chief turned in his chair and looked at Jason.

"She put up a hell of a fight sir, a hell of fight."

The chief hesitated, unable to say the words. Jason nodded sadly.

"Prepare to abandon ship," Jason said quietly. "All crew to the escape pods. Helmsman, before you leave, try and bring her around for a run straight back on that carrier, but I want everyone off this ship when I take her back in."

"Jason!"

He looked up as Doomsday scrambled up the ladder onto the bridge.

"Well, buddy, if you want to play out your death wish just stick around with me, otherwise get into one of the escape pods."

"Damn it, Jason, the other carrier's closing in."

"I know."

"No, you don't. Didn't you get the tail end of Grierson's message?"

Jason looked at Doomsday, not understanding.

"Grierson knew you were finished, communications and defense shot, another hit and you'd be lost. That's why that crazy bastard turned back, to pull the fighters off and buy some time."

"Well, we're going to join him," Jason snapped, "so either shut up or get the hell off this bridge. You keep talking about getting yourself killed; well today's the day."

"Damn it, sir!" Kevin shouted, shouldering in past Doomsday.

"That other carrier, it's the *Concordia*!"

"What the hell are you talking about?"

"It's *Concordia*! They masked it with a Kilrathi IFF transponder. Her fighters will be here any minute. She was broadcasting a message in the clear for us to hang on. Just hang on, damn it!"

Stunned, Jason could not even respond.

"Helmsman, can you steer us towards that other carrier?"

"We've lost all outside data."

"Well, damn it, steer to where you think she is and for God's sake don't put us in the asteroid field!"

"Aye, sir."

Jason stepped off the bridge and out on to the flight deck. Fires continued to sweep the bay, fire retardant swirling in a blizzard of foam. Directly beneath the bridge an emergency aid station was set up and dozens of casualties were laid out, med teams struggling to save the wounded, the ship's chaplain with them, kneeling over a dying marine and praying with him. As Jason watched, the chaplain made the sign of the cross and then pulled a flight jacket up over the marine's face and then went to kneel by the next casualty.

Jason walked past the aid station to stand directly in front of the airlock door.

He finally saw them, tiny pinpoints of light that

within seconds took form. A squadron of Broadswords flashed by, torpedoes glinting evilly under their wings, escorted by Sabres and Rapiers. Four Rapiers broke off, circling around to take up escort positions; and on their wings were the markings of their ship—*Concordia*.

"That old bastard Tolwyn wouldn't leave us out here to die," Jason said quietly.

"I guess not, sir," Kevin said, and Jason looked over at the pilot and grinned.

"I knew we'd make it," Doomsday said, slapping Jason on the shoulder and hugging him with exuberance, and for the first time in all the years that he knew him, Jason heard Doomsday laugh.

"Yeah, sure," Jason whispered. "Me, too. I knew it all along."

• CHAPTER XII

"So I am to take the blame for your failings and that of your decrepit grandfather."

Prince Thrakhath looked up angrily, wishing more than ever that he had been allowed to simply kill the Baron. There was too much pressure from the family now against a blood feud, for though all were seeking blame for the fiasco, all of the royal blood also feared that the minor families might turn against them, especially now that the home fleet was crippled. Five carriers lost at Vukar, two so seriously damaged that it'd be a standard year or more before they would be active again, and then the loss of six more in the construction yard. Unthinkable, just unthinkable.

"You at least are alive, not like Rusmak and Gar."

"They were both fools and deserved to die. Vukar was a disaster. Gar was far too confident and eager to close. If he had held off and waited on the landing effort, as I advised him to do, he would have not been caught with his landing fleet out in the open when their fighters jumped us, unable to return in time to his transports. He died and deserved it, the tragedy is that forty thousand of our best died as well and we still have not retaken Vukar.

"We don't need to now," Prince Thrakhath continued quietly. "We just received a surveillance report.

Confederation marines abandoned the planet this morning. They have left it a wrecked hulk, destroying everything before departure."

"I told you from the beginning that it was a senseless campaign, launched to retrieve a ruined palace that a beggar would have turned his nose up at even before it was destroyed."

"How dare you speak such of the Emperor's mother?"

"I dare because someone must," the Baron snapped, and Thrakhath was shocked by his anger. For the first time in his life he had heard the normally effete Baron raise his voice in anger.

"Your grandfather, my step-uncle, has led us into a disastrous war. You are too young to even remember that before this war started I warned that we should first seek an accommodation with these humans. Send our ambassadors in, establish our spies, lull their people with promises of our heartfelt desire for peace and disarmament, and then strike. One can always find fools who will listen to such drivel and do half your work for you—establishing friendship committees and lulling them with soft words. Easier to kill a fleet through lack of money because it must be spent on peaceful activities, than to have to destroy it in battle. You and your grandfather have never learned the inner truth that peace and war can be one and the same, the pursuing of a policy that in the end, no matter what the means, can lead to ultimate victory. All you ever see is the path of the sword."

"That is now ancient history and the talk of cowards. The fact that you, a Kilrathi of the royal blood, could even think in such a way is beyond my comprehension."

"Ah yes, our Kilrathi pride. We have never lost a war, we do not talk, we take what is ours, our rightful destiny to rule the stars. But now we have met a match to our pride. These humans are worthy of our study, and not our mindless disdain. It is only through knowing them that we will eventually defeat them."

"Do you now whine for peace?"

"Far from it. It is a war to the death, either them or us. But war must be waged with cunning and clear thought, which your grandfather lacks."

"I will not listen to this treason."

"Dare call it treason, cousin? Not if it prosper! I call it clear thinking. We believed them to be nothing but a warrior made of paper, one push and they would tear apart and float away on the winds of our storm. Well, they have endured over thirty years of war and within the last ten days have destroyed five of our fleet carriers and six which were nearing completion, a reserve which I remember you promising would be the strength that would bring this war to a conclusion before the year was out."

The Baron walked over to a side table and poured himself a drink. He looked over quizzically at Thrakhath.

"No, I will have none."

The Baron hesitated.

"It is not poison, my blood oath upon that."

The Baron nodded and emptied the goblet.

"Cousin, I know you not to be a fool. I know as well your ambition to be emperor. But I warn you, do not discount the cunning, the intellect, the warrior spirit of these humans. Too many empires in the past were destroyed by enemies whom they laughed at."

"Is that all, Baron?"

He nodded.

"I do not go lightly into this exile. The truth of the real blame of Vukar and the fiasco at Kilrah will come out. This little exile buys me the time to indulge my readings of the ancient classics and the translations of human works which far too many of our people view with disdain. I'll have that, at least, along with my study of art and music. And I assure you, I will be back. I do not hate you, cousin, but I also think that you are no longer fit to be our Emperor if you allow that old shriveled up corpse to sit on the throne that either you must seize, or I will take. For if one or the other of us does not take it, someone outside the family will."

"Get off my ship and I hope you rot in your exile."

The Baron smiled.

"The feeling is mutual, cousin. If you wish, though, I would be happy to lend you the scribe of my clan. He is most proficient in writing up rubbish that tells of stirring victories, his lies so convincing that no one ever discovers the truth. For that is how I see what we are doing. We live in a fantasy, and until that changes, until we study these humans and learn to think as they do, this war will drag on and on."

With a mocking salute the Baron left the room.

Prince Thrakhath stood up and went over to pour himself a drink as well, first activating the poison scanner built into his signet ring to check if his cousin might have slipped something into the decanter. It was clean.

He nursed the drink, returning to his desk to review the casualty and damage reports. Any hope for an offensive to smash straight through to Earth and end this war was now lost, at least for the next year. It was again back to a bloody stalemate. Perhaps he could organize some form of a raid straight into the heart of the Confederation the same way they had done it. The Baron was right on that; they had to more closely study their enemy to learn how he thinks. That was evident in how he twice misjudged his opponent's intentions in battle.

Yes, the Baron was right, as he almost always was

on all things. That was why he was willing to listen, and that was why he feared him as well.

"You damn fool, I should bust you straight out of the service."

Admiral Tolwyn stood defiant in the middle of Banbridge's wardroom, a thin smile creasing his features.

"Without my knowledge or approval you jump out, abandoning the mop-up after Vukar. You haul your butt straight into the guts of the Kilrathi system, placing a carrier at risk. Damn it, man, you are insane."

"When we picked up that coded Kilrathi signal with the information that *Tarawa* had gone through jump point One-F, it was obvious that he had to come out at Jugara and I knew I could get there at about the same time—if I moved at once—and help pull them out. There wasn't any time to check with you Wayne. Your commlinks were all shot to hell from the battle."

"Don't give me that bull," Banbridge snapped. He stood up and came around from behind his desk, coming up to Tolwyn and putting a finger into his face.

"We won Vukar by the skin of our teeth. We lost the *Trafalgar*, and *Gettysburg* will be in dry dock for a year. That just leaves *Wolfhound* and *Concordia* for this entire sector and you take half of our assets and go gallivanting off. Damn it, man, you almost took our victory and turned it into a disaster."

"But I didn't lose *Concordia*, and I did get *Tarawa* out," Tolwyn said quietly.

Banbridge, his features beet-red, turned away.

"You're a loose cannon, Geof."

"But you can't argue with success, Wayne. We've dealt out a victory that reversed the tide of this war, at least for the moment. Vukar was brilliant; we took down six carriers—though I doubt that sixth kill claim—crippled another, destroyed at least four imperial legions, along with twenty other ships, a dozen or more transports and support vessels, for one carrier lost, one seriously damaged, and seven escorts." Then he paused. "And ninety-six good pilots. You did a hell of job out there."

"Don't try and kiss my butt out of your troubles, mister."

Geof laughed and shook his head.

"We go back a long way together, Wayne. You know me better than that, so don't insult me."

Banbridge turned to look back at Tolwyn.

"What those kids on *Tarawa* did wasn't just the icing on the cake," Tolwyn said, "it was another whole damned cake. You just saw the holo playbacks. They killed six carriers under construction. Killing them in the hangers is a hell of a lot cheaper than killing them in space and losing a lot of good pilots in the process. They smashed up their construction facilities, took down one cruiser, two orbital bases, four corvettes, and at least ninety fighter craft. But it's not just that. The moral impact is incredible. People are going nuts all over the Confederation, first Vukar and then word of this. Morale hasn't been this high since we took back Enigma. And think about it from the Kilrathi side. I wouldn't be surprised if they aren't on the edge of a palace coup, or at least a damned good purge.

"And I'll be damned if we were going to leave them out there, Wayne. They made Vukar possible; we owed them a chance to get out alive. I just wish the hell I had gotten in there twenty minutes earlier to save Grierson."

"Grierson saved your butt, too. If he hadn't gone in and slowed them down, they would have ripped you apart as well."

Banbridge stalked over to his desk and grabbed a comm sheet and waved it at Tolwyn.

"Damn you, I agree with all that about saving them. It's this that has my blood boiling!"

Tolwyn grinned slyly.

"To send out a false communication, under my signature, stating that *Concordia* was detailed for the rescue effort under my orders is fraudulent and a court-martial offense."

"It makes you the hero of it all," Tolwyn said quietly. "Risking all to save the brave crew of *Tarawa*."

"You've got me in a corner and you know it, Geof. I've just been recommended for a medal of valor with diamonds for this whole thing. You're slated for one as well. How the hell am I supposed to turn around now and say the whole thing was a massive act of disobedience?"

"You can't, Wayne, and you know it. It's turned out all right. Everyone's a hero and history will record it that way. Hell, it'll be a holo drama playing in every theater within the year. I wonder who they'll get to play you? I can just imagine the scene when you look up from your desk and say, 'Geof, we've got to save those kids no matter what; the Confederation owes it to them. Go in there and get them out.' "

Banbridge exhaled noisily and sat down on the edge of his desk.

"All right, damn you, you've got me over a barrel. You were doing it to me twenty-five years ago in the Academy when I was your instructor, and you're still doing it now."

"And I'll continue to do it, Wayne; it keeps both of us on our toes."

Banbridge nodded.

"If you had failed though."

"I'd be dead, but I still think it would have been worth it. Damn you, Wayne," and his voice went cold, "you've forgotten what this war is being fought with. It's not ships, it's men and women, most of them not much more than kids, hanging their hides out on the line and getting precious little thanks. I was not going to leave those kids out there to die alone. They deserved better than that. We've got a hell of a long war yet to be fought; we can still lose it. When those kids sign on the dotted line to join the fleet, they've got to know we'll stand behind them no matter what. I tell you this, I'm never going to allow our people to become throwaway cannon fodder. I'd rather lose and go down fighting than to allow that. A country, a civilization worth fighting for, will risk everything to bring its warriors back."

"All right then. Is he still out there?"

"Waiting to see you."

"Show them in."

Tolwyn went to the door and pulled it open.

"Come on in, you two."

Jason, with Merritt by his side, came into the room. They started to come to attention but Banbridge motioned for them to stand at ease and then to their surprise it was Banbridge who came to attention and saluted them before coming forward to shake their hands, a friendly grin lighting his features.

"Damn it all, it's good to see you alive."

"Thank you, sir," Jason said quietly, "it's good to be back alive."

"Both of you are bloody heroes. I'm personally signing your medal of honor reports. The entire confederation's talking about you two. The holo news stations are killing each other to try to get the first interviews. Your faces are on every screen in the Confederation."

Jason could not respond and stood silent.

"Brigadier General Merritt, I just got word from your boss that you're being promoted to command First Marine Regiment."

"What about Gonzales, sir? That was her job."

"I'm sorry, you didn't know?"

Merritt lowered his head.

"She bought it on Vukar during the Kilrathi bombardment."

"She was a damned good officer," Merritt said softly.

"We lost a lot of good people, but at least we got you back."

"How's Big Duke?" Merritt asked.

"Lost an arm, but they'll regen him another, and he'll be back in the fight in no time."

"Good news on that," Merritt replied with a smile. "They can't keep him down."

Banbridge looked over at Jason.

"And you, son. Interested in a new command? I was talking with commfleet and there's a new light carrier coming on line next month. Either that or I need some damned good people on my staff."

"I'd rather stay with *Tarawa*, sir."

"She's heading to the bone yard son. She's finished."

"Like hell," Tolwyn snapped. "When word of that decision gets out, the public will go mad. *Tarawa*'s going to be refitted and rejoin the fleet."

"All right, all right," Banbridge replied. "That will cost more than rebuilding from scratch but you can keep your ship, Captain Bondarevsky."

Jason nodded his thanks.

"We've got a lot of debriefing to go through. My intelligence people are looking over your computer records and holo data right now. You're the first damned warship to get into Kilrah and back out alive. I'll see you again after some of those debriefings to go over details. By the way, commfleet intelligence just informed me that you were facing Prince Thrakhath out there."

"So he wasn't at Vukar then?" Jason asked.

"Don't rub it in," Banbridge said quietly.

"If I'd have known that, I might have pressed the attack and killed that carrier. I'm surprised he held back and retreated when we came in. It's not like him," Tolwyn said.

"Element of surprise, his own fighters were depleted, and I guess he wanted to cap his losses," Banbridge replied.

"You pulled Thrakhath's beard son; be proud of that," Banbridge said and he went back to his desk, signalling that the interview was over.

Jason and Merritt saluted. Jason hesitated, then couldn't resist.

"Thanks for giving that order to pull us out, sir."

Banbridge looked up at Jason, smiled coldly, and said nothing.

Smiling, Jason walked out of the office, Tolwyn by his side.

"You must be exhausted, Jason," Tolwyn said.

Jason nodded woodenly. After *Concordia* had opened the line of retreat they had flown straight out, and throughout the flight back into Confederation space, it had been a struggle to keep the ship alive. Fires were still flaring up, hull ruptures leaking air to the point that by the last jump the crew was wearing pressure suits, a most unpleasant experience when you were in one for thirty-six hours straight. As they cleared into Confederation territory a team of damage control experts rendezvoused with the crippled ship, a supply tanker anchoring alongside, pumping in air, fuel, and supplies, and offloading the wounded. One of Banbridge's staff officers had loaned Jason a uniform for the interview, along with a quick shower which had helped a bit, but the shock of it all was still burned deep within him.

He could not escape the mental images, the last call from Svetlana, Grierson turning to buy those few precious minutes, and the hangar full of the dead, wounded, and dying. There were only fourteen pilots left out of the forty-four that he had called pups only weeks before.

"Would you care to come over to *Concordia* with me, get some sleep?" Tolwyn asked, putting his hand on Jason's shoulder. "My steward can cook up a hell of a steak along with a good stiff double whiskey, and there's even a small tub there to soak in."

"No, sir. I'd better get back to my ship."

It felt strange to call it that. My ship. He remembered his first Ferret, calling her that, "My ship," beaming with pride when his crew chief had painted "Bear" under the cockpit, complete to a small cartoon character beneath it. And now he was a carrier commander, and he would be ready to kill anyone who dared to say a word against the *Tarawa*, or any escort carrier for that matter. They were, after all, the best damned fighting ships in the fleet.

They walked out onto the flight deck of *Concordia*. It looked so big now. It was clean, immaculate, not like the tight quarters which were home.

Jason looked over at Merritt.

"Take care, marine."

"You too, pilot."

They shook hands warmly.

"She was one of the best. I'll never forget her," Merritt said quietly and Jason nodded, unable to reply.

He looked over at Admiral Tolwyn.

"And, sir, we've kind of got a hunch about the truth in all of this. Thank you."

"It's the other way around," Tolwyn said quietly. "Thank you, and it was an honor to be out there with you."

He hesitated for a moment.

"And Jason, thanks for my nephew as well. I saw your preliminary report, and Doomsday filled me in as well. He can't say enough about him—it's the most I've ever heard that man talk. You took Kevin out a spoiled little rich boy and brought him back a man that I'm proud of."

"I kind of felt, sir, that if given the chance Kevin would finally prove himself."

The two shook hands and Jason went over to his Ferret and climbed in. It felt wonderful to be back at the controls of a fighter again. The inside of the cockpit smelled of scorched wiring, the tactical display screen still cracked from a hit. He had a flash memory of Janice at the controls of her Ferret, turning in towards the torpedo. He pushed the thought away.

He taxied over to the launch line, took the clear signal and powered up, clearing the airlock and kicking on a touch of afterburner, pulling a quick roll for the pleasure of it. The flight was only a five-minute hop and as he slowed down and took the clearance for landing he first circled around his ship. The repair transport was still strapped alongside, a snakelike cluster of umbilical cords going from one to the other, pumping in air, energy, and fuel. A group of welders, in EVA garb, were swarming over the torn-off forward bow, spot welding durasteel plates on. The ship was a battered wreck from stem to stern, armor plating torn up, paint blistered off, the communications and surveillance instrument arrays tangled wreckage.

And yet there was a touch that made him swell with pride. On the port side of the ship, near where the bridge used to be located, a work crew had repainted the name of the ship "CVE-8 TARAWA." Underneath was stenciled the traditional symbols representing her kills, and emblazoned in golden letters the proud statement FIRST TO KILRAH.

He swung around and lined up on the airlock door, coming through easily and touching down to a stop.

As he opened his canopy Sparks was there to greet him, her forehead still wrapped with a bandage.

"How's the wound, Sparks?"

"Still a bit sore, sir. Thanks for asking."

"I was worried about you, getting knocked out like that."

"You were worried about me?"

"Sure I was."

And she flashed him a radiant smile.

"Sparks, how does it feel to be a lieutenant now and head of all ground crews?"

"An officer, I never thought I'd see the day, sir. Thanks."

"You deserved it for the work you did. We got through that fight thanks to your turning those fighters around."

"I'm proud to be part of the team, sir, especially since you're leading it."

She smiled again and then stepped off the ladder.

He alighted onto the deck and saluted the far bulkhead wall, which had been riddled to shreds by the Kilrathi mass driver shots. A section of durasteel taken from a wrecked fighter had been pasted over the holes and a new flag painted on to it.

"Captain coming aboard."

Two sweat-soaked non-commissioned officers came up to Jason and saluted.

"Permission to come aboard," Jason asked.

"A pleasure to grant it, sir," and the two returned Jason's salute.

The ceremony over, Jason turned to walk over to the makeshift bridge.

Doomsday was standing by the ladder leading up to the bridge, watching as a new sheet of plastiglass was being lifted up to replace the one blown out in the final attack.

"How'd it go with the old man?"

"I think he's all right with Banbridge. Hell, they can't shoot a hero can they? Anyhow, while I was over there I got word on you."

"Oh, now what?" Doomsday sighed.

"Your promotion's been confirmed as wing commander for this ship, along with that medal of honor recommendation."

"Yeah, thanks. Thirty new pups to train, all of them trying to get me killed."

"Undoubtably."

"Hope they don't try and kill me the way you did."

Jason laughed and walked away.

As he crossed the flight deck he saw the two pilots that he wanted.

"Round Top, Lone Wolf."

The two, hunched over inside the weapons bay of a Rapier, looked up, their faces streaked with grease, and came over to Jason, shaking his hand.

"How'd it go over there, sir?" Round Top asked.

"I'm staying with *Tarawa* and word is that those decommission stories are bunk. She'll go back for repairs, refitting, and back out for more action."

"Great, sir, it's what we wanted to hear about this old lady."

"Chamberlain, I want you to take over as squadron commander for the Ferrets."

Chamberlain grinned.

"Thanks, sir."

"Kevin, let's talk for a minute."

Kevin fell in alongside Jason and they walked across the deck.

"I got an offer from one of Banbridge's staff people while I was waiting to see the old man. I wanted to pass it along."

"What is it, sir?"

"Banbridge wants you as an adjutant on his staff. It's a top position, Kevin. Serve with Banbridge, do your job right, and you'll move on to commfleet. You'll be hot property there—a red combat tab on your dossier, a confirmed ace with a silver star with gold wings which I'm recommending you for; headquarters staffers love that type of record for their people. You'll climb quickly, Kevin. Hell, you could be my boss in five years time."

"Thank you, sir."

Jason looked at him, noticing the frown.

"Aren't you excited?"

"Honestly, sir?"

"Sure, go ahead."

"Tell them to stuff it. I can't stomach those types of officers. I'd rather be out here flying with you and the rest of the crew."

Jason grinned.

"How about a job aboard an escort carrier as a squadron commander?"

"Here, sir?"

"Sure, right here. I'd like to make your assignment permanent and have you run the Rapiers."

"Sir, I'd love it."

Smiling, Jason slapped Kevin on the shoulder.

"We'll talk more about it later."

Grinning with delight, Kevin raced back to Chamberlain, the two laughing and slapping each other on the back.

Jason turned and walked away.

As he reached the doorway into the main corridor leading aft he stopped for a moment to look at the roll of honor.

Two hundred and eighty-three names were on the list. So many of them he didn't even know, so many were just barely remembered faces and names, learned in the heat of combat. He could not even recall now the names of his young and so attractive combat information officer, the lowly cook who had dragged the wounded out of a shattered corridor, finally pushing a jammed airlock door shut, with himself on the vacuum side, or the deckhand who had waded into a wall of fire to shut down a ruptured hydrogen fuel line and died saving the ship. So many names, so many letters to write in the days to come.

He walked down the corridor which was blackened from fire, squeezing past a work crew, realizing that he still had on a borrowed uniform which was now stained and filthy.

He reached his cabin in the flight crew quarters and looked around. Fourteen people left. The other rooms now empty, quiet, personal effects stowed and waiting to be shipped home.

He went into his room and closed the door.

The bed seemed to float up and he collapsed upon it, not even bothering to undress. There was still a faint scent of perfume to the pillow case and the memory of it all brought the tears close to the surface.

"Damn this war," he whispered.

He only sighed her name once, and then, blessedly, Captain Jason "Bear" Bondarevsky drifted off into a dreamless sleep of peace, from which he would awaken the following day—ready to return to the war against the Kilrathi.

PRAISE FOR
LOIS MCMASTER BUJOLD

What the critics say:

The Warrior's Apprentice: "Now here's a fun romp through the spaceways—not so much a space opera as space ballet.... it has all the 'right stuff.' A lot of thought and thoughtfulness stand behind the all-too-human characters. Enjoy this one, and look forward to the next."
—Dean Lambe, *SF Reviews*

"The pace is breathless, the characterization thoughtful and emotionally powerful, and the author's narrative technique and command of language compelling. Highly recommended."
—*Booklist*

Brothers in Arms: "... she gives it a geniune depth of character, while reveling in the wild turnings of her tale. ... Bujold is as audacious as her favorite hero, and as brilliantly (if sneakily) successful."
—*Locus*

"Miles Vorkosigan is such a great character that I'll read anything Lois wants to write about him. ... a book to re-read on cold rainy days." —Robert Coulson, *Comics Buyer's Guide*

Borders of Infinity: "Bujold's series hero Miles Vorkosigan may be a lord by birth and an admiral by rank, but a bone disease that has left him hobbled and in frequent pain has sensitized him to the suffering of outcasts in his very hierarchical era.... Playing off Miles's reserve and cleverness, Bujold draws outrageous and outlandish foils to color her high-minded adventures."
—*Publishers Weekly*

Falling Free: "In *Falling Free* Lois McMaster Bujold has written her fourth straight superb novel. ... How to break down a talent like Bujold's into analyzable components? Best not to try. Best to say 'Read, or you will be missing something extraordinary.'" —Roland Green, *Chicago Sun-Times*

The Vor Game: "The chronicles of Miles Vorkosigan are far too witty to be literary junk food, but they rouse the kind of craving that makes popcorn magically vanish during a double feature."
—Faren Miller, *Locus*

MORE PRAISE FOR
LOIS MCMASTER BUJOLD

What the readers say:

"My copy of *Shards of Honor* is falling apart I've reread it so often.... I'll read whatever you write. You've certainly proved yourself a grand storyteller."

—Liesl Kolbe, Colorado Springs, CO

"I experience the stories of Miles Vorkosigan as almost viscerally uplifting.... But certainly, even the weightiest theme would have less impact than a cinder on snow were it not for a rousing good story, and good storytelling with it. This is the second thing I want to thank you for.... I suppose if you boiled down all I've said to its simplest expression, it would be that I immensely enjoy and admire your work. I submit that, as literature, your work raises the overall level of the science fiction genre, and spiritually, your work cannot avoid positively influencing all who read it."

—Glen Stonebraker, Gaithersburg, MD

"'The Mountains of Mourning' [in *Borders of Infinity*] was one of the best-crafted, and simply best, works I'd ever read. When I finished it, I immediately turned back to the beginning and read it again, and I can't remember the last time I did that."

—Betsy Bizot, Lisle, IL

"I can only hope that you will continue to write, so that I can continue to read (and of course buy) your books, for they make me laugh and cry and think ... rare indeed."

—Steven Knott, Major, USAF